Stormbreaker

Matt Sconce

Dedicated to my beloved wife, Heather,
and my precious children, Makenzie and Kaden.
May we have many epic adventures together,
in this life and beyond...

Preface

When I was young, I had a love for all things fantasy. I was constantly fighting shrubbery dragons in the front yard with plastic swords and sometimes my friends' faces as well. As I grew up, my love for stories turned into screenwriting. To date, I have produced seven feature films, three of which I directed and wrote or co-wrote with my father.

For the last fifteen years, I have been slowly working on a story I truly love ... an epic adventure of good versus evil ... a merging of fantasy and reality.

I hope you are ready for an action-packed, epic thrill ride through a modern fantasy world because that is what lives in these pages.

Let your imagination take flight and, if you enjoy this, please tell your friends.

Two more things... If you want to listen to the music I listened to when I wrote this story, listen to the albums "Invincible" and "Archangel" from the movie scoring music group Two Steps from Hell. It makes reading epic battle scenes even more epic.

Lastly, if you do not own a sword you will probably buy one after reading this. I recommend a folded, Damascus steel katana, electroplated red.

Prologue

The startled doctor stared at his stomach, his white clothing becoming overwhelmed by an expanding red stain. The second shot hit him squarely in the chest. His body flipped over the instrument table, scattering medical equipment onto the white tile floor. A second doctor, clothed in blue surgical scrubs, cowered in the corner.

The attacker, a taller man, growled at the doctor. "Deliver the baby!"

"What are you going to do to it?" the doctor asked timidly.

A bullet tore through his left instep and he screamed in pain. Without another word, he hobbled to the woman lying unconscious on the operating table. Bending gingerly to the red splattered floor, he picked up the fallen scalpel. His associate's glazed eyes stared accusingly at him and he shivered involuntarily.

Slowly, his gaze wandered across the other bodies strewn about the room. The floor was becoming slippery with blood. He looked up at the killers. Their eyes were cold and hard. He knew they would not hesitate to kill him too. An incision later, the doctor lifted a baby into the air, its crying breaking the silence that had settled upon the room. With a gun to his temple, he handed the naked baby boy to the tall man in black.

"It is not such a grand thing," muttered the man in black. The newborn blinked at the bright light and gasped its first breath. Its cries echoed in the cold room.

"Does it have the mark?" asked the other. The man holding the baby straightened its arm out so he could inspect its wrist. On the front of its wrist, directly below the baby's palm, he saw what he was looking for—the green mark of a cross. It shimmered emerald green as he turned the baby's wrist back and forth. Without a word, he lifted the gun to the baby's head and fired.

The terrified doctor jumped away, tripping over one of the bodies and falling to the ground. He slid for several inches on the bloody tile. The tall man tossed the murdered baby onto the floor and walked toward the operating table. The doctor scrambled backwards, his hands slipping and sliding, providing little stability. The tall man walked directly to the unconscious woman, raised his weapon, and fired one shot into her chest. Her breathing slowed then stopped altogether.

The doctor noticed his mouth was open. He faintly heard the scream of horror coming from his own lungs. The attacker turned the gun on him and he felt the burning impact of the bullet in his stomach. He saw the world reel as he slumped, his blood beginning to mingle with that of his friends. The room began to grow very cold.

Outside Rockefeller University Hospital, the NYPD's police cars swarmed to the front of the hospital. The two men watched from the shadows of an adjacent building as the police charged through the front doors, M4s at low ready position.

With a slight smirk, the tall man turned into the darkened building followed by his comrade. They had accomplished their mission.

Inside the hospital, the bleeding doctor pulled himself to his feet. He knew he was losing too much blood but did not have time to stop the flow. The pain from each step threatened to sever his link to consciousness, but he continued forward. He had to reach the woman.

The New York Police officers encountered a grisly scene when they entered the maternity operating room. One of the officers, overwhelmed by the gore, rushed to the corner of the room and emptied his stomach. Slipping through the blood, a second officer gave a cry and rushed out of the red-stained tomb through another entrance. A smeared trail of bloody markings ran down the entire length of the long, sterile hallway, disappearing under a door near the end.

A single bloody handprint intermittently appeared beside the trail. The officer slowly approached the door. The sign on the door read, "Neo-Natal Intensive Care Unit."

Chapter 1: The Underdog

"Mackinsi Wrighton!" The teacher's voice rang out loudly as his mind jerked to the present. He was known for being the "fantasy geek", the boy who spent more time in his daydreams than in the real world. "Mac-kin-si!" His English teacher, Ms. Hubby, loomed over his desk.

"I'm sorry, Ms. Hubby," Mac stammered. "I didn't hear you."

The classroom was silent as Ms. Hubby snatched the notebook from Mac's desk. She read a sentence loudly. "The large Orc swung his rusted blade toward Trace." She rolled her eyes. The class tittered with laughter. Mac felt his face reddening. "You will go to the principal's office immediately, young man. You need to learn how to focus, and I am sick of your attitude."

Mackinsi tried to respond, tried to tell her it was just for a writing contest he had entered, but the mocking eyes of his peers bored into him.

Their continuing laughter was grating and he felt his face grow hot. The people at Lathim High School had always looked at him as a "freak".

When he turned eighteen, Mac had somehow thought things might be different. Perhaps his senior year would bring the acceptance he hoped for … or at least an end to the cruelty. He had been wrong on both counts.

He stood up and slid his backpack over his shoulder. It was filled with books and very heavy. Mac wondered when he would fill out. At 6 feet, he only weighed 150 pounds. His muscles had not caught up to his bones yet, or so his mother told him. Whenever he mentioned his dilemma to his father, his dad only shrugged and stated confidently that it would change with time. That didn't change the fact that his nickname had become "Scarecrow".

The door closed behind him muting the raucous sounds of the classroom. The hall was empty and, at that moment, Mackinsi felt very alone. Sighing, he made his way down the quiet hall, turned a corner and came face-to-face with the last person he wanted to see.

Stockton Brown was a thug and a star running back for Lathim High's football team. At 6 foot 3 inches and 250 pounds, he was all muscle. Mackinsi believed even his brain was muscle, which would explain a lot. Since the first days of high school, Stockton and his toadies had targeted Mackinsi. Stockton had been suspended for bullying many times but had never been expelled. His father's money took care of that. His most recent suspension came after several teachers' windows were broken in the faculty parking lot. Someone had told the school administration that Stockton had done the act. That someone had been Mackinsi Wrighton.

"Well, look who we have here," Stockton growled. He punched Mac hard in the stomach. Mackinsi doubled over onto the floor of the empty hall, gasping for air, as Stockton Brown stepped over him.

"Are you going to tell your mommy about this, Scarecrow?" Stockton laughed deeply as his two friends walked up beside him. Zach Johnson and Chet Wilson were always by Stockton's side, the rotten icing on the cake.

Mac rose to his feet regaining his breath. His mouth was dry and he noticed his knees were wobbly. "Just let me by. I'm sorry I bumped into you."

Stockton smiled devilishly at Mac. "You don't know how sorry you are going to be!" He shoved Mackinsi roughly into the door to the men's bathroom. "Get in there." Mac saw the other two press in closely behind Stockton and noticed a glimmer of bared steel in Stockton's hand. Stockton lowered his voice, glancing to make sure the coast was still clear. "Come on, Scarecrow … if you give me the money in your wallet, I may not cut you up… It's up to you."

Mac felt his pulse racing. His mind spun frantically, landing suddenly on an idea, his only chance. Slowly, he pulled his wallet from the back pocket of his jeans. "You … don't need the knives." Mac lifted the wallet slowly. He felt the butterflies attempting to tear a hole through his stomach. "You can have my wallet… Here…" Mackinsi lifted the wallet to face level then hurled it as hard as he could, hitting Stockton directly between the eyes.

Mac turned and bolted for the exit door at the end of the hallway. His breath came quickly as he exploded through the doors, hearing the shouts behind him telling him the pursuit was already on. He did not know where he was going, but he knew that his pursuers had knives. His lanky frame wobbled awkwardly as he turned the corner onto the sidewalk. "Help!" he shouted, but the street was empty. *Of course people picked this day to sleep in*, he thought ruefully. He saw an alley ahead that looped back to the school. A light of hope blossomed in his heart. *I can make it!* He knew he could not outrun the star running back for long.

"Stop running, Scarecrow!" Stockton had blood running from his nose.

"The more you run the more we'll hurt you!" Zach shouted.

Mac turned into the dark alley at a full sprint. Two seconds later, the others turned into the alley behind him. Stockton's laughter followed him. "Now we've got him."

Overflowing garbage cans lined the walls of the alley, their spilled contents moldering around their bases. A homeless man lay sleeping by the entrance. Stagnant water pooled across its length.

Mac's footsteps pattered across the puddles as he ran. Then he saw the fence. The other end of the alley had been fenced off. He was blocked in. *He knew I was trapped,* Mac thought. He looked behind him. The three large seniors had stopped running and were walking toward him, waving their knives in front of them. "Where are you going to go?" asked Chet. Zach laughed. "Maybe he can get carried away by those elves he's always reading about … or a unicorn!" They laughed scornfully.

Mac desperately searched the ground around him for something to use to defend himself. He felt tears welling up in his eyes. *Stop that. That's what they want. You cannot cry!* He frantically looked around and his eyes came to rest on some trashcans near the fence. The broken handle of a broom sat next to the nearest can. He raced to the wall, taking the broomstick into both of his hands like a bat.

The broken part of the shaft sat two inches below his left hand and his right hand gripped tightly above that. He turned to face his slowly approaching attackers. He felt a bead of sweat run down his cheek, dropping into a puddle of water. The ripple the drop created distorted the reflection of the sky above. Through his rapid breathing, Mac felt his knees stop shaking. He searched inside for his previous fear and was surprised to find it wasn't there. The broomstick felt good in his hands.

Stockton slowed slightly. "Ooh... Careful, boys, Scarecrow's got himself a little stick."

He looked smugly toward his toadies.

Mac felt a calm wash over him. *I will not let them hurt me.*

Stockton stood for a moment, glaring at Mac. "I'm sick of you, Scarecrow." He looked to the others. "Cut him up."

Zach attacked first, thrusting his knife savagely at Mac's stomach. Mac reacted swiftly. The broom handle slashed from his right shoulder downward toward the ground.

The knife skittered away into the heap of garbage. Continuing the fluid movement of the handle, Mac brought it back across Zach's face. The tall boy dropped like a stone from the strike and lay unconscious at Mac's feet. Stockton's eyes bulged in surprise and rage. "Get him!"

Running toward him, Chet plunged his knife down toward Mac's head. The broom handle swiftly rose to meet the thug's arm. Mac braced the impact with his left hand, palm open, at the top of the handle. Shifting to his left, he swung the handle horizontally into Chet's stomach, knocking the wind from him. The wooden pole continued in its arc to come down with a crack on his head. Chet dropped on top of Zack, joining him in slumber.

With an enraged yell, Stockton charged Mac. The thrusts of Stockton's knife stabbed harmlessly into the air as the gangly senior parried the attacks with unexpected skill and grace. Mac raised the tip of the handle, jabbing Stockton painfully in the throat. The large bully stumbled backward, struggling to breathe. Mac followed forward quickly, crouching low. The handle came hard across Stockton's knees.

With a cry, the bully tumbled to the ground. His hair clung matted to his forehead, wet with stagnant water. As his knife flashed toward Mac's leg, the broom handle came down across his jaw. Stockton's vision blurred. His last recollection, before unconsciousness took him, was Mackinsi standing over him and a homeless man applauding wildly.

Mac stepped back from the three unconscious men. His mind reeled. What just happened?

"You okay, son?" The homeless man was on his feet.

Mac took inventory of himself. "Yeah... I think I am."

Chapter 2: Encounter

Days passed quickly at Lathim High School for Glenn Cross. He was arguably the most popular senior in school. He was the starting quarterback for the varsity football team and, at the towering height of 6 foot 3 inches with large muscles and blond hair, he was a ladykiller. Glenn's days consisted of school and parties. Nothing more could hold his interest. Not that school really ever held it in the first place. He just did well without trying. At the moment, it was dark outside and he was in the middle of the greatest party he had ever been to—and that was saying a lot.

The music blared as the beer flowed freely. "Glenn!" Zach Chester yelled from across the room. "Come play a game or two!" Glenn glanced quickly toward Zach. The black and blue bruising around his face had finally begun to dissipate. Rumor had it that Zach, Chet and Stockton had been pretty messed up a week earlier.

No one knew who had done it. The guys weren't talking and the police had not found anyone except the thugs in the alleyway by the school. Glenn smiled to himself. He wished it had been him.

"I'm living it up, Zach. You couldn't win anyway." Glenn was the champion of beer pong but somewhere along the way it had lost its appeal. "Fine." Zach sulked off. Glenn glanced again at the layout of Stockton's house. His family must be extremely wealthy to afford such a mansion. He estimated that it probably had at least 20 rooms. The rooms were what he was interested in of course … the rooms and some company. He sauntered toward the foyer where he saw a large group was playing spin the bottle. Of course, this was not the normal game of spin the bottle. The girls sat in a circle and, one at a time, the guys took turns spinning the bottle. It was a hook-up game.

The girl the bottle pointed at went up to a
bedroom with the lucky guy who spun it for an
uninterrupted half-hour. He had enjoyed many half-
hours in his high school career. He scanned the
ladies in the circle and noticed a newcomer. A
slender girl with shoulder length, dark hair and pale
skin sat near the opposite wall from him. Glenn
whistled quietly. She was the most beautiful creature
he had ever seen. She caught his gaze and returned a
smile. He smiled back. He would definitely play a
game of spin the bottle. There was talent involved.
With the right force, you could make the bottle point
right where you wanted...

***

A cloaked figure entered the enormous doors
of Stockton's house. The figure was tall and slender
but all else was hidden under his flowing green
traveler's cloak. Nobody said a word to him. The
crowd seemed to melt out of his path as he made his
way toward the stairs.

***

In the upstairs room things were going nicely for Glenn. The girl he had seen in the foyer was more beautiful than he had previously thought, especially in her red, lace underwear. She wouldn't tell him her name, and he found that all the more exciting. She had ripped the buttons off of his shirt in her hurry to remove it and seemed very interested in his wrist. It was odd to him, but all women seemed to like that cross birthmark. He looked up at her on top of him and smiled. Her body was perfect. This was the life.

As he lifted his eyes to look at her face, he thought he saw it flicker. Flicker was the only way he could describe it. Her face seemed to shift for a brief moment into something else. He gasped in surprise.

"Don't worry, Glenn," the girl crooned, "I'll be gentle."

The image of the girl flickered again, but this time the shifted image remained. The girl's face was rotting. Her jagged teeth resembled fangs and her skin was gray, peeling and slimy. Her hair hung in a tangled mess behind her. Her eyes were bright yellow with flecks of red. A long, curved dagger was in her hand. She moved the blade in small circles as she smiled crookedly. Flicker. The girl was back to the soft-skinned beauty. Glenn felt his blood run cold. Her eyes had not changed back. They were the same hideous yellow. Glenn screamed.

With a howl, the girl plunged the dagger at his heart. He deflected the blade to the side, taking a slight cut to his arm. Frantically, he tried to throw her off of him but found that he could not move her. The dagger plunged toward him again as he twisted his body to the side. The dagger tore a hole in the mattress below him. *I am going to die*, his mind screamed. *This can't be real!*

As the girl raised the dagger again, the door to the room exploded open, falling off of its hinges. Halfway through the fall, it stopped, as if frozen. Glenn's eyes shot involuntarily toward the clock and saw that its second hand had stopped as well. The girl on top of him was motionless too, caught in the freezing of time, but then the world shifted again. The girl's eyes became their normal brown as some … thing leapt out of her. Like a picture that had been hiding behind another, a corpse like woman slid from within the girl. The dagger went with her and her stringy drool pooled onto the ground. She rushed toward the window. The figure in the doorway did not give her time to escape. Before she had taken two steps, he loomed before her. He held a Japanese-style sword, a katana, in front of him. Its blade was slender, curved and at least five feet long. With a cry of rage the creature flung herself at the cloaked figure. He easily shifted to the side and brought his curved blade down in a lightning swift arc. The creature's head flew from her body, screaming as it fell with a thud. Her dagger flipped downward embedding itself into the carpeted floor, and her head rolled to the side of the bed. When the head stopped rolling, the creature's eyes turned black and the screaming halted abruptly.

The cloaked man walked toward Glenn, pulling back his hood. He was a strong looking man with night-black hair. His eyes were green and his face was sharp with hard angles. He deftly bent and retrieved the dagger, putting it into a pouch under his cloak. Glenn could not speak. He stammered slightly, and the cloaked man turned his eyes toward the girl. With a touch of his hand, she became aware of her surroundings. Her eyes grew wide as the man placed a hand on her head. Her body went limp. The man then lifted her off of Glenn and tucked her under the covers next to him.

Glenn finally was able to form a complete thought. "Wha ... what is going on?" His voice stuttered, sounding tight. He looked at his arm, seeing the reality of the situation for the first time. He frantically scrambled out of bed away from the girl.

"Don't worry, Glenn, she is no danger to you now." The man's deep voice calmed Glenn slightly, and he turned to face him. "What is going on?" he asked.

"My name is Michael, and that is all you need to know of me for now. Follow me." As they walked down the stairs, Glenn stared in confusion at the frozen scene around him. "This has to be a dream…"

The cloaked man chuckled quietly. "They all say the same thing."

Glenn quietly followed Michael past the motionless partygoers and out into the night.

Chapter 3: Discoveries

Mac lifted his father's bow carefully from its resting place behind the coats in the closet. His dad had told him stories of hunting bear with the bow but Mac had never seen him use it. He took a deep breath of determination, gathered the arrows and walked into the backyard.

A weathered bale of hay now leaned against the wooden fence across the yard from him. His dad's quiver hung snugly on his back. It was definitely not made for someone thinner than his father. Fitting an arrow on the string, he drew the string back to his ear. He had placed a paper plate in the middle of the hay bale. He hoped he could hit it. He let out his breath and released the string.

The swish of the bowstring came a fraction of a second before the arrow pinned the plate to the hay bale. With a smile, he drew another arrow, drawing and placing it in a single movement.

The pull was swift and the release was sure as the second then the third, fourth, fifth, sixth, and seventh arrows sunk into the hay bale. He looked at the plate and laughed. The arrows formed a smiling face on the piece of paper. He was right.

Ever since the fight in the alley, he had been trying to understand the amazing improvement in his reactions and he had come up with a theory. Each time he had an opportunity, he attempted another battle skill. He suspected he would be good at each one.

Launching into a somersault, he drew an arrow and let it fly. He dove to the side, laid on the ground, and fell onto his back, all the while launching a barrage of arrows. He never missed the target.

An hour later, a sweating Mackinsi walked into the house, replacing the bow and taking his mother's block of kitchen knives. By the time his father arrived home, Mackinsi was in his room reading a fantasy adventure novel. His father smiled and sat down in the living room to watch television. Sometimes he wished his son would be more active.

Mac sat in his room watching the sun set over the city. In the weeks following the alley incident, he had made a friend ... the first in a very long time. He had previously only known Glenn Cross as the quarterback of the football team and the ultimate party boy. It seemed everyone was always talking about Glenn's prowess under the covers, on top of the covers, on the floor, in the movie theater or in the back seat of a car. The thought made Mac blush. He also longed to be close to a woman but he wanted that woman to be his wife.

Despite the differences between them, the two had been spending long hours together talking fantasy and weaponry.

Stockton was no longer at school. Stockton's father had decided not to pay for his son's mistakes because money was thin. Rumor had it that he was involved in a lawsuit regarding a seventeen-year-old transfer student found in his bed after a party. Her parents had filed charges against him. The girl could not remember how she had gotten there and the press was having a field day with the story.

Zach and Chet had gone their separate ways after their leader had been expelled. And now, with the discovery of hidden talents, life was looking up for Mackinsi Wrighton.

***

The party at Chet Wilson's house was raging but the familiar face was not in attendance. Glenn lay in his bed, lost in thought. After the incident several weeks earlier, Michael had led him to the center of a darkened park, where he had told him more. What he had seen was a Dimlock. The memory of the rotting face and yellow eyes sent chills along Glenn's spine. Michael explained that the creature had been sent to kill him. He told him he was special, even dangerous. Glenn liked that thought. He wouldn't mind being dangerous.

Michael advised him to find Mackinsi Wrighton and befriend him. He said it would be very important in the future, and that he would know why when he found him. It had taken Glenn several days of asking around but he finally found out who Mackinsi was. When he shook hands with him in introduction, Glenn understood why he had to get to know Mackinsi. They had a connection.

Mac sat in his room. He had put the book down and was staring at his wrist. He had always wondered how he had acquired the interesting marking on it. He turned his wrist in the lamplight and saw it glimmer green. As it glimmered, the room seemed to flicker. There was power in that mark. He knew that now, but he did not know what it was or why he had it. Glenn promised they would talk to a friend of his soon who he promised had some answers. Mackinsi closed his eyes, his thoughts swirling. Answers were exactly what he longed for.

Sitting on a tree branch outside of his window, Michael smiled. The boy was strong. Creator had been right to choose him. He watched as the room flickered in and out. The boy was beginning to awaken the power that was within him. Soon it would be time.

Chapter 4: Michael's Tale

The night was cold as Mackinsi and Glenn made their way through the dark. The lamps along the sidewalk cast eerie shadows across the closed business doors. The streets were surprisingly empty. That was very strange on a Friday night in New York City.

Mac's mind was spinning. The promise of answers was all consuming. When he was young, the mark on his arm had been an interesting topic of conversation, and as he had entered high school, he had accepted it as a mystery in his life that he would never solve. Recently, the mystery had become overwhelming. As he realized his hidden talents, he became increasingly certain that the mark on his arm had something to do with them.

The first hope of answering the questions about his origins came to him several weeks earlier when he shook Glenn Cross's hand. They shared the mark: the flickering, shimmering, green cross on their wrist.

The mark flashed back at him. The night seemed to flicker. The people and cars seemed to stutter in their movement like the skipping of a scratched CD-ROM. Glenn smiled at him knowingly.

Mac glanced over to regard Glenn. He trusted Glenn, but still felt an anxious churning in his stomach at the thought of the upcoming meeting. Answers were important to him, but the source of the answers mattered as well. How could he trust the knowledge he would gain was the truth?

The man, Michael, sounded like a character out of a fantasy novel. Glenn had told him the story of how they met. New York was full of strange characters but men in traveling cloaks, battling monsters with katanas were not a usual occurrence at high school parties.

"There it is." Glenn's voice pulled him back to the task at hand. "That's the park Michael took me to after he saved me."

Walker Park sat in the middle of a large square of skyscrapers. The park was large and poorly lit. Interesting characters roamed its shadows, their eyes flitting nervously around.

A police siren pierced the chilly air and, for several seconds, the park was awash in blue and red flashing lights as the patrol car passed by.

"Where do we meet him?" Mac asked.

Glenn continued to stare after the police car. "He said to meet him by the statue at the center," he mumbled.

"Isn't that the statue that was on the news the other day?"

Glenn smiled at the question. "Yeah, someone knocked old General Walker's head off."

Mac shrugged his shoulders. "The statue needed to be repaired anyway. If the statue of the old general had been alive, he would have drowned in spray paint."

A movement caught his eyes and he realized they were within sight of the graffiti covered, headless statue. A tall figure in a flowing, green cloak glided from behind it like a ghost. As he let his large, green hood fall, Mac could make out his face. His sharp features matched the breadth of his shoulders.

The man was larger than Glenn, but moved as if gravity held him in a lighter grasp. Several homeless men passed the cloaked man without a glance. Mac thought it was odd that such a large man in a cloak would attract no attention. He looked at Glenn and saw excitement in his eyes. The cloaked man spoke.

"Hello, Mackinsi Wrighton."

His voice was low but was not harsh. It seemed to carry wisdom at the same time as a smooth confidence. Mac stared too, and he knew what the cause was. The guy was straight out of Middle Earth.

Michael was still looking at him, expecting an answer.

"Hello, Michael."

Michael smiled.

"I hope you are prepared for what I will share with you tonight."

Mac felt the hair on the back of his neck stand up. Goosebumps spread across the surface of his skin. The promise of answers had given him a chill the cold night had not been able to bring.

Michael led them toward the shadows around the decapitated statue of General Walker.

Suddenly, Glenn grunted, and Mac felt his mark burn like fire. Time slowed and flickered all around them. An arrow burst into view in front of Mac and whizzed passed his ear. He then noticed that Michael held a bow and was looking past them. Mac had not known the strange man had a weapon on him, much less seen him fire an arrow. Simultaneously, Mac and Glenn spun to look behind them. Several feet from them, what appeared to Mac to be a zombie writhed on the ground and then laid still, an arrow in its throat. Mac felt his adrenaline rush and then jumped back as he noticed a man in a hooded sweatshirt next to him holding a knife.

He rapidly backpedaled away from him until he realized the man was not following him. He was holding still as if frozen in mid-stab. In fact, the cars in the road next to the park were motionless as well. Mac jumped as he felt Michael's hand on his shoulder.

"A second later and you would be dead." Michael turned him by the shoulders and his green eyes bored into his own.

"You already have the weapon but do not yet know how to use it."

Glenn stood staring at the fallen corpse-like monster. "A … another one?"

Michael nodded solemnly as he turned and walked into the shadows "Quickly now… They are rarely alone and it's past time you learned."

The shadows hung heavily around Mac as he stood next to Glenn. Despite himself, he glanced around for any other monsters in the dark.

"Listen and learn!" Michael's deep voice seemed to echo off the skyscraper, though he spoke just above a whisper. The two youths grew silent as Michael, with simple words, pulled the carpet from beneath their reality.

"In the beginning, Creator made seven dimensions, each a reflection of the others. Within each dimension he placed mankind."

"For thirty thousand years the balances Creator established held back the evil created by human selfishness. Then, ten thousand years ago, the balance in the second dimension shifted. It became quickly apparent that evil was hungrily taking hold in a world primed for dark conversion."

"Selfishness became murder and anarchy and, through this corruption, there appeared a being named Destroyer. With him came an army of darkness. The foot soldiers of his army are the Dimlocks."

He pointed to the creature he had shot and Mac felt another chill rise from the ground and travel up his spine.

"Dimlocks were given the power to exist a step outside of time. With that power came the ability to possess human beings."

Michael paused for a moment to look at the headless statue.

"All purposeful evil deeds have a Dimlock behind them. Their goal is to use humans like pawns, controlling them from the inside, to ruin the tide of the morality in a dimension.

"When Destroyer had conquered the second dimension, he tainted it. He drained all of the good, mixed it with the suffering he had caused, and fused it into a black sphere called the Heartstone.

It was through the power of the Heartstone that Destroyer gained the ability to assimilate dimensions. Methodically, he led his armies into dimension after dimension, tipping the scales of good and overcoming the good with evil. When the balance shifted enough, the dimension went insane, falling into the Heartstone and merging with the other dimensions already pulled inside."

Glenn interrupted. "You said there were seven dimensions created?"

Michael nodded, and Glenn continued, hesitation growing with each word. "How many are left?"

Michael's hard expression softened slightly.

"This is the last free world. This is the Seventh Dimension."

Mac couldn't hold the question back any longer. "Where do we fit into this? Can't we do anything to stop him?"

"That is a two-fold question, my young friend, and I will answer both parts."

Again, Glenn interrupted. "We're not children."

Michael chuckled deeply.

"Glenn Cross, you are eighteen years old. To you, that age is an eternity. I, on the other hand, am over two thousand years old."

He paused to let the fact sink in.

"To me, eighteen years is a blink of an eye."

Mac realized his jaw was hanging open and closed it quickly, noticing Glenn do the same. Before either of them could say a word, Michael casually continued to speak.

"As to where we fit into this, I'll begin at the beginning. With the creation of the seven dimensions, Creator introduced a power into the bloodline of some humans. It was to be known as the Power of Light. The power passed itself on, sometimes skipping generations, but perpetually introducing defenders into the human population.

The defenders of the dimension were born with a mark of a cross on their wrist. They were called the Stormbreakers, named for their job of stopping the coming storms."

Glenn's eyes lit up. "So we are Stormbreakers... Does that mean we get special powers?"

"The Power of Light first manifests itself when the Stormbreaker is in great peril. When the Power of Light comes upon a Stormbreaker, it is called the Covering."

"What does this covering do?" Glenn asked.

Michael took a step backwards and fixed his eyes on Glenn. He flared his cloak and turned in a circle.

"Do I have any visible weapons on me?"

"No," Glenn replied.

In a fluid movement, Michael's katana blade rested on Glenn's shoulder. The startled senior's mouth moved without tangible words as he tried to form a response. Mac spoke first.

"So your weapons come into existence when you need them?"

"Actually," Michael answered, "they are always with us. They are just unseen."

He slid the blade into the air on his left and it disappeared.

"It is now re-sheathed. Feel the back of my cloak, Mackinsi Wrighton."

Mackinsi slid his hand along the back of Michael's cloak and was surprised to feel something unseen beneath his fingers.

"Your bow?" he asked.

"Yes. For me, the Covering gave the katana and bow and the arrows never run out in my quiver. That was my gift along with the cloak of a Stormbreaker."

"I don't need an old cloak. This isn't Halloween," Glenn muttered under his breath, but loud enough to be heard.

Mac was surprised at his friend. They were learning the meaning of life and, if he did not know better, he would have said Glenn was impatient for more. Michael must have seen the same.

"Patience, Glenn Cross. All things are learned in time. But if you try to wrench knowledge and strength from the universe instead of accepting the rate at which they are given, you will fail. You will either gain nothing or gain more than you can handle. Both have the same end."

Glenn looked down at the ground but his brow remained furrowed. Michael turned his gaze to Mac.

"The cloak is what allows us to function amongst society unnoticed. It is a powerful tool. It can transform itself into clothing with a thought and can get you into many places you otherwise could not enter."

As he spoke, his cloak wrapped around him becoming a black Armani suit. The next moment, it changed back into a flowing cloak. Glenn's brow lifted and he seemed a bit more interested.

"What else can it do?" he asked.

"The greatest gift of the cloak is the ability to move unseen. When people's eyes cross the cloak of a Stormbreaker, it registers as empty space like a fleeting mist that disappears with the first rays of sunlight.

The cloak puts us in the blind spot of the human eye. It is not that we are invisible but that people simply look past us."

"With the Covering comes the knowledge of weaponry and agility as well as many other things. But I am guessing that for you, Mackinsi Wrighton, that knowledge has already come."

Mac felt his face grow hot. He had not told Glenn about his backyard exploits. How had Michael known? Glenn glanced suspiciously toward Mac.

"Why should Mac be different? Aren't all Stormbreakers the same?"

The question had also been in Mac's mind.

Michael continued to look at Mac. Mac felt as if the man could actually see his thoughts.

"Mackinsi Wrighton is an enigma," Michael said a little softer. "Some would have the Stormbreakers believe hope is not lost. They would tell us that, before the bloodline ran out, one was born who could stand alone against Destroyer."

"What do mean, the bloodline ran out?" Mac asked.

"Destroyer has been attempting to kill every person who could pass on the gift of the Stormbreaker bloodline. For years he has been hunting them down and systematically executing them and their children. His goal was to stop the production of any more of Creator's warriors so he could conquer this final dimension more rapidly. The story was the same in all of the other dimensions. The only difference here is that we prevented him from accomplishing this goal for many more years than the Stormbreakers from the other dimensions."

"What was the point of stopping Destroyer if you knew he would succeed eventually?" Glenn asked skeptically.

"We were trying to maintain the bloodline until the prophecies were fulfilled," Michael said softly, seeming lost in thought. "Almost two decades ago, the last of the bloodline was killed along with her newborn son. The child indeed had the mark of a Stormbreaker.

It was a very tragic day. When we discovered there were two Stormbreakers, only eighteen, at Lathim High, our curiosity was sparked. No Stormbreaker should be so young, unless they had somehow survived the last execution or were unknown to us. That would make them the last in the line of the Stormbreakers."

"But you said yourself that the baby was killed," Glenn pointedly reminded the cloaked man.

"One of them was," Michael answered cryptically.

The weight of his proclamation hit Mac like a bucket of ice water. He thought about his parents, who he in no way resembled, and wondered if Michael spoke the truth. Could he be adopted? He forced the thoughts away. He wanted more answers and he had come tonight ready for anything. Let the answers come!

"The prophecies speak of a Stormbreaker that will battle Destroyer to save mankind," Michael began but was interrupted again by an outburst from Glenn.

"You think that's Mackinsi?" Glenn asked incredulously. "Look at him! I'm twice as big as he is. How could anyone believe he is the savior of the world?"

Mac felt the sting of the words but also acknowledged their validity. He was not as strong as Glenn and had always been gangly. His self-deprecating thoughts were interrupted as Glenn's outburst rambled on.

"If anyone could be the one to save the world, why not me?"

Michael's face tensed with the first hint of a frown Mac had seen on it. Michael's eyes seemed to be shutting Glenn's mouth with the intensity of their glare. His words were measured and low.

"The Covering changes many things, but some things it will never change. Whether or not this belief holds true will be seen with time. It is possible the bloodline was stopped before the prophecy was fulfilled. If that is so, then our world, the last remaining dimension, has fallen into doom."

Mac realized his palms were sweaty. He wiped his clammy hands against his brown jacket. Saving the world was a bit more responsibility than he was ready to take on. He looked at Glenn. The senior's large frame held more muscles than he thought were possible. He knew that Glenn was probably right. He was much more qualified to save the world. He noticed Michael's face had grown serious.

"The Stormbreakers in the other dimensions failed to stop Destroyer and he has been in the Seventh Dimension for many years … thousands of years before I was born. His pattern is simple yet powerful. He attains power and control through manipulation and deceit. All the while, his outer appearance is radiant and spotless. If he appears in public, as he almost never does, the causes he publicly supports would rally the world to support him."

"How could Destroyer appear good in person when he is a monster?" Mac asked.

"He has taken the form of a Resident."

Michael paused, seeking the right words.

"There are things allied with Destroyer much more deadly than a Dimlock."

Mac felt as if the night grew darker. He saw Glenn shift his stance nervously as well.

"When a Dimlock possesses a human, it rips control away from them and uses the body for evil, but if a human being willingly accepts the Dimlock's possession, the two are fused into one creature: a Resident. This is the form Destroyer has taken in this world. But he is a more powerful being than a simple Resident. The Resident maintains a human appearance but has three to four times the strength of a Dimlock. Moving out of time has no effect on them because they exist as a whole both in and out of time. They can never again separate into human and Dimlock; they are forever Residents, ageless but mortal. Kill the physical body and you kill the Resident."

"So the same applies to Destroyer," Glenn stated.

"No," Michael responded smoothly, "Destroyer can fuse and un-fuse with a human at will. This makes him very hard to locate."

"Why don't you guys, I mean the other Stormbreakers, buy some firepower and level any Resident we come across?" Glenn quipped.

The frown returned to Michael's face.

"I see you still have much to learn, Glenn Cross. Guns and weapons of mass destruction were created by Destroyer to further his agenda. Light cannot wield darkness. The weapons we use are given to us by Creator at the Covering. Their sole purpose is to destroy evil."

Glenn glowered at the ground.

"It seems like it still might be a good idea," Mac heard him mutter.

Michael raised the volume of his voice slightly.

"Destroyer has pulled the strings of evil from the platform of good for thousands of years, always with a new name. I believe Destroyer is fused, for the time being, with someone in New York. There are several large corporations here that have the billions of dollars needed to fund his campaign for assimilation."

The shadows around him grew lighter and Mac realized that dawn was rapidly approaching. He had not realized they had reentered normal time.

"So what now?" he asked.

Michael stepped closer to the two of them.

"Your Covering could come at any time. Make sure your lives are pure and ready for its coming. I will research into the powers in this city and will return to you in several days. Until then, watch and wait."

Michael stepped back into the shadows and vanished as the sun's rays glinted softly across the sky. Mac and Glenn quietly walked across the park and toward their homes. Mac's world had just been turned upside down, yet he felt at peace. Somehow, he had known this day would come and now his questions had been answered. He was a Stormbreaker.

Chapter 5: The Man of Power

In a large conference room at the top of Leviathan Corporation's skyscraper in New York City voices were buzzing. Suggestions, criticisms, and random input were flying from the mouths of six men and six women positioned around a round table. Photos of humanitarian efforts around the world lined the stark white walls, injecting the warmth of children's smiles into the room.

The faces of the board of trustees of Leviathan had obviously never suffered a single day from hunger, yet the corner of their eyes held the aged lines that only happy lives can bring.

A man in a large, black suit spoke: "We will be much more profitable if we invest it in a country that can pay us back."

Some other members nodded in agreement but an older lady interjected.

"John, the mission of Leviathan is to help the people of the world. We want world peace, not profit."

John's eyes turned down reluctantly.

"I want peace too, Judith, but we can't continue without funds. We're scraping the bottom of the barrel for cash right now, regardless of what the books say."

All of the board members became quiet. Silence hung in the air like a hammer waiting to fall. Every person in the room was aware of the problem with the books. No matter how much money the corporation pulled in, it never appeared again. It was if someone had punched a hole in their pocketbook and anything they put in drained out. Their books, of course, did not reflect this. The corporation would go under if the investors or the Internal Revenue Service ever found out about the constant outflow of cash.

The big man shuddered.

The doors to the large room opened quietly and a man in a black suit entered. The big man rose to acknowledge him. "Sir."

The man in black nodded to acknowledge him. "John."

He sat down in the empty chair at the table, regarding each face around the table. Their smile lines were less visible now that he was in the room. The stress of their financial problem was getting to them.

"John, how is the humanitarian aid program coming?"

John knew the correct response... "It is coming along nicely, sir. The flight rotations are working well, and the price of rice has actually dropped significantly. This is allowing us to ship more food to the countries in need."

"Excellent." The Man of Power's voice was silver, smooth as silk.

"You are doing well, John."

The man's face brightened slightly. The Man of Power turned to Judith.

"How are our after-school programs?"

Judith's eyes did not brighten much.

"They are fine at the moment, sir." The older lady sighed resignedly. "I estimate though, sir, that the program will run out of funding within the year."

The Man of Power's eyes narrowed slightly.

"Are you telling me that the financial leak has not been remedied? How can Leviathan help the world when we can't even help ourselves?"

Everyone's eyes became busy regarding the table in front of them. The man continued.

"Find the leak, keep your programs running, and let me know when you have fixed the problem."

An audible volley of "Yes, sir" answered.

The hallway echoed with his footfalls as the Man of Power left the conference room.

"Fools! Blind lapdogs!" He chuckled to himself.

The elevator opened to the 50th floor and he continued down the hallway toward two large, wooden doors with brass latches. They swung open as he reached them, and he entered a very different conference.

Candlelight flickered across the stone walls of a throne room and across the faces of the ten gathered men. Their matching black suits seemed to melt into the darkness. Their eyes were hard, but each softened slightly at the sight of the man who entered. Each of the men at the table had killed hundreds of people.

They were Residents, gathered to confer with their master. All of them knew the Man of Power could crush them and would crush them at the slightest provocation and each valued their vile existence.

"Master." A large Resident at the head of the rectangular table stepped aside and offered him a large, cushioned chair. Without hesitation, the Man of Power took it.

He spoke immediately: "Who is in charge of hiding what we do from the humans in the corporation?"

At the end of the table, a Resident rose.

"That is my job, Master."

Despite his show of confidence, his voice shook.

Like an acrid wind, the master was around the table and clutching the creature's throat. His legs kicked futilely as he dangled from the master's hand.

"Don't kill me," the Resident rasped.

"How can we continue to operate in the world if we are observed?" Destroyer growled.

His hand continued to tighten. The Resident's cries became weaker and his struggling slowed.

"No! You will not die today."

Destroyer hurled the Resident across the room, and he slammed into the stone wall.

"You will solve the problem. And if you do not, you will die tomorrow."

The Resident rose to his feet, bowed, and returned to the table. It would take more than being hurled into a wall to kill him.

Destroyer took his seat again at the head of the long, oak table.

The throne room was immense. Its soft, red carpeting and stone walls dwarfed the large men around the table. To one side of the room, opposite the wooden doors, was a raised platform and on it an ornate, golden throne. Each armrest was a sculpted dragon with eyes of ruby. The feet of the throne seemed to grip the carpet with claws that glittered like razors. The back of the throne was like a finely worked needlepoint: thin strands of gold intertwined with others. It was the throne of kings.

Beside the throne sat a golden pedestal with a small, cup-shaped indention on the top of it. Resting in the indention sat the Heartstone, the foundation of so much of Destroyer's power and the key to ultimate dimensional domination. Candles lined the walls of the chamber. Destroyer preferred the flickering luminescence to electricity. It brought back memories from ages past.

Another Resident general spoke: "Master, our efforts in creeping gradualism are succeeding well. The more violence we feed to society the more they demand. The more they observe the more they seem to need. Their moral line is slipping. They believe in nothing except themselves. They will soon be vulnerable."

The Residents murmured softly at the declaration; they could taste the power almost within their reach.

"Excellent." Destroyer smiled to himself. "What of the weapons programs?"

Another general rose.

"The biological and chemical weapons are being produced at an incredible rate. The nuclear weapons programs are moving at a slower pace but are on track."

"Invest more into the program. It will not serve our purposes if it is not at the ready."

Another Resident stood.

"Master, our army is being organized and should be completed, trained, and mobilized in several months."

The Resident hesitated, and then went on: "Two of our numbers have disappeared. I believe there is a Stormbreaker in the city."

The Man of Power's smile fell.

"Where there is one there are others. Warn the other Dimlocks and increase training. Gather the Fiends together as well. They will soon be needed."

"Yes, Master," the Resident replied, and sat down.

"Send the hunters to find and kill the Stormbreakers, unless one of them is double marked. If you find the one with two marks, bring him to me alive."

Destroyer needed the Stormbreaker who was double marked. He knew that now. He had been hasty in the killing of the woman to end the bloodline. He should have waited until after he had found the destined one before summarily ending the bloodline Creator had begun. What if he had stopped the line before it had borne the Chosen One? The legends told of a woman who would bear a son who would save his people. Destroyer laughed and the Residents stared at him. Creator thought his warrior would defeat him. How could he know that Destroyer desperately wanted him to come? The sooner he found him the sooner he could get the artifact he needed to obtain the power of the heavens. The Heartstone was powerful indeed, but the power of Creator could not be attained without the Aquillian scroll, and the double-marked Stormbreaker was the only one who could discover its location and activate its power.

"Someday I will find it," Destroyer growled, "and this world, and all the dimensions, will be mine!"

Chapter 6: The Covering

Mackinsi sat at his desk. His right arm was resting palm up, his mark flickering like green fire. The past several weeks had been strange and had passed slowly. He had not seen Michael since their meeting, and Glenn had begun to distance himself from him ever since they had left the park. He guessed it had something to do with the interest Michael had shown in him. Maybe Glenn was jealous. Whatever the reason, he was once again lonely. His books could no longer hold his interest. Knowing about reality somehow dwarfed their fictional capability of entertainment. Every day he expected the Covering and every day it failed to come. He was beginning to wonder if it ever would. His marking grew brighter with each day that passed and he was beginning to understand the power it contained. It was the Power of Light.

He thought about his family, if that is what they truly were. *No!* He chastised himself.

Even if he had been adopted, they were still his family. True family was not defined by blood. The thought eased his mind and caused him to think of their wellbeing. He had been successful at hiding his new capabilities from them but he did not know if it would be possible after the Covering. What would the Covering bring? Would he be a sword wielder or be given a staff? Would he receive a bow or knives? He knew it was up to Creator and this thought put his mind at rest. The Covering would come when it was time and he would work out a way to stay with his family.

Glenn had been on his mind a lot recently. The way he had acted with Michael confused Mackinsi. Before the meeting, Glenn had been calm and amiable. Mackinsi had felt like he had a friend. Yet, after it, Glenn seemed like a different person.

Mac had only been able to get in contact with him once and that had been on the telephone. In that conversation, Glenn had only been able to talk about the Covering, the stupidity of the notion that Mac would save the world and what he would be able to get away with using his cloak. Many of those ideas involved women.

Mac had not known him before they had met in the school hall. Maybe this was how he used to be. He hoped things would someday turn around. It had been nice to have a friend.

Rain began to splatter against his windowpane, gaining intensity with the rising of the wind. A clap of thunder sent a chill through his body. He was glad he was inside tonight.

***

Two men stood under the downpour. They were dressed in black trench coats and were staring up at the window. The short man nodded when a faint green glimmer flashed at him from the room.

"Definitely one of them," the tall man declared in a solemn voice. "We've lost other hunters to vermin who have seemed weaker. Our plans will not change."

As the hunters approached the front door, the night seemed to come alive behind them. Yellow eyes with red flecks bobbed in the darkness as drool fell onto the cement, mingling with pooling rain.

A faint noise caught Mac's attention … a creak on the stairs.

Another creak caused goose bumps to rise on his arms. It was the sound of someone sneaking. Slowly, Mac crept toward his bedroom door. His heart pounded. He reached toward the doorknob and froze. Someone or something was turning it from the other side. Fear tasted sour in his mouth as the door swung open. He scrambled backward toward his bed as he realized what was standing in his doorframe.

Long, matted, black hair hung wetly against the creature's rotting, grey flesh. Its mouth was open in a smile, and its teeth shone yellow, matching its wild yellow stare. Lightning flickered.

Frantically, Mac's mind reeled. He could not face a Dimlock alone, not yet. The covering had not arrived in time. He quickly scrambled toward the window. He had to run.

As he reached the window, he remembered his parents asleep in their room. That stopped him in his flight. He couldn't leave them.

He spun again toward the door to see that several Dimlocks had entered the room along with two men in black trench coats.

He felt a burning sensation in his wrist and saw the floor around him was glowing, pulsing with green light that must have been coming from his mark. He felt a fire begin to flow through his veins. The burning sensation increased on his wrist, and the glow in the room became a bright light.

With a bark, the hunters screamed orders. The Dimlock on his right drew a sword and leapt toward him. With a concussive force, the window shattered. A burst of wind hurled the glass into the leaping Dimlock. Black blood splattered the wall behind it and it fell gurgling to the floor.

The wind became a column, spiraling around Mac. His hair whipped and tossed with the force of it. He felt another burning on his left wrist and looked down to see pinpoints of green appearing.

The next Dimlock that tried to jump onto him was flung across the room by the wind, its head exploding against the wall. The air whipped Mac around to face the window. He noticed that it seemed like time had slowed. Each raindrop moved slowly toward the ground. A bolt of lightning slid lazily down to hit a lightning rod on the house across the street.

Despite the miracle in front of him, something else caught Mac's attention. Wisps of green light spiraled through the black clouds like spirits dancing in the storm. They existed outside of time like the wind around him, rocketing across the slow moving backdrop. The trails of green light spun together and shot toward him. His left wrist screamed in pain and he looked down to see both wrists glowing with a green cross. The wind lifted his arms and the green light engulfed him.

Cloth and metal brushed his skin as he was lifted off of the ground. He vaguely noticed he was screaming. His wrists pulsed in time with his heart.

Wind and light moved across his face and down his body. He felt heavier but filled with strength. Power coursed through him like rushing water and the green light changed to blinding white.

All at once, as quickly as it had begun, the wind was gone, leaving only the sound of the storm.

The Covering had come.

Mac pushed himself up from the ground. He did not recognize the arms in front of him. Each muscle was strong and defined, rippling with the slight exertion of pushing himself to his feet.

Soft cloth brushed his arm. He looked down to see the edge of a forest-green cloak.

With a cry, the shorter hunter threw himself at Mac, his gun aimed at his head. As Mac turned, his marking flickered. He felt knowledge of battle flowing through him. The double marking flashed green at the hunter, and he hesitated, shock apparent upon his normally emotionless face.

In a fluid movement, Mac's left arm intercepted the gun and his right hand whipped out, impacting the Resident's windpipe. The Resident's gun bounced out of his hand, onto the desk and out of the window. The Resident stumbled backward, drawing a short sword.

Mac pulled his cloak back, revealing the long hilt of a katana. The handle was marked with two crosses. The tall hunter's eyes bulged. Mac drew his sword. The blade showed layered lines proving it had been forged and folded and shone an electroplated crimson. The short resident screamed an order. The Dimlocks at the door exploded to life amidst the cries of the tall man.

Like a razor wind, Mac moved. His sword spun and dipped, thrust and parried. Black blood flew as the Dimlocks dropped. Like a dancing tiger, his movements were the embodiment of grace and death. In several seconds, only the hunters remained standing.

They were both backed against the door frame.

"Remember your orders," the tall hunter barked. "You do not want to anger the master."

The other hunter danced to the side, his sword still pointed at Mac.

"His orders contradict our purpose," he spat.

Mac had heard enough. He leapt toward them and sounds of metal upon metal echoed around the room. Both hunters were attacking and they were very good.

Mac's sword slipped and bobbed as his body ducked and pivoted. He moved by instinct, as if he had sparred with his opponents many times before. His mind anticipated their attacks to the extent that, as they lunged, he had already avoided the attack, his sword slicing back toward them.

The two hunters' trench coats flared and slid like scales on a serpent as they relentlessly attacked Mackinsi.

Outside, a straggling Dimlock picked up the hunter's pistol and began to climb the side of the house. His master would be grateful for his weapon's return.

The battle within the room was still raging despite the fact that the raindrops were frozen in midair.

Mac saw the tall hunter's broadsword thrust toward his side. Spinning to the left, he parried the blow, counterattacking with a diagonal slash. The tall hunter barely blocked the attack, and Mac's razor sharp blade cut a deep wound in the side of his neck. The hunter gave a cry and staggered back to the wall, holding his neck to stop the bleeding.

Mac's blade turned toward the other attacker. Sparks flew as short sword met katana. Mac's thrust was met by a downward deflection, and the hunter's upward slash fell short as Mac leapt backward. The battle could go either way, and Mackinsi knew it.

A sound at the window caught his attention. Yellow eyes appeared over the edge. He turned back toward the hunter to see a foot cover his vision. The impact of the kick to his head sent him flying across the room. As he flew, he saw the Dimlock throw the pistol toward the hunter. His grip tightened on his sword's hilt as he crashed into the wall. Picture frames fell from the impact, their glass shattering as they hit the floor. He felt the air leave his lungs, but kept his grip on his sword.

The short hunter caught the gun and spun toward Mac, grinning. "No!" the tall hunter roared. Mac saw the pull of the trigger, tasted the powder of the bullet, and heard the deafening roar of the semiautomatic. He was on his feet, his sword rising. The bullet spun toward his face as his sword stopped vertically in front of him. The bullet met the katana's razor edge and lost the battle. It split in two, passing an inch away from both of Mac's ears and into the wall.

The hunter's eyes went wide and his mouth hung open. He looked surprised as the knife Mac had slipped from inside his sleeve imbedded itself into his chest.

Looking up from his chest, the short hunter again raised the weapon, but Mac was no longer there. He turned just in time to feel the blade of a katana meet his neck, and then he felt no more.

The tall hunter backed up with a gasp as his associate's head tumbled across the floor in front of him. The decapitated Resident's body slumped heavily to the ground. Red blood pooled in the carpet at Mac's feet.

With a cry, the tall hunter turned and fled. The Dimlock at the window did the same. After several moments, the rain began to once again fall to the ground as the storm raged on. Mac was left alone with his adrenaline and his thoughts.

Chapter 7: Headhunting

The next hour was the hardest Mac had ever faced. It was more painful than the years of ridicule he had endured and more difficult than the battle.

Mac signed his name to the letter and set it gently on the dresser next to his parents' bed. He was thankful he had the power to move outside of time. The battle had taken place without his parents hearing a sound. They were safe, and that was what mattered. His cloak flowed like water as he moved across the room, down the stairs and out the front door. The letter explained it all and also explained why he had to go. Whether or not his parents believed it did not matter. What did matter was that he had told the truth. Even if the police tried to find him, they would be looking for the boy he used to be. He ran his large hand across his jaw and felt stubble. The Covering had changed many things.

The storm still pounded the ground around him, and lightning lit up the sky. Without realizing it, he longed for a raincoat.

Instantly, he was wearing one, his cloak's surface changing into smooth plastic. In his surprise, he looked down at his glowing wrists. Why had a second mark appeared? If it was something that came with the Covering, why hadn't Michael mentioned it? Before leaving the house, he called Glenn. He had not mentioned anything about the Covering, but Glenn had told him Michael wanted to meet with them. Mac was glad because he had some questions for the ancient Stormbreaker. With a last look at his home, he walked into the storm, his tears mingling with the rain.

The rain had begun to fall harder by the time Mac reached Walker Park. The shady characters, thugs and dealers were strangely absent. The storm had driven them into the holes they had crawled out of.

The lightning flashes illuminated the headless general. Paint streamed down his body. Some graffiti artist had used water-soluble paint. Wonders never ceased.

Mac approached the two figures behind the statue. Their conversation halted as they noticed his approach.

The dim lights surrounding the park were bright enough to show their reactions.

Michael's gaze flickered down then up, and he smiled. Glenn's reaction was quite different.

"Mac?" Glenn's mouth hung open and his eyes opened wide.

Mac's concentration wavered and his raincoat flowed back into his cloak. Glenn's eyes grew wider.

"The Covering," he whispered. "This is what it does?"

Mac remained silent. Something in Glenn's eyes troubled him.

"What weapons did you get?" Glenn asked.

Mac pulled the corner of his cloak back, and his double-marked sword flickered into appearance. He willed it to vanish just as quickly. Glenn ran a hand along the back of Mac's cloak.

"A bow and quiver," he whispered.

Michael interrupted the awkward interaction.

"Glenn Cross, there will be time to gawk later. Now is the time to listen."

Glenn's arm pulled back from the invisible bow as if bitten, and his slightly sullen look returned.

"I have called you here for an important reason. Mackinsi Wrighton, I am sorry for the decision you had to make. You are correct in your actions. They will be safe without you there."

Mac looked down at the water-soaked grass. He felt a vise clamp around his heart every time he thought about his decision to protect his parents by leaving them.

"The storms are rising, my young friends. The folly of the Stormbreakers of the other six dimensions was that they were randomly spread about the earth. When the time came to engage Destroyer, they did not have the unity needed to face him."

As Mac listened to Michael, he felt a knot growing in his stomach. Michael was going to leave them. His cloak flowed back into a raincoat, and Glenn stared.

"I have been called to unite the Stormbreakers. It will not be easy to do."

"I must send a call through the mark that draws Stormbreakers from around the world to the location of the meeting, and it must be done in complete secrecy.

"Once the meeting is complete, we will have a plan in place of what to do when the storm comes."

As the thunder boomed overhead and rain pounded off of his raincoat, Mac tried to envision what a storm of evil would be like. He guessed it would be worse than anything he could imagine.

"What are we supposed to do while you're gone?" Glenn asked.

A gleam appeared in Michael's eye.

"I have investigated companies throughout the city and believe I have found the one."

"The one?" Glenn asked.

"The corporation Destroyer uses as a front to gather together his armies," Michael firmly replied. "Now that I am leaving, I will need someone to research deeper into the company."

He turned his eyes to Mac.

"By deeper, I mean higher up. Our goal is to unmask the man or woman in charge of Leviathan. If we do this, I believe we will unmask Destroyer."

Glenn smiled. "That will be fun." Michael's expression did not change as Glenn lauded his connections and qualifications that would help with the assignment.

"We'll find out who the head honcho is but, by the time you get back, you won't need this army. We will have already defeated him."

Michael glided closer toward them, invading their space. Mac could almost feel the intensity of the Stormbreaker's focus.

"You will not confront Destroyer! To confront Destroyer now would be like trying to stop a tidal wave with a single outstretched hand." Michael's voice grew harder. "You will wait until the Stormbreakers are united. It is only then that we will have a chance of stopping him."

Glenn glanced at Mac and quickly responded.

"But if I have received my Covering, surely Mac and I … you know … coming from both sides and all, might surprise Destroyer."

Michael was cold steel.

"If you confront Destroyer now, you will both die and"—he glanced at Mac—"that would turn the tide of history in Destroyer's favor."

Mac looked at Michael's face. Rain ran from the top of his hood, driven away from his face by the convenient folds of his cloak. Mac thought he could see worry in his eyes. Anything that would cause Michael to worry terrified him. He would heed the warning from the ancient warrior. Despite the power he felt coursing through him, he was pretty sure if he tried to defeat Destroyer he would be squashed like a bug.

"Where do we begin?" he asked.

Michael's expression lifted at the mood shift in the conversation. Curiosity was much safer than arrogance. He stepped back to give the two their space.

"There is one who knows a lot about Leviathan. The Stormbreaker lives in the inner city and will be difficult to find, so just wander the streets and I'm sure they will find you. Once your paths have crossed, begin to conduct research. When I return, I hope you will have the identity of Destroyer, and I will have an army of Stormbreakers. At that time, with the help of Creator, we will defeat the creature once and for all."

There was fire behind Michael's eyes. He placed a hand on each of their shoulders.

"Remember this… If all seems lost, return to this park."

His eyes darted to Mac's wrists and back.

"The answers you will be seeking will begin here."

"What do you mean 'if all seems lost'?" Glenn asked.

"You will understand when and if the time comes."

Michael could see that Glenn was not happy with that answer, but he pushed it no further. He turned to Mac.

"Mackinsi Wrighton, I know what you have accomplished and am proud of your survival, but you should know that hunters never give up. Be very aware of your surroundings."

"I will," Mackinsi replied. As he answered, he felt the icy grip of fear he had felt earlier well up inside him once again. Looking up from the base of the paint-smeared statue, he started to thank Michael, but he had already disappeared into the night to fight the coming storm.

Chapter 8: Unexpected Meeting

The morning air held a crisp, cool bite as Mac and Glenn stepped out of the cab and into the streets of Brooklyn. Mac felt warmth grow inside him.

"I think I can feel the presence of the other Stormbreaker."

Glenn did not look up. He was staring at the sidewalk.

"Maybe you can, and maybe you can't," he muttered. "I won't know until I get the Covering." He looked down at Mackinsi's glowing wrists. His eyes seemed stagnant and distant. "If it ever comes."

"Don't talk like that," Mac replied. "Michael said it would come, and it will. You just have to be patient."

Glenn finally glanced up into the crowds passing by.

"Patience has never been one of my virtues." He glanced at Mac. "Do you ever get the feeling the cards are all falling your way?"

Mac thought about his family and the years he endured teasing.

"I don't think so, Glenn. I think life is like a roller coaster. Sometimes you are at the bottom but you are always on your way up."

"I feel like I'm stuck at the bottom."

Glenn's focus shifted to the passing cars.

"I know that I have potential to be one of the greatest Stormbreakers of all time. I can feel it, but the Covering will not come!"

The crowded sidewalk felt like an ocean of bodies as they weaved their way through them.

"Creator doesn't like me, but he seems to really like you." Glenn growled.

Mac was surprised by the edge in Glenn's voice. He could not choose when his Covering came any more than Glenn could. Michael had told them that the Covering was a gift from Creator but that it came when it chose to.

"Creator sends the Covering to the world, but he doesn't choose when it happens to us. That is something it does on its own," Mac said.

Glenn's voice rose. "Creator still favors you!"

"Creator favors us all!" Mac shot back.

It was then he noticed the difficulty Glenn was experiencing. Each individual that passed Glenn bumped into him or brushed against him. He was like a salmon trying to swim upstream. Ahead of Mac, the crowd parted smoothly. Their eyes drifted passed his cloak and kept moving. None of their eyes registered his presence, but they subconsciously avoided him. They were moving out of the way of an invisible man. He began to understand why Glenn was jealous. Glenn's whistle startled him.

"Whoa," Glenn said quietly.

Mac saw her immediately. Walking gracefully through the crowd was one of the most striking women he had ever seen. The curves of her slim figure were accentuated by the short, red, form-fitting dress she was wearing. Her blonde hair swayed back and forth, just below her shoulders. Her blue eyes met his and then quickly looked away.

Mac felt the warmth grow inside his stomach. Had she seen him? How was that possible?

As she passed him, she caught his eyes again, and the faint curve of a smile painted her delicate lips.

Glenn turned, following her with the flow of the crowd.

"Hey there!" Glenn called after her.

She didn't slow as she turned down an alleyway. Glenn turned and winked at Mac and then disappeared after her.

The warm feeling remained, and Mac smiled in understanding. Turning smoothly, he glided into the alleyway. If his suspicions were correct, Glenn was not going anywhere.

"Mac!"

Glenn's voice was high and tight. Mac stifled a laugh. He had been correct.

Glenn's back was pressed against the grimy brick wall and his eyes were wide. A blade was pressed against his neck, and a dagger was under the inseam of his pants. The blade against his neck was attached to the end of a polished oak staff. The elf-like woman in red held the weapons.

Her blue eyes glittered as she smiled.

"It seems I was being followed."

Glenn started to explain but stopped as her blade pressed closer.

"It appears so." Mac returned her smile.

Glenn abandoned caution and broke in. "Mac! Do something! She is going to kill me!"

"Are you?" Mac asked.

The woman's laugh was like a soft wind chime: gentle and soothing. Even Glenn's shoulders relaxed a little.

"I had thought about it," she said frankly. "Obviously, he was imagining me naked ... but perhaps I should feel flattered?"

The sarcasm was evident in her tone and she turned her gaze back to Glenn. Her blade moved away from his neck and he swallowed, his Adam's apple finally free once again.

"Actually," she continued, "I had thought of another solution to his problem."

The blade between his legs lifted, and Glenn rose to his tiptoes.

"But then I saw this." With a flash, the dagger was away, and her pale-skinned hand was holding Glenn's right wrist. His cross mark flickered green. Stepping back, she addressed both of them.

"Why are you here?" she asked.

The impending threat to his manhood gone, Glenn's courage returned.

"Why should we tell you anything after you treated us like that?"

In the blink of an eye, the woman's red dress shifted into a red cloak with its hood down. Her right wrist flashed green, and she smiled.

Glenn's sullen look returned as his right hand rubbed his throat slowly.

"My name is Anaiya Lynn." She turned to face Mac. "You must be Mackinsi Wrighton. Your reputation precedes you. The community of Stormbreakers has been stirring recently about your victory over one of the hunters. The feat is not accomplished often. Stormbreakers usually meet their match when facing them."

Glenn stared daggers at Mackinsi.

Anaiya continued. "I have encountered a hunter twice in my life. Both times I barely triumphed, and that was only due to Michael's teachings. He trained me for 20 years after my Covering, which came when I turned 23."

Mackinsi noted her weapons, as they had remained visible. She had been given the bladed staff at her Covering. Its white shaft looked thin and fragile. Anaiya seemed to read his mind.

"The staff is blessed by Creator. By itself, it could break stone. Combined with its curved blade, it is a force to be reckoned with." Her gaze flickered down to Mac's wrists and her eyes filled with tears. "So, it is you... I have dreamed of you many times."

Mackinsi's face flushed deep red.

"And what of me, woman?" Glenn growled. "Have you not heard of Glenn Cross?"

Anaiya's laugh tore the intensity from Glenn's statement, breaking the mood.

"I just have," she said and chuckled. "Thank you for introducing him to me, though you should inform him to have more respect when speaking to his elders."

She tried to suppress her smile. Sometimes the arrogance of young Stormbreakers astounded her. It was true; they were powerful Stormbreakers, but true skill came from experience … usually. She glanced again at Mackinsi. Never before had one so young defeated a hunter.

Mac's curiosity got the best of him. "So, how old are you?"

Anaiya smiled playfully. "Now, Mac, you should know a lady does not discuss her age." Then, leaning close, she stated in a confidential tone, "But, if you must know, yesterday was my hundredth birthday. That was a lot of candles…" She laughed as Mac gawked.

Glenn grumbled under his breath as they walked out from the alley. Once again he felt alone as the crowds ran into him but melted around his two companions. Why was Creator delaying his Covering? He wanted the power now.

Anaiya dipped and swayed gracefully as she led the way down the crowded sidewalk.

Mac looked down to his double-marked wrists. They flickered back at him with unspoken promise.

***

Anaiya's home was two stories tall and was sandwiched between several other houses of similar design.

The constant thrum of the cars was somewhat muffled when she closed the front door, and Mac immediately felt at home.

The furniture was stained oak and appeared warm and inviting under the room's soft lighting. Impressionist paintings hung about the room. One in particular caught Mac's attention. A brilliant sunrise exploded over a green meadow surrounded by evergreens.

"This is beautiful," he said in wonder.

"Thank you, Mackinsi," Anaiya said, her cloak now a shimmering evening gown. "I painted it five years ago after a visit to the Sierra Nevada."

She turned to Glenn.

"May I take your jacket?"

He handed it to her.

Mac noticed his jaw was hanging open and quickly closed it.

"You painted this?"

Anaiya laughed. "Of course I did. I love to paint."

Mac realized he liked her smile.

Ten minutes later they were situated on the beautiful furniture in front a friendly fire.

"The two of you have come at an opportune time," Anaiya began.

Glenn interrupted. "Before you tell us what we are supposed to do, how about you tell us a little about yourself? Why should we trust you?"

Mac's stared hard at him.

"A fair question." Anaiya seemed to have maintained her calm, but her evening gown again became a cloak.

"I was born in California," she began, "in the mountains of the Sierra Nevada. I grew up in the forest all of my young life. I guess you could say I was a mountain girl."

Mac suddenly understood why she could paint nature with such perfection and delicacy. It was her world.

"I lived in the mountains until I was 18 then headed here, to New York, for college."

Mac noticed Anaiya's gaze shift from them to the soft-carpeted floor. The fire flickered and danced in her eyes.

"I returned home after graduation to visit my mother and father."

Her voice grew quieter. "One day, when I returned from the grocery store, I found our front door wide open. Three men were inside in black masks."

Her voice began to waver again. The wall had broken.

"As I walked through the door, I watched one of the men shoot my father in the face and turn the gun on my mother."

A single tear fell from Anaiya's eye to be enveloped by the brown carpet.

"That was when the Covering came. It was unlike any experience I have ever had. I felt as if all the light on Earth was flowing into me. It was then I received my staff. The power we receive is breathtaking but it does not rewind time. I still lost my parents."

She looked up quickly, startled by her own self-disclosure. Her cloak smoothly flowed back into an evening gown.

Glenn had been listening intently. The Covering, and the power it would bring him, was something he longed for above all else. As he listened to Anaiya's tale, he found he was enjoying himself.

"Enough about me." Anaiya forced a laugh. "Let's talk about why we should be concerned about Leviathan."

An hour passed quickly for the three Stormbreakers as Anaiya recapped the information Michael had already touched upon. At the end of the hour, the fire had burned down and the room had grown darker. Mac swirled the ice in a glass of water Anaiya had given him. The condensation felt cool against his hand.

Leviathan had its claws in everything. Each involvement was just below the public's view. Some relationships seemed above board but the amount of power they brought was undeniable.

Anaiya's blue eyes sparkled in the dim light as she continued.

"I have been hard at work lately and have made several connections within Leviathan." Her faint smile hinted at what Mac was thinking. He would bet money her connections were male. Her staff was not her only weapon.

She paused to light several lamps. The room grew brighter as did Mac's spirit as Anaiya unfurled her plan.

***

Several days passed before Anaiya's plan could come to fruition. She was the highlight of many hours for Mac but for Glenn the waiting seemed to bring only gloom. His attitude grew darker each day he awoke without the Covering. Mac tried to approach him several times to talk about it but was always turned away with insults or shouts. It took effort not to resent his former friend.

With Mac's Covering came an increased maturity. He held deep conversations with Anaiya about life and love. He came to understand that wisdom had come with the physical changes of the Covering.

Each time Glenn exploded, Mac wished the Covering would come quickly for his troubled friend. Glenn desperately needed an infusion of wisdom.

Mac heard the front door slam as Glenn stormed into the night. Anaiya entered the room and sighed, settling onto the couch next to him and leaning her head on his shoulder. "Thank you."

Butterflies danced in Mac's stomach. "For what?"

"For being you." Anaiya smiled up at him.

Mac smiled. "I try… I try."

Anaiya's voice grew serious. "I just don't know if he is ready … he is so angry."

Mac sighed. "I know."

They enjoyed each other's company in silence, both thinking about the following day. It was the moment of truth … the day Leviathan was throwing its charity ball. Anaiya saw Glenn return just before daybreak. He was smiling.

Chapter 9: The Dark Covering

Morning came without the sun. Grey clouds roamed the sky over Brooklyn, dropping water onto the streets like a leaky shower.

Mac awoke at 7 AM, joining Glenn and Anaiya in preparations for the day to come.

Anaiya's connections had given her three tickets to Leviathan's charity ball. It would begin at 8 PM and would run through the night.

She had explained their purpose over the last several days. Michael suspected Destroyer was dwelling inside a person, the man behind Leviathan. Sources told her he was going to make an appearance and the ball would provide an opportunity to get a look at him. She had labeled him the *Man of Power*.

"Good morning," Anaiya said cheerfully as Mac and Glenn entered the dining room.

"Eggs and pancakes to prepare you for the day."

Even Glenn smiled at Anaiya's announcement.

Breakfast went smoothly and the remainder of the day was spent planning for the covert operation. When evening rolled around, the three Stormbreakers were brimming with excitement. With the knowledge of the Man of Power's identity, the Gathering army of Stormbreakers would have a focused target at which to strike. This was Michael's plan to stop the coming storm.

With a flick of her wrist, Anaiya slid back a closet door, revealing a rack of tuxedos. With a glance at Glenn, she pulled a tuxedo from the closet. 44 long. He left without a word to put it on, knowing it was exactly his size.

"So, Mackinsi—" Anaiya waited expectantly "—where's your tuxedo?"

Mac smiled, his cloak flowing into a perfectly fitting tuxedo. He smiled confidently at Anaiya and was surprised at her laughter. Her blonde hair swayed as she held her stomach.

"Rookie," she mumbled through laughs.

Mac looked down and realized the source of her laughter. He had transformed his cloak into a well-fitting tuxedo but it was still forest green.

"Don't you know how to change the color of your clothing?" Anaiya asked, controlling her laughter.

"No," Mac answered, smiling. "I thought this was just the color of cloak Creator gave me."

"Oh, the cloak is forest green," Anaiya assured him. "A Stormbreaker's cloak remains its original color until it is shifted into clothing. Once there, all it takes is concentration."

With a smile, her evening gown became a dazzling blue, matching her sparkling eyes.

Mac put the image of a black tuxedo into his mind then looked down. He was wearing a perfectly fitted black tux. He caught Anaiya's approving nod as Glenn walked into the room. He looked like he had not slept well.

It had indeed been a long night for Glenn. For a while, he had noticed himself slipping toward the edge. What it was the edge of he couldn't say, but he knew that, if he went over, there was no coming back.

He knew it was not Mac's fault the Covering had not come to him yet but he needed to blame someone, and Mac was a convenient target. He felt rage bubbling inside him once again and tried unsuccessfully to push it back down.

"Stop smiling at me!" he snapped at Mac.

He could see hurt in Mac's eyes and his mind waged war with his conscience.

Anaiya took up Mac's faded smile.

"You look amazing, Glenn! You should look in the mirro—"

"Shut up!" Glenn barked then turned his eyes to the floor. "You're nothing but Michael's whore anyway."

He expected a reaction. Surely Mac would stand up for Anaiya. He knew they had become friends. Yet, when he looked up, all he saw was pity in their eyes. With a growl, he stormed out of the door.

Anaiya gave Mac a sad smile and followed Glenn out. Mac fought the rage growing inside him. How dare Glenn insult Anaiya!

She had accepted him and had treated him with kindness! Mac noticed he was feeling the smoldering beginnings of rage. He could not harbor hate; Anaiya had showed him that. With a sigh, he slowly let the anger go. A burden lifted from his shoulders, and he felt light again. Smiling, Mac closed the front door behind him.

Outside, a taxi arrived, and the three well-dressed people ducked inside. Glenn was still livid. Maybe he could not blame Mac, but Creator could not escape the blame. *The Covering will not come,* he thought to himself. Creator favored Mac. Glenn felt the heat swirling around his heart. Why should he serve Creator when Creator would not serve him? He balanced, boiling upon the razor edge.

As the taxi pulled to a stop, Mac inhaled loudly. The mansion they were parked in front of loomed tall, glittering with gold-lined pillars and marble walls.

"Are you sure this is the place?" he asked Anaiya.

"Yep, this is the one," she answered.

Anaiya paid their fare, and the three accompanied one another through the twelve-foot-tall entryway doors. Each had their assignment.

They were to socialize, fit in and work their way into enough confidences to discover the identity of the Man of Power. Once they had learned this, they were to make a graceful exit and rendezvous at Anaiya's house.

Glenn smiled immediately as he entered the immense ballroom. His eyes took in the crystal chandelier hanging above the large dance floor. Everywhere on the dance floor couples waltzed. Against the wall, a line of women waited, swaying to the music and hoping someone would ask them to dance. His expert eye could also see that some of them wanted to be asked to do more than dance and he was just the man for the job.

***

The music floated through the room as Mac stood at the refreshment table. He sipped his water as he watched Anaiya. She twirled and dipped gracefully to the music.

Her dress shimmered under the soft lights. She was dancing with her tenth partner. The men could not get enough of her. Mac saw her mouth moving as she talked to each partner throughout the dance. She was a pro. The men would never suspect her intentions. All that was on their minds was the beautiful woman in their arms.

I better get back to work, Mac thought to himself.

He turned to the table where several men and women were busy drinking yet another glass of champagne. They had already emptied one too many and Mac laughed along with them, prodding them gently with questions, leading them subtly into giving him the answers he desired.

***

Anaiya watched Mac as she spun around the dance floor. She hoped he was getting some answers. Despite her attempts, she was not getting far. She honestly believed the men she had danced with did not know the name of the person behind Leviathan.

Knowing this, she had begun to turn her questions in a different direction. She was now dancing with John Branch, who sat on Leviathan's board of directors.

"You dance beautifully, Mr. Branch," Anaiya said quietly as the large man spun her around the dance floor.

Branch smiled at her.

"Please, call me John."

They completed another three step of the waltz and he continued.

"What should I call you?"

"Please, John, call me Anaiya," she answered softly.

She watched his eyes drift down past her chin. After several more revolutions, she knew the time was right to begin her work.

***

Mac had learned quite a bit from his new friends. He made his way through the crowd surrounding the refreshment table and stopped at the open bar. He had discovered the older woman swirling her drink thoughtfully was named Judith Penny.

He had also learned that she was on the board of directors of Leviathan and, at the moment, she was unhappy.

"May I sit here?" he asked.

Judith glanced up absently.

"Oh, sure."

Her tone was distracted and heavy. Her grey hair was pulled into a bun, and her smile lines showed the cloud of gloom floating around her was not an everyday occurrence.

"My name is Mackinsi Wrighton."

***

Glenn had been busy as well. Several young women's phone numbers were in his pocket, and they had bluntly told him what he could do with them when he called. He smiled to himself. Let Mac and Anaiya do the work tonight; he would have the fun.

A dark-haired, slender brunette stood against the wall at the end of the line of wallflowers. He had noticed her refuse several dance requests, all the while looking into his eyes.

Her black dress was thin, almost transparent and it clung to her body, showing every curve. Her green eyes sparkled with a playfulness that Glenn understood well. He ignored the other wallflowers and approached her.

"Hello, I'm—" Glenn began, but the girl quickly cut him off.

"Glenn Cross," she finished. "I have friends at Lathim High. Your reputation precedes you."

She took his hands in hers and slid them around her waist, inching them downward. Glenn could feel her skin through her dress. She was smooth and firm with not a hint of undergarments. Glenn smiled. The night was going perfectly.

The girl pulled him towards her until their bodies were pressed together.

"My name is Melanie," she whispered into his ear. "Do you want to go upstairs with me?"

Glenn could feel her breasts pressing into his chest.

"Lead the way."

***

Mac was just saying his goodbyes to Judith when he saw Glenn ascend the curving stairway with a dark-haired woman. From their body language, Mac did not have to guess the couple's intentions. He found Anaiya on the dance floor and quickly cut in.

After several turns, Anaiya smiled. "Who taught you to dance?"

Her question caught him off guard. In his haste, he had not even realized he was dancing.

"No one … this is my first time." He reddened slightly under Anaiya's gaze. His mind recovered and he jumped immediately to the point. "I think we have a problem. I just saw Glenn go upstairs with a woman."

Anaiya finished his thought. "Not to talk, I suppose."

Mac nodded in agreement.

"Then we do have a problem," she whispered.

Another spin brought them to the staircase Glenn had disappeared up.

"The Man of Power is definitely here and that means Destroyer is as well," Anaiya said quietly, pulling Mac off of the dance floor. "It's time to change clothes."

With a quick glance around to make sure no one was staring at them, she allowed her blue dress to shift into her deep red cloak.

Mac quickly followed suit and sighed at the comfortable brush of his forest green cloak against his arms.

"How many rooms are upstairs?" he asked.

"This is a strange house, Mackinsi." Anaiya answered quickly, glancing up the stairs. "There are four stories to it with over 100 rooms. Glenn could be in any of them."

Mac looked at the stairway with resignation.

"Well, let's go find him before he gets himself and us into trouble," he said.

No one in the ballroom even glanced toward the stairs as two cloaked figures disappeared upward into the shadows.

"Just a little farther," Melanie crooned, pulling Glenn by the hand. "We'll have the master bedroom all to ourselves."

Glenn smiled at her sparkling green eyes. He was going to enjoy himself tonight, he just wished they would hurry up and get to the room she was taking him to. They had turned down too many hallways and ascended three staircases. He was sure he could not find his way back alone. He pulled Melanie back against his body, sliding his hand into the top of her dress. Her skin was so soft. He felt her shiver under his touch.

"Soon, baby." She giggled, pulling away and leading him onward.

He sighed and followed her.

He imagined Mac downstairs, still talking to the old hag at the bar. The fool just didn't know how to have a good time. Life was all about living for the moment. If you paused too long to reflect on the morality of your actions, amazing opportunities passed you by.

Glenn thought about his high school life. He had lived his philosophy to perfection, and it had taken him places. He had become one of the most popular people in school, the captain of the football team, and a legend with the ladies. His mind wandered to one in particular.

She had been so nervous. She told him that it was her first time. How he had relished watching her face as he took her innocence. He tried to remember her name, but could not seem to bring it to mind.

He remembered ignoring her through the next week at school. He remembered her tears. *Oh well*, he thought to himself, *she doesn't matter anyway*. Quickly dismissing the unwelcome memory from his mind, Glenn saw that they had stopped in front of a large double-door at the end of a long hallway.

Melanie opened the door and simultaneously slipped the spaghetti straps of her black dress off of her shoulders. The thin material dropped lightly to the red-carpeted hallway. Glenn stared at her naked body, and Melanie, beckoning to the open door, quietly whispered, "After you."

***

Mac felt it before he saw it. He couldn't explain how, but he knew from the way the hairs on the back of his neck stood up that something very evil was near.

He and Anaiya had quickly and methodically searched the second floor of the immense mansion and had almost finished searching the third. The stairway leading to the fourth floor was faintly visible at the end of the long, candle-lit hallway he and Anaiya were standing in. They just had to reach it.

The unexplainable sensation of evil grew with each passing step forward. Mac apprehensively looked behind him only to find empty air. Anaiya sensed his wariness and joined him in readying her weapon.

In the shadows, bulbous red eyes watched the two Stormbreakers hungrily.

Their spirits are strong, the Reap thought, a fanged grin spreading across its triangular face. It watched the man turn and stare right at it then look way. The Reap laughed within itself. It wore darkness like a cloak. The man had made the mistake of many dead victims and assumed it was just a shadow.

The Reap saw the Dimlocks attacking at the same time the humans did.

Oh well, it thought. *Let the petty creatures have their fun.* When they were done, regardless of the outcome, the Reap would have its meal.

"Dimlocks!" Anaiya shouted, moving against the left wall of the hallway. Together, the Stormbreaker's wrists glowed brightly as time slowed to a stop.

Mac moved against the right wall, quickly glancing behind him once more, unable to shake the feeling they were being watched. The horde of Dimlocks fell upon them like a thunderstorm, their twisted, rusting blades hacking and slashing. Anaiya had planned for this and Mac remembered the plan well. Slowly, he and Anaiya began to circle in opposite directions, pinning the Dimlocks between them then pressing inward.

A Dimlock holding a chipped broadsword rushed at Mac, trying to escape the trap the Stormbreakers were laying. Its blade fell heavily against Mac's katana. The force of the blow from the broadsword blew Mac backward but he was able to remain standing.

The Dimlock leapt at him with a squeal of glee, dropping the same strike at his head, but Mac was a Stormbreaker, and he didn't make the same mistake twice. As the blow fell, he pivoted gracefully to the right, letting the momentum of the strike carry the corpse-like creature's blade down past his left shoulder. The surprised Dimlock went with it, its balance destroyed. Suddenly, it saw the world spinning and, before the world went black, the Dimlock saw its headless body fall to the ground, still clutching its useless weapon.

Anaiya's staff moved as if guided by a supernatural precognition. The Dimlocks' strikes rained down upon her but her staff met every one. Her long blade at the end of the staff danced and darted. It was already awash in black, tar-like blood.

She spun to her left, her blade catching an ambushing Dimlock through the throat. Droplets of black splattered the pale skin of her face but her blue eyes showed no hesitation. She knew the Man of Power would have known the horde of Dimlocks could not defeat them. She struggled to come up with the reason they were sent.

She buried her blade into the chest of another attacker and launched it off its impalement with a right front thrust kick.

Were they a distraction, sent only to stall them, or were they something more? The thought swirled through the back of her mind and she looked at Mac. His sword skills were impressive. She marveled that they had come naturally with no formal training. Her blue eyes moved away from him to the shadows behind him, and her questions found an answer. One of the shadows was too dark.

"Mackinsi!"

She pushed her way through the Dimlocks as she attempted to warn Mac. Her eyes were wide in the darkness.

"There's a fiend behind you!"

Mac leapt to the left without turning and rolled to his feet. A slimy, black tongue shot out from a writhing cloud of darkness and hit the Dimlock in front of where Mac had been. The Dimlock was instantly surrounded in a pulsating, purple glow and lifted high into the air.

It flailed as what color it had faded away with its scream. The purple glow disappeared and the dead husk of the Dimlock thudded heavily to the floor. The Reap howled in rage at missing its intended target. It spun toward Mac, its tongue rocketing out. Mac's reaction saved him as he bent backward, arching his back and reaching for the ground. The tongue smashed a hole in the wall and was quickly retracted. Anaiya cut down the last Dimlock, and she and Mac turned to face the fiend. Three arrows flew swiftly from Mac's bow, all finding the center of the darkness. To his dismay, they continued out the back of the shadow, imbedding into the wall. The Reap laughed a deep, rumbling laugh and advanced toward them slowly.

"What is it?" Mac cried out, dodging yet another thrust of its purplish tongue.

"It's a Reap," Anaiya answered solemnly. "While it is covered in shadow no weapon can harm it."

Mac sensed fear in her voice.

"There's more to this, isn't there?"

"Yes," Anaiya shouted. "Every Stormbreaker who has ever faced a Reap has died."

Mac felt the chill that accompanied her statement seep into his bones.

"Come to me." The Reap's rasping voice resonated through the room.

Mac felt a tug inside him to do just that.

"No!" he yelled, and saw Anaiya fighting the same inward battle.

Anaiya felt the Reap's powerful words pulling at her mind.

"No," she mumbled, but took a step forward before she could stop herself.

As she stumbled over one of the fallen Dimlock's corpses, the Reap's slimy tongue shot out and wrapped around her.

Mac exploded into action before his mind could catch up. Before the purplish glow could appear around Anaiya, his katana had severed the deadly tongue. The shriek of the powerful monster echoed down the halls, but the people downstairs would never hear it because, for the warriors, time was standing still.

Anaiya felt relief rush through her as she dropped to the ground, tearing the severed tongue off of her. What remained of the Reap's tongue shot back into the dark shadow where it was safe.

Mac felt his wrists pulsing with green fire. They would not die by this fiend! *I will not let it kill Anaiya!* he thought savagely. With a cry, he hurled himself into the darkness surrounding the fiend and disappeared from view.

Anaiya screamed as she watched him leap into the black shadow of the Reap. Torrents of emotion exploded inside of her, but she could not pinpoint a single one. She did notice her eyes had filled with tears.

The shadow lurched about the hall, slamming into walls. Sounds of the battle rang out from inside the darkness, and the thunderous cries of the fiend threatened to deafen Anaiya. All she could do was wait and hope.

Darkness swirled around Mac. The green beacons on his wrists were the only light he could see except for the Reap's red eyes. Claws met steel as the two waged war in complete darkness.

Mac had never fought without sight before, but it felt natural to him. His razor sharp, red blade rose to meet each strike the Reap threw at him. His sword moved swiftly and surely. The movement of his arms was visible only by the trails of green they left in their wake. Spinning to the left, he brought his blade up, slicing off another section of the fiend's tongue. In light, he was a force to be reckoned with, but in darkness, Mac discovered he was a master.

The Reap's bulging eyes widened in disbelief, their red glow growing in intensity as they peered through the darkness. It could clearly see the Stormbreaker, but it could not seem to touch him. The man moved as easily as if he was in the light of day. The Reap saw the green glow from both wrists and trembled. The double marked… This had not been a part of the bargain. The fiend sought one blow, one fatal blow that would end it all. After it had defeated this one, it would feast on the woman.

Mac was startled by the thoughts that pressed into his mind but immediately knew the source. "You are fighting a hopeless battle." The words slithered through his mind. "Give yourself to me."

Mac felt the tug of compliance weighing on his heart, and this only made his wrists burn brighter. In the glow of the green, he suddenly could see the beast.

The fiend recoiled at the sudden light. Without its darkness, it was vulnerable. It vainly tried to summon the darkness back to it but instead found the human smiling at it, his eyes blazing with ferocity. "Afraid of a little light?" In desperate terror, the Reap shot what was left of its tongue toward the human's head.

In the green glow of his markings, Mac had no trouble avoiding the tongue. The Reap felt the human grab its extended tongue and pull with all his might. Despite its 300 pound body, it was pulled from its clawed feet. As it fell toward steel death, all the Reap could see were the blazing double crosses.

Anaiya felt her heart leap as the darkness dissipated, leaving Mac standing over his fallen enemy. The Reap's tongue twitched once then was still. Its body instantly decomposed into fetid ooze then vanished altogether in a cloud of dark fumes.

Before she could stop herself, Anaiya was wrapped in Mac's arms in a tight embrace. Her tears fell wetly onto his forest green cloak. Mac returned the hug warmly. They had faced death many times in the long hallway and somehow they were still breathing. It was okay to take a moment.

***

As he stepped through the doors, Glenn's eyes became accustomed to the low level of light. He was surprised when he saw another person in the room.

"What's going on?" he asked the naked girl evenly.

Melanie only smiled and waltzed over to lounge on the king sized bed fit into the corner of the large room. Three long, vertical windows showed a view of the city. Large, red drapes hung across the window, suspended by lengths of fine, white rope. The room was fit for a king. Glenn felt the hairs on his neck rise as he glared at the stranger.

"Maybe I can answer your question," the stranger said as he stepped out of the shadows.

Glenn was immediately struck by the immense power surrounding the man.

"Who are you?" he stammered.

"What's in a name?" the stranger replied smoothly. "My name is not what matters, Glenn Cross. What truly matters is what I can do for you."

"You're the man behind Leviathan," Glenn whispered then jumped at the fact that he had spoken aloud.

The Man of Power eyed Glenn thoughtfully.

"I see you have the mark of a Stormbreaker."

Glenn tensed, ready to be struck down. He let his wrist relax from the position he had been keeping it in to hide his mark. He opened his mouth, but no words came out.

"Don't worry, my young friend." The Man of Power strode suddenly forward, placing a hand on Glenn's shoulder. "I am not here to hurt you. I am here to help you."

Glenn looked at Melanie, hoping for some answers, but the woman simply sat on the edge of the bed, smiling.

The Man of Power's voice brought his mind back to the gravity of the situation. "I see you have not yet received the Covering."

Glenn felt humiliation creeping into his cheeks.

"It is nothing to be ashamed of," the Man of Power quickly added. "It is not your fault that it has not come."

Glenn looked up hopefully.

"Creator has never and will never favor you. He will never trust you with *his* Covering. On the other hand, I offer a Covering of my own."

Glenn glanced up warily. Who was this man to offer a gift of the same magnitude as Creator's? Did he think he was as powerful as Creator himself? Despite his doubts, Glenn continued to listen. If, for some reason, the man's words were true, he did not want to offend him.

"You do not believe I have the power." The man laughed as Glenn stammered and stuttered. "Watch and believe."

Melanie whimpered and pushed back against the pillows as the man's voice grew into a deep growl. The candles in the room roared into columns of flame. Shadows pooled on the ground all around the man.

They slowly began to melt upward and form shapes. The temperature of the room rose rapidly as the candle infernos did their work. The melting shadows continued to take shape, and Glenn finally saw them for what they were… Dimlocks.

Glenn was torn in that instant, in that moment when Destroyer rose halfway out of the Man of Power, laughing in deep growls and unfurling his black wings. He could run and hope for Creator's blessing or he could remain and surely receive the gift of the Covering. The power is what he longed for, and that is why he remained, with knees trembling, to hear Destroyer out.

"I am Destroyer, conqueror of dimensions!" the enormous beast bellowed.

Its black wings took up the entire width of the room. Its head was like a dragon's, as long as Glenn was tall. The sight of Destroyer was impressive to say the least. Both the Man of Power's and the creature's mouths moved in unison:

"Do you believe I have the power now?"

Glenn nodded in terror and the monster continued.

"I offer you the world!" Destroyer cried. "You will sit at my right hand to rule the nations. Your life will be eternal and your pleasures endless."

Glenn noticed Melanie was passionately kissing his neck and exploring his body with her hands. How long had she been there, he wondered. A surge of excitement worked its way through the fear inside of Glenn. The fantasies Destroyer's words brought into his mind were more than he had ever imagined, but he had grown up in New York City. Struggling against the fear of death and pleasure from Melanie, he asked the deciding question…

"What's the catch?"

After hearing Destroyer tell him what he must do, Glenn nodded and Destroyer's voice rang out.

"Come!"

With the word, Destroyer returned fully to union with the Man of Power, and he stepped into the darkness, leaving Glenn to wonder about the growing clouds. When they had arrived at the mansion there had not been a cloud in the sky.

***

Mac and Anaiya had ascended the stairs to the fourth floor when they heard someone or something shout a command. Pinpointing the possible source of the cry, the two raced down the intersecting corridors. They didn't have much time.

***

Glenn watched fire dart around the storm clouds. He had never known lightning could appear as fire. A heavy wind pounded into the window, threatening to shatter it at any moment. Then the moment came. With a crash, the windows exploded into the room. The gale of wind poured in and the fire came behind it. Fire and darkness poured into Glenn's mouth and all around him.

***

The Stormbreakers rushed to the door at the end of the long hall. Glass had shattered inside.

***

Glenn was immersed in darkness. No, he was the darkness. He felt the brush of cloth against his arms and grinned. A bolt of flame fell from the clouds and exploded into his chest. He felt searing pain then knew no more.

***

Somewhere far away, Glenn awoke, or seemed to wake. He was on the desert floor in a barren wasteland. Miles and miles of desert stretched in every direction, yet he felt at peace. Despite the location, he felt no sun upon his neck. Looking up, he noticed the clouds were swirling by. The heatless sun dropped swiftly behind the mountains then immediately rose again in the east. Despite the miracle, it felt natural to him. Perhaps he was dreaming. Something stirred in the sand before him, and he jumped backward in surprise. He watched in horror as what could have been his identical twin rose before him. His alter ego wore a black cloak and held a wickedly crafted scimitar.

Glenn looked down to find he was naked and unarmed. With a thought, a brilliant blue cloak appeared upon him with matching tunic and pants; a silver lined scimitar glittered in his hand.

"Who are you?" he asked of the mirror image.

"One of us will be you when this is over," the image replied wickedly. "But you are at a disadvantage. I have been winning this battle for months."

"Do we have to fight?" Glenn asked.

"You serve Creator in your heart," the image replied, beginning to circle Glenn. "I serve Destroyer and will someday rise even above his power. We cannot both exist together. One of us must die!"

With a cry, the doppelganger's scimitar cut toward Glenn. He rose to meet it, and their cloaks of blue and black swirled in the dance of battle upon the sand. Each gained advantage and lost it again as the sun completed another revolution in the sky, dropping the desert into momentary night and then back into daylight. Twice more darkness fell as the two waged desperate war. Three times Glenn's blade almost found an opening against the dark other. Three times Glenn almost redeemed his soul. As the sun dropped the third time toward the horizon, both men saw their opening and swung hard. A single scream rippled through the desert that was Glenn's consciousness.

***

The candles still blazed as Glenn stood. His black cloak seemed to pull light into it. His half smile widened as he held the cruel black scimitar up to reflect the candlelight. His wrist shimmered green with his cross mark. His dark laugh startled even the Dimlocks behind him. Destroyer's word had held true. He had the power to give a Covering. Power surged through Glenn's veins, and he looked up expectantly as the door burst open.

The heat assaulted the cloaked Stormbreakers as they entered the room.

Mac saw Glenn and then the Dimlocks surrounding him. "Glenn!" Mac cried. "Behind you!"

His warning caused no movement in his friend. A moment later, Mac realized the truth.

"They're with you," he stated somberly.

Anaiya walked to stand next to him, her weapon now pointed at Glenn.

Glenn remained silent, grinning.

Mac saw Glenn's dark cloak and his weapon.

"He received the Covering."

"He has received a Dark Covering," Anaiya corrected.

"A Covering is a Covering." Glenn grinned coolly. "I have tasted the fires of the heavens and will someday rule them. You two can't stop me."

Anaiya stepped forward. "Because your Covering was brought on before its time, Creator's blessing is not with it. There is a difference. We can help you attain that blessing."

Glenn smirked. "Why do I need Creator's petty blessings when I can sit at the right hand of Destroyer and rule the world?"

Mac saw no light in Glenn's eyes, save the blazing orange of the fire.

"Glenn has lost his battle," he said quietly to Anaiya. "He is no longer, and never again will be, our friend."

Anaiya's shoulders sagged slightly at the truth of Mac's words. Despite his grating attitude, she had grown to care about Glenn's wellbeing. Now he was a rogue Stormbreaker and in the service of their enemy.

"Where do we go from here?" she quietly asked Glenn.

The black-cloaked Stormbreaker sneered at her sympathy and raised his scimitar.

"To the grave."

***

Three floors below the master's chamber, the dance was still going in full swing. The music droned on, and Judith continued to sit solemnly at the bar. It had been nice to talk to the young man earlier. He had been kind to her and listened to her worries. She wished more people were like him. She cocked her head to the side.

"What's wrong?" asked the bartender.

"Nothing," Judith said, staring back into her cup. "I just thought I heard something."

***

The master chamber was awash with the sound of clashing metal. Heat rippled in waves around the bodies of the combatants, fed by the blazing torches on the wall. Once again, Anaiya and Mac circled their opponents and closed in. Glenn stood in the center of a ring of Dimlocks, sneering at Mac and Anaiya. He feigned an impressed expression each time one of the creatures fell under one of the Stormbreaker's blades. Melanie laughed at the sight as she lounged on the bed. This would be a great show.

A Dimlock roared only inches way from Mac's face. Its hot, stinking breath hit Mac's nostrils like a truck, and his blade struck back with equal force, tearing the creature's face from its body. Mac's double-marked katana swirled through the Dimlock ranks, clearing a path toward Glenn. Mac could feel the power flowing from the dark Stormbreaker. Looking up, he saw Anaiya was doing even better than he was. In seconds, she would confront Glenn. Mac knew it would take him more time. He hoped Anaiya could face Glenn alone.

A female shaped Dimlock spat at Anaiya as they squared off. Its yellow eyes searched for an opening in her defenses. The blonde-haired human had not looked formidable when the battle had begun. The Dimlock leader had thought the fragile looking woman would fall immediately. It had underestimated her, to its demise.

Its snake-shaped blade barely intercepted Anaiya's staff before she brought it down heavily in a blow that would surely have split the Dimlock's skull.

The thin, white shaft of the Stormbreaker's bladed staff had been a surprise. Despite its appearance, the weapon had shattered several Dimlock blades.

The Dimlock leader saw Anaiya's thrust coming and moved left to avoid it, but Anaiya had expected this, and her thrust suddenly flicked to the right.

Anaiya shifted her weight into the attack and felt the blade cut through the Dimlock's ribs and find its heart. The Dimlock's eyes glazed over and it fell sideways. Anaiya turned swiftly to find herself facing Glenn Cross.

***

The sounds of battle rang out behind him as Glenn smiled darkly. He had hoped for this moment. Anaiya had denied his advances and humiliated him. She thought she was Creator's gift to the world. Glenn laughed under his breath. He knew better. Creator did not hold the reins of the universe. That power belonged to Destroyer.

With a perverted glee in his heart, Glenn stalked toward Anaiya.

His first barrage of attacks fell harmlessly against her staff as she struggled. For the time she had known Glenn, her mission had been to protect him. Despite his fall, he was still a fellow Stormbreaker. Mac had told her he was lost to them, but she was not so sure. Through her parries, she decided to try one more time.

"It's not too late, Glenn Cross," she said in between breaths. "If you just ask for forgiveness, Creator will take you back."

"It is I who will not take him back!" Glenn snarled, hacking at Anaiya with the razor edge of his scimitar. "He abandoned me, woman ... just like you!"

He spun with another flurry of deadly blows that Anaiya blocked just as quickly.

"I owe you nothing," he snarled.

Emotions bled through Anaiya's voice.

"Please, Glenn. Don't take this path."

Glenn greeted her words with laughter. "That decision has already been made!"

It was then that the battle truly began. In the moment when Anaiya realized the futility of her words, Glenn unleashed the full power of the Dark Covering. His black blade glowed with red fire as he relentlessly rained blows down upon Anaiya.

The sudden blaze of skill surprised her and set her off balance. She felt her staff knocked aside then saw the blade descending toward her. She saw the blazing fire of hate burning in Glenn's eyes then felt an inferno ignite within her. The world went black. She vaguely realized she was falling.

***

The Dimlocks had fallen in a steady line under Mac's blade but not fast enough. He was still battling three of the creatures when he saw Anaiya reach Glenn.

Hope leapt into his heart as he saw her holding her ground but, despite her prowess, he sensed she was holding back.

"Fight him!" he screamed. Mac knew Glenn would not give her a second chance.

He slew two more Dimlocks, moving closer to Anaiya. And then, despite the fact that it was already standing still, time seemed to move even slower.

Mac saw Glenn's blade ignite with flame and saw him throw Anaiya off balance.

"No, Glenn!" he screamed.

Mac shoved the Dimlock out of the way, taking a slash across his left arm from his stumbling opponent. He returned a fatal blow, but the Dimlock's blow slammed him against the wall, jarring his field of vision. As his vision cleared, the flickering orange light cast a grim scene.

Anaiya's mouth moved in silent attempts to breathe as she tried to pull Glenn's blade from her stomach. The flames licked hungrily at her hands. Glenn drove the blade deeper into her body, bringing him closer and allowing him to kiss her lips. The horror abated, and white flames glittered fiercely in Mac's eyes. He would kill Glenn Cross.

Glenn pulled his blade from Anaiya savagely and laughed as she staggered backwards. Then, like a puppet whose strings have been cut, Anaiya crumpled silently to the floor.

By the time Glenn looked up from her fallen form, Mac was upon him. His katana showed no mercy as it fell again and again toward Glenn's vital areas. The rogue Stormbreaker regained his composure quickly and met Mac's attacks with attacks of his own. Scimitar and katana shimmered in the low light as the two former friends gracefully moved to the rhythm of their deadly dance.

A sound caught Mac's attention over the din of the battle. It was a single gasping breath from behind him. *She's alive!* his mind screamed. The steel lifted from his mind, and his purpose shifted.

Like a tidal wave, the power rose inside of him, exploding through his technique. His attack rate doubled, overwhelming the black-cloaked Stormbreaker's flashing scimitar. Mac's strikes fell one on the tail of the other, keeping Glenn on the defensive and preparing him for what Mac had planned. Mac struck low, drawing Glenn's parry toward his ankles, and then launched his surprise attack. His left spinning hook kick slammed into Glenn's head, flipping him onto the ground. His sword fell several feet away from him and he lay motionless.

A screech echoed up the hallway outside the door. More Dimlocks were coming. Frantically, Mac looked around for a means of escape. The large window overlooked a four-story drop to the pavement below, and the only other exit was the doorway they had come through.

Mac saw Glenn's eyes flutter open as the first rotting creature rounded the doorframe. He was out of time. The sneer returned to Glenn's lips as he reached for his scimitar. The first Dimlock bolted toward Mac, a cruel dagger in its hand. An image of a thin, white rope flashed into Mac's mind. The curtains! His arrow caught the rushing Dimlock in the throat, launching it backwards into the others. With a leap, he caught the white rope and pulled it from the wall. The red curtains slid quickly downward to the floor.

The Dimlocks had recovered their balance and were up and pressing in again. Mac was grateful that they did not have any guns. Daggers from his boots dropped the two leading creatures with enough force to flip them onto their heads.

He noticed Glenn was staggering to his feet. He had to act now. In a movement as fluid as if it had been rehearsed hundreds of times, Mac tied the rope to the arrow, drew the heavy pull of his longbow, and fired the arrow through the broken window. He was thankful Creator had gifted him with the marvelous weapon when he saw the arrow drive halfway into his targeted telephone pole.

Tying the rope off, he scooped Anaiya's limp body into his arms and rushed toward the open window.

Glenn had regained his balance and bolted to intercept them. But the years of running from danger gave Mac the edge he needed and he reached the window first.

He threw his cloak over the rope, catching the other side and clenching it in his fist. The loop of his cloak slid smoothly as he launched himself and Anaiya out into the night. They slid down the rope toward the street below.

Glenn raised his cloak to follow but, to his surprise, the rope went slack before he could throw his cloak over it.

He looked out the window to see Mac land gracefully on the street below. The fool had cut the rope behind him and had swung onto the street. A growl escaped his lips. Glenn glared downward with a fevered gleam in his eyes. "You can't run forever!" He spun to face the Dimlocks. "Get moving!" he screamed. He would not let the pathetic boy get away. Anaiya's stare of death had thrilled him and he wanted to see the same sad stare from Mackinsi Wrighton ... the supposed chosen of Creator.

***

Mac landed lightly on the street and raced off into the night. He could not afford another battle. Anaiya was hanging on the edge of life and death.

Chapter 10: Betrayal

Michael sat stoically in Gilder's Café, deep in the heart of Los Angeles. His dark green cloak flowed over his shoulders to the floor and he slowly drummed his fingers across the smooth, wooden table as he reflected on the past several days.

Upon his arrival in L.A., he had released the awesome power of the beacon. Even now, he was recovering from the drain it had put on him. The beacon consisted of a mental projection to the minds of all Stormbreakers, informing them of the details of the Gathering. The beacon had spanned the globe, but had taken several hours to do so. Michael had maintained concentration throughout that time. He sighed, still feeling the strain of those long minutes. Soon, all the Stormbreakers of the world would converge on Los Angeles and the war would begin. A large figure sat down across the table from him.

"It is nice to once again see the legend in the flesh."

Michael smiled and turned to look on the dark-haired Stormbreaker. The man's dark purple cloak wrapped around him tightly but his hood was pulled back revealing his smiling face. Michael was glad he had arrived.

"James Morgan, it is nice to finally see you again. How are things going in Africa?"

James' smile grew tight.

"Not as well as we would hope."

Michael's fingers stopped drumming. He had expected as much. As the other Stormbreakers arrived, he knew he would hear similar reports.

"The Dimlocks are massing?" Michael preemptively guessed.

James nodded solemnly. It was time to tell the large African leader the status of the world.

Several hours later, James left the café with a gleam in his eye. Yes, the world was growing thick with Dimlocks and, yes, a battle was coming, but the Stormbreakers were gathering for the first and hopefully last time in history. He knew the amazing power the warriors of Creator could wield in that number. James' imagination whirled. Maybe the gathered army could even defeat Destroyer himself.

In the café, Michael's eyes held more weight. His experience had taught him that Destroyer was not an enemy who could be simply swept under the rug. Even with the entire Stormbreaker army united, Michael was unsure of victory. Perhaps he had waited too long to unite Creator's army. Perhaps it was too late. His thoughts drifted along that gloomy train of thought until they ran into a gleam of hope. Mackinsi was a ray of sunlight in the darkness of the slow spiral of despair. He was the double marked! How long had he been waiting. A double-marked Stormbreaker meant the end was near.

With a renewed spirit, Michael rose and swept out of the café. The world sometimes seemed dark but Creator had always had a plan, and Michael knew he had one now.

The American Airlines 767 touched down gracefully at LAX. The flight had been uneventful, and Glenn was happy his long journey was finally over. As he walked down the stairs to the tarmac his black suit transformed back into a cloak.

Security did not even blink as he walked around the checkpoints. He noticed several Dimlocks staring at him from their host bodies. They were no longer a threat but an ally. He served a new master now. Closing his eyes, Glenn looked at the directions glowing in his mind. The beacon had made his task so much easier. It would lead him straight to the Gathering.

***

"Room 813," Glenn announced to a balding, middle-aged man behind the hotel desk. Several seconds later, he was in the elevator, headed to the eighth floor.

The hallway was thickly carpeted and ornately decorated. Glenn smiled as he approached the master suite.

His key card opened the door to reveal an immense room and a familiar figure sitting in a chair against the back wall.

"Glenn Cross!" Michael said, rising from his chair. His grin broke the normally stoic lines of his chiseled face as he wrapped his young friend in a tight embrace.

Glenn played along. "Hello, Michael!" He returned his smile twofold. "I hoped I would run into you before the Gathering but I didn't expect to find you in my room."

Michael's grin remained as he stepped back to take in the changes in Glenn. "I see you finally learned patience," he stated, noting Glenn's cloak. "Creator's timing is always perfect."

Glenn nodded and replied smoothly, "It is nice to finally feel like one of you."

The next hours passed swiftly as Glenn fabricated the story of how he came to receive the Covering and what he, Mac and Anaiya had been up to since.

As Michael listened intently, he felt a chill race along his spine. He pulled his cloak tighter around him. Even as he did so, he realized the chill was not from a draft. His mind shifted focus. No longer was he simply listening to what Glenn was saying; he instead began to weigh and measure each phrase, each syllable. His eyes also began to move over Glenn's equipment.

It had been Glenn's attitude that had sent the chill into Michael. The last time he had seen the young man, Glenn had been bitter and unfriendly. Had the Covering brought the positive change in his attitude? If Glenn still harbored the anger he had previously possessed, why was he pretending everything was okay? The ancient Stormbreaker continued his analysis as they talked late into the night.

Glenn smiled to himself as he closed the door behind the leader of the Stormbreakers. His facade had successfully fooled Michael. It was just as Destroyer had foretold. He glided gracefully across the large room and settled into an overstuffed, black leather chair, picking up the phone.

He had a master suite, and a night all to himself. He wanted some company.

***

Michael crouched atop the building across from the Hilton. The moonlight cast eerie shadows all around him but his was nowhere to be found. His cloak did more than simply hide him from human eyes.

He watched three scantily clad women get out of a taxi and enter the hotel. After several minutes, he saw Glenn rise from his overstuffed chair, his cloak becoming a black tuxedo, to let the women in. Michael turned away, the chill once again sliding down his spine. Despite the Covering, Glenn seemed the same as he had been before. Something was wrong but Michael would sort it out later. At the moment, he had a gathering to organize.

***

The Gathering rapidly approached as Michael made his rounds. He visited the many Stormbreaker leaders who had arrived in the city. All of them spoke of a rise in Dimlock activity … of the coming war. None of them knew any disturbing details about Glenn Cross.

Several days passed and Michael spent a lot of time with Glenn. Despite the frequency of his late night escapades, Glenn had made no actions that would show him to be a fraud. Besides, Michael reflected, he did have the Covering. In all his years on Earth, Michael had never seen Creator give the covering to someone who could not be trusted.

He knew people had bad habits and he hoped Glenn's womanizing was simply that … a habit … something that could be broken. The tales of Mac and Anaiya made Michael smile. So, the two had feelings for each other. He had guessed that outcome from the beginning. Glenn told him that the two were close to discovering the Man of Power's identity and had sent him to be a support to Michael as he organized the Gathering. As each day went by, Michael began to trust Glenn more. It was true that Glenn had his problems … but didn't everyone?

Each night, Glenn felt more and more comfortable in his role. He knew Michael had been suspicious of him at first. It had been a challenge winning him over. He laughed inwardly. He had been winning people over all of his life. It was late as Glenn sat alone in the master suite. Well, not quite alone. He looked over to the large, four post bed where his recent conquest slept, and imagined who might be there next... If she had not forced him to kill her it may have even been Anaiya.

He chuckled darkly. Her death would have gnawed wonderfully at Mackinsi. Despite the darkness, Glenn left the lights off. It was the third night in a row he had been visited by Destroyer's presence. He knew the master did not prefer electric lights.

Glenn was amazed at Destroyer's power. Every time he witnessed it, he longed for the same. The last night had been what had made up his mind. Destroyer had appeared to him in what seemed to be a shimmering mirror. It had appeared in the middle of the room and Glenn had been able to see into the Man of Power's throne room. He had seen the Heartstone. He had felt the power of the black, glowing sphere emanating from within the shimmering portal and Glenn knew then that he must have it. With the stone, he could become the most powerful being on Earth. It would be he, not Destroyer, who conquered the Seventh Dimension. No one would be his master!

His final thoughts sent his mind spinning and a confident smirk to his lips. He hid it quickly as the mirror appeared. He would bide his time.

***

"L.A.'s own Marcus Stone." Michael smiled warmly and bowed low to his old friend.

"Michael, it is good to see you." Marcus laughed. "How long has it been?"

Michael put his strong hand on his friend's shoulder and led him down the sidewalk.

"Only a short one hundred years."

Pedestrians separated like the tide for the two cloaked men.

Marcus was a large, African American man with broad shoulders and large forearms. His smile was his most striking feature. It traveled from ear to ear. His broadsword hung casually at his hip and his confident stride showed it was for more than show.

Michael had enjoyed many sparring matches against Marcus Stone. He smiled as he remembered that his slender katana, Whisper, had always won the day.

Marcus led the faction of Stormbreakers in Los Angeles. The area was one of the greatest hot spots of Dimlock activity on Earth. Every blade of Stone's men knew well the taste of Dimlock blood.

"Your people tell me it's been unusually quiet around here."

Marcus regarded the ground thoughtfully. "The calm before the storm, my friend … the calm before the storm."

"That's what I've been hearing. We all believe a storm is coming. The question we will address tomorrow night is how to best prepare for it."

Marcus smiled. "How many Stormbreakers are coming tomorrow night?"

Michael paused in thought. "I expect at least 15,000, and in truth I expect it will be many times that number." Michael smiled as Marcus' jaw dropped.

"How will we hold them all?"

"Leave that to Creator." Michael laughed along with his friend as they made their way through the streets they knew would soon become a battleground.

***

The mirror darkened in the large room at the Hilton then disappeared into a shimmering cloud. Glenn watched the images of Michael and Marcus vanish and smiled inwardly.

He was glad Destroyer had shown him the power of the mirror. He now fully understood the gravity of his mission.

***

The oddities of Glenn Cross did not even cross Michael's mind as he prepared for sundown. 50,000 Stormbreakers had come to Los Angeles. In his long life he had only witnessed one other gathering. It had been during World War II. The Stormbreakers had united against the growing evil. Now they were uniting against the greatest evil of all, Destroyer.

Michael approached Warehouse 220 in L.A.'s industrial district. From the outside, the warehouse seemed much too small to hold 50,000 Stormbreakers but Michael knew the truth of Creator's power. Approaching the door, he clapped his hands together. His cross marking began to glow, shining brighter and brighter. He closed his eyes and stretched his right arm toward the metal-sided structure.

The air seemed to ripple between his hand and the warehouse, and then all was still. A faint shimmering around the doorframes was the only sign something had changed.

Night fell swiftly upon Los Angeles as the column of cloaked figures wound its way through the industrial district and into the warehouse.

Glenn stood with Michael at the back of the line of warriors. Despite himself, he was impressed by their power. They exuded it as surely as the Heartstone. He looked ahead and in the distance could see the warehouse. Almost all of the Stormbreakers had entered and there still seemed to be room for more.

Glenn looked inquisitively at Michael. "What magic is this?"

Michael looked at the door with the awe he always experienced gazing upon Creator's power. "It is no magic, my young friend. Step inside and experience the power of Creator."

It was with anxious reluctance that Glenn stepped through the glowing door. What he encountered took his breath away.

A sea of cloaked figures greeted his unbelieving eyes. The area of the inside of the warehouse was infinitely larger than the perimeter allowed. How was it physically possible? "The power of Creator," he whispered to himself. As he gazed upon the miracle, he briefly reconsidered his allegiance, but the moment passed. They deserved this... No one would ever forget the name of Glenn Cross.

A warm glow illuminated the entire warehouse despite the fact that no light sources were visible. A large platform rose from the ground in the center of the sea of cloaks and every face rose to regard the man on top of it. Marcus Stone, his blue cloak hanging heavily around his shoulders, stood tall above the sea. Glenn noticed Michael standing stoically behind the large man, dwarfing even him. He also noticed Whisper was now visible, hanging at Michael's side. He had not noticed Michael move to the pedestal.

Marcus opened his mouth and, throughout the immense room, his voice lost no volume despite the fact that he was not using a microphone.

"Brothers and Sisters!" Marcus boomed. "We all know why we have answered the beacon's call, and have gathered here tonight." Heads nodded in solemn agreement. "A dark time is coming. Destroyer's armies are gaining momentum and will soon break upon the world. We know the threat he poses to the Seventh Dimension, the final obstacle between him and absolute power. We understand the consequences of failure." Marcus paused for effect. "I am here tonight to pull our army together into a united front. Separated, we will not have the numbers to stop Destroyer's massing force. Together, he cannot stand against us."

Stormbreakers around the room stood taller at Stone's statement. It was the truth and the foundation of their confidence.

"I now give you the leader of our army and the oldest amongst us."

Marcus moved back and Michael stepped forward. His cloak fell about him as silently as the footfalls of his knee high, brown boots.

"Despite his size, he seemed to glide into position as lightly as a stalking cat. Whisper's hilt was visible and gleamed in the soft light.

A thunderous sound greeted him as every Stormbreaker pulled their closed fist to their heart in salute.

Glenn slipped, unnoticed, closer to the center of the room, all the while keeping his eyes locked onto the powerful Stormbreaker beginning to speak. From his head to his toes, Glenn's body began to tingle. It was almost time. His wrist pulsed with power. He had released a beacon of his own.

From atop the platform, Michael tensed. The hairs rose on the back of his neck as if lifted by a breath of frigid cold. His eyes darted around the massive crowd as he attempted to discover the source of the sensation.

The power surging through Glenn's body rose in intensity. His wrist felt as if it was burning with a flame of ice. Destroyer's plan had been a success! He allowed a smirk to spread across his face. Any second Destroyer would be here! His confidence plummeted as his eyes drifted back to the uplifted platform. Michael was staring directly at him with Whisper drawn and ready.

The eye contact was all Michael needed to confirm his suspicion. Energy was flowing from Glenn Cross in powerful amounts. It was the pattern of the energy pulses that disturbed him the most. They were the pulses of a beacon.

"We are betrayed! Evil approaches!" Michael cried, leaping from the platform. Before even his feet left the platform the ceiling exploded inward allowing an enormous, black shape to descend upon the surprised Stormbreakers. The shadowy behemoth landed heavily atop the upraised pillar and stretched its black, leathery wings.

The shout, "Destroyer!" spread like wildfire throughout the massive crowd as the sounds of weapons being drawn rang off the high walls. The wrath of Destroyer fell upon the cloaked army like the tide upon the shore. Glenn watched in awe as flames engulfed a hundred Stormbreakers attempting to climb the pillar. They fell in ashes, lighting those below them with the fatal flames. Glenn noticed a Stormbreaker had his back to him and swiftly drove his scimitar through his spine and into his lung.

The man gasped in a desperate attempt to draw breath then slid off the cruel blade onto the ground. Glenn laughed maniacally as several Stormbreakers, who had witnessed the murder, came at him, blades rotating rapidly. The seasoned Stormbreakers could not understand it when the impertinent youth easily slashed their throats. They had never battled a Stormbreaker who had received the Dark Covering. Blade cutting savagely, Glenn cleared a path toward the exit. His role was over. He had acted as a homing beacon for Destroyer. Now all he desired was to leave the slaughter safely. It was not compassion or guilt that motivated him, but the pressing memory that one had escaped him. Wrighton was still alive somewhere out there. He wanted to remedy that unfortunate truth.

Before he could reach the doors, a stream of black trench coat wearing Residents poured into the building. The sound of metal on metal rose in volume and gunshots deafened him. The Residents blew through the first lines of Stormbreaker defense, the element of surprise aiding them in their whirlwind of slaughter.

The flood of Residents did not diminish and Glenn realized he would not have a clear path to leave the battle. "Oh well," he muttered, "I might as well join the fun."

After the initial surprise, the Stormbreakers rallied their defenses and the battle became give and take, or would have if not for Destroyer, Glenn, and Michael. A ring of smoldering bodies surrounded the pillar where Destroyer rained down flaming death. It was not simple fire killing Creator's warriors. If the flames had been earthly the cloaks given by the Covering would have turned them away. But the fire was a weapon of evil, the embodiment of Destroyer's murderous will, and no Stormbreaker's cloak could repel it.

Michael watched another hundred Stormbreakers scaling the pillar and hundreds more firing arrows at Destroyer. Destroyer's deep, booming laughter echoed around the immense room as the arrows ignited when they came in contact with a shield of flame. Their ashes were the only things that made it through Destroyer's protective sphere.

Another wave of evil flame rolled down the pillar, incinerating the Stormbreakers scaling its sides. With a rush of his mighty wings, Destroyer leapt down from the pillar and into the melee.

Michael's thoughts were torn from Destroyer as a bullet whizzed past his right ear. At once he was running. The years Michael had weathered had honed his reflexes and he had learned to trust them.

Glenn's scimitar spun and dropped methodically as he led the flowing wall of Residents across the battleground. Far to his left, he saw Destroyer, towering with his flaming swords blazing. Through the blur of frantic battle, Glenn noticed a tall man cutting a path toward the Dark Lord, Whisper gleaming with each blast of Destroyer's fireballs.

A movement caught his eye and his blade rose just in time to parry the thrust of a broadsword. He fell back into a ready stance, locking gazes with Marcus Stone.

"Traitor," Marcus growled. He shifted his broadsword slowly as he circled. "Michael brought you under his wing, trusted you with the fate of mankind, and you used that friendship to stab him in the back?" Marcus' tone held death but his eyes showed a profound sadness. "You've doomed your own world!"

Glenn snarled back at Marcus. "It was Michael's ineptitude that allowed me here. Your destruction lies solely upon your own shoulders."

With a cry, the men melted together. Their movements perfectly complimented one another. Each thrust was parried; each slash met only empty air or metal. Back and forth the two warriors fought, neither gaining any advantage upon the other, as the battle raged only inches away.

Michael had no trouble clearing a path to the mighty beast. Bullets missed him by mere millimeters, but they were calculated millimeters. His experience with Residents had taught him many things throughout the years.

He instantaneously calculated where the Residents were aiming as they pulled the trigger and chose not to be there. To the Residents, he was a ghost, a specter they couldn't touch. He cut a smooth path through their numbers and soon stood before the evil monster.

Destroyer smiled wickedly. This was the moment he had waited for.

Near one of the entrances, a unit of Stormbreakers formed a wedge formation. They drove through a group of Residents, only to be stopped in their tracks by an organized formation of attackers. Throughout the entire room, the scene was pandemonium. Stormbreakers cut Residents down, only to be killed by others from behind. The walls of the warehouse were on fire and, as a wave of Dimlocks poured into join the battle, pools of drool ignited on the cement floor.

The sound of battle was deafening as Glenn and Marcus continued to try to find an opening in the others' defenses. Out of the corner of his eye Marcus saw Michael confront Destroyer. His heart soared. Maybe the ancient Stormbreaker could defeat the beast.

Perhaps there was hope after all. Marcus felt the newly acquired hope surge through his veins, giving him renewed strength. Fire flickered in his dark eyes.

Glenn saw the change in his opponent and wondered if this challenging battle might not go his way. He met an overhead blow from Marcus with an upward block. The force of Stone's mighty broadsword knocked him back several steps. Glenn brought his scimitar in slashing arcs, each lightly parried by the enraged man in the blue cloak. He felt his body shudder as he blocked another mighty swing. He knew the fight could go either way.

Michael lowered his head and was immediately surrounded by a faint, white glow. Without hesitation, he stepped through the sphere of flame Destroyer was ensconced in. The evil flames grabbed hungrily at his flesh and clothing but hit the faint, white wall of light surrounding him. He entered the sphere unscathed. Behind him a drooling Dimlock saw the back of the ancient enemy and thought it had gained an easy kill. It leapt with a gurgling snarl at the man who had just walked safely through what it had thought to be a wall of flame.

Too late, it realized its error. Only ashes fluttered into the sphere behind the sword master.

Destroyer smiled, truly pleased with the convenience Michael had afforded him by confronting him out of his own volition. Destroyer had believed he would have to pursue the fool, but his prey had come to him. He straightened his 30-foot-tall frame, glaring down at Michael. "Michael, Michael, Michael … why do you continue to fight me? Have you not the intelligence to see the futility of it all?"

Michael took a step nearer to the beast. Despite the flaming swords at the creature's sides, he showed no fear. He called up to the beast.

"Creator will not let you have the Seventh Dimension. The end has already been written. He has shown me. You lose!"

"Fool!" Destroyer bellowed. "I already have all of the cards! Your army is being defeated even as we speak. The end is being written as each second passes. Look at the piles of your dead warriors." Destroyer waved a flaming sword in a circular fashion. "They are vastly outnumbered and cannot win. All of you are doomed!"

A smile spread across his beastly face, and he laughed with glee.

"This is not the end," Michael stated, "and you do not have the control you believe you do!"

Destroyer's scimitars leapt to life, each massive blade falling heavily toward Michael. Whisper had joined the battle. The slim blade flicked back and forth against the seven foot long blades. The nearest Stormbreakers, Residents, and Dimlocks alike stopped warring to observe the incredible spectacle. They could not tear their gaze from what they saw.

Each time the opponents' blades crossed, sparks exploded onto the floor. Destroyer and Michael moved like the wind. Their battle resembled an intricate dance. The 6-foot-5-inch Stormbreaker and the 20-foot-tall denizen circled each other. Rapidly, their blades moved almost faster than the human eye could comprehend, cutting downward, parrying, and thrusting. Michael rolled between Destroyer's legs to come up with an upward thrust. Destroyer spun swiftly, his right scimitar cutting horizontally, deflecting the thrust.

His left scimitar followed behind the parrying blade. Michael dove over the potentially mortal strike. His roll brought him to his feet, just in time to take the brunt of a gust of wind from Destroyer's wings. The ancient Stormbreaker allowed the wind to flip him backwards, sheathing Whisper as he tumbled. As he flew through the air, an arrow flew from under his swirling cloak. Destroyer roared as the arrow pierced his shoulder. Michael landed on his feet gracefully, his longbow in his hand. He would not get another shot. Tearing the arrow from his shoulder, Destroyer rushed toward him. Michael quickly drew Whisper but the momentum of the large beast bowled him over. As he rolled head over heels, he lashed out. Whisper cut a deep gash in Destroyer's calf. Rising from the roll, Michael leapt high into the air. His cloak trailed behind him with a life of its own as he plunged Whisper deep into Destroyer's thigh. With a great roar, Destroyer hit Michael with a mighty backhand. Whisper flew from his grasp, and he hit the ground hard.

The Stormbreakers were suffering great losses. Each was now fighting an impossible battle and was subsequently falling under the mass of bullets and blades.

Marcus parried one of Glenn's attacks, his right front kick snapping out under the traitor's jaw and sending him onto the ground.

As Glenn fell, Marcus caught a glimpse of Michael plummeting heavily to the ground. Everything inside told him to rush to his friend's aid, but Glenn's flashing scimitar held him like an anchor. The evil Stormbreaker was back on his feet and into the battle again.

Marcus' broadsword rang down, each clash echoing across the support structure at the top of the building. Despite the danger of Glenn Cross, his thoughts were focused on the most important battle. He listened intently for the fall of Destroyer, and Michael's victory.

As Michael pulled his body up from the ground, blood flowed freely from his mouth. An alarm of pain went off in his head as he stood, confirming one of his legs was broken.

Destroyer's back fist had nearly finished him … but he had survived. With a cry, Michael called to Whisper and the great katana materialized in his hand. Destroyer growled in surprise and launched both scimitars into a flowing attack.

A fresh surge of energy within his body nearly overwhelmed Michael as Creator's power coursed through him. The blood stopped dripping from his lip as Whisper met the vicious attack with one of its own.

To Destroyer's horror, the broken adversary parried his attacks and leapt high into the air. Michael's leg had been healed. Destroyer felt the slash of the razor sharp blade across his chest. He felt it slice through ribs seeking a way to his evil heart. With lightning speed, he pushed Michael away, leaping back with a flap of his wings. The Heartstone called out to him and he heeded its advice.

Michael saw the change in tactics as Destroyer dropped his right scimitar, lifting his large, clawed hand so his palm faced Michael. Michael threw Whisper into his left hand and simultaneously lifted his right.

The explosion of flame temporarily blinded everyone in the large building, leaving them staggering to regain their footing. A column of sizzling, orange flame flew from Destroyer's hand and was met by a dazzling column of white flame from Michael's.

The columns of flame merged in a brilliant display with the intensity of the sun. The spray of the flames colliding with each other stretched from the floor to the ceiling and the wall of fire thundered and flashed in a standoff between the two warriors of power. The vision returned to the armies and the battle in the room resumed its brutal escalation. Each side was bolstered by the spectacle of their leader's potential victory.

Across the battlefield, Marcus kicked Glenn in the throat, dropping him to the floor. He then turned, sprinting toward the battle being waged in the center of the room.

Sweat beaded on Michael's forehead. The heat of the flames rippled off the ground between him and Destroyer. The power of Creator flowed through him and into the column of pure white fire. His entire body was shaking with the effort to sustain the flame. Destroyer's concentration was intense, and Michael could feel Destroyer slowly winning the battle.

Michael sighed in acceptance. He had known the outcome of the night as soon as he sensed Glenn's beacon. His goal had been to slow Destroyer down, to keep him focused on this personal battle so as many Stormbreakers as possible could escape slaughter. He felt hope. Even now, he trusted Creator. Even now, he remembered Mackinsi and once again felt the surge of excitement at the name. It would be up to the young Stormbreaker now to stop the coming storm. The Aquillian scroll could not fall into Destroyer's hands. Michael pushed the jumble of his last thoughts away. All that mattered was delaying Destroyer even for just one more second.

Glenn saw his chance for escape as he regained his footing. The air felt cool to him as he walked out of the slaughterhouse. He laughed to himself quietly and wiped his sword on the cloak of a fallen Stormbreaker. After the gore and triumph of the night, he would call his sword Bloodletter.

He had seen the battle nearing its end. No doubt, the ancient Stormbreaker would fall and with him his army. What held Glenn's thoughts was the Heartstone. He had seen it hanging beside Destroyer during the battle … had felt its immense power. "Destroyer would be nothing without that stone," Glenn muttered to no one in particular. "But I would be everything with it!" Melting into the night, he focused on his next desire—to kill Mackinsi Wrighton, and gain even more power.

**

Michael felt his arm growing weak under Destroyer's fiery barrage. The point at which the flames merged was only inches from him now. Soon, his millennia long life would end.

Michael pondered the strange thought for a moment but the sight of Marcus rushing toward him sent it flying from his mind. Michael realized his friend's peril instantly. In his rush to help Michael, Marcus would be incinerated by the protective shield of fire around Destroyer.

"No!" he shouted to Marcus. "Go back!"

The defender of Los Angeles didn't slow and barreled toward Destroyer, sword swinging at his side. "Michael!"

Michael saw the futility of Marcus' path. He thought of Mackinsi Wrighton and Anaiya Lynn. "Creator," he whispered, "keep them safe." With that said, he did the only thing left for him. Pulling Whisper to his heart in a salute, he let Destroyer's flame overwhelm him. The pain was excruciating as Michael was blown across the room. Destroyer ran after him, roaring with glee. He quickly left Marcus behind as he maintained the blasting fire on his fallen foe.

Michael had stopped feeling the pain of the fire and now could see only the Heartstone at Destroyer's side. It slowly filled his vision then Michael closed his eyes for the last time.

"No!" Marcus screamed as he saw Michael's body disintegrate into ash. He felt hot tears filling his eyes as he realized his next required action. He was the leader of the Stormbreakers now, and in the face of such overwhelming odds he had only one choice.

His voice was carried by Creator's power to every ear in the immense room as he shouted for the retreat. All about the room, the limping, wounded, and exhausted Stormbreakers escaped through the enchanted doors, melting into the night. 50,000 Stormbreakers had entered the warehouse. Little more than one hundred made it out alive.

Chapter 11: Waiting

Mac opened his eyes, taking in the white speckled ceiling. On instinct he reached his right hand out and felt the familiar warm body. Smoothly, he rolled from atop the covers. He breathed a little easier seeing the beautiful Anaiya breathing deeply, still deep in healing slumber.

Has it really been a month? Mac pondered to himself. The battle with Glenn, who had once been his friend, seemed as if it had only happened yesterday.

No, Mac thought. Anaiya's recovery alone reminded him it had been a month. The worry and confusion he felt on that night once again assaulted him. He had been betrayed and had almost lost his only friend.

After landing from the rapid descent from the window, Mac had carried Anaiya up roads and down alleyways, finally discovering the direction to the hospital.

Anaiya's blood flowed freely onto his hands, spilling to the ground, and pushing him into a state of panic. Anaiya drifted into consciousness long enough to dissuade him from the hospital and, instead, she weakly directed him to a safe haven she had prepared for an occasion such as this.

Mac looked at her sleeping form and again was amazed she had survived that night. When they had arrived at the apartment Anaiya had been deathly white and her breathing had been shallow. Mac had seriously questioned the decision to avoid the hospital as he laid her broken body on the bed. Weakly, Anaiya had told him to get something from the nightstand. He had retrieved a small vial of blue liquid and, after being directed, had gently poured it into her mouth. The change had been subtle, yet immediate. Her bleeding had stopped and some color had returned to her delicate cheeks. Sleep had come immediately to the battered woman, leaving Mac alone with his anxious thoughts.

Several hours had passed, but to Mac it felt like years. Finally, he had convinced himself she would live through the night, and had drifted into an uneasy sleep.

Sometime later, he had been awakened by her cries. Rushing to her side, he found her in the midst of a nightmare. As he crawled onto the bed next to her, she had opened her eyes.

"Don't leave me," she had whispered, and Mac hadn't. He had held Anaiya every night since. He was content sleeping with the warmth of her beside him. It let him know she was alive.

Several more nightmares had assaulted her during the following nights, but Mac's reassuring presence had soothed her.

Glancing at the sleeping woman again, Mac felt the familiar flutter in his stomach. It had spread to his heart over the past month. He wasn't really surprised by that. He had felt something the first time he had seen her.

Michael. The name calmed Mac's mind, helped him concentrate on the task at hand ... waiting. Michael would come for them.

"Is the weight of the world on your shoulders again?" Anaiya's voice sent relief washing over Mac. Each word she spoke meant she was doing better. She could read him like a book.

"I'm just thinking things over," he replied.

"You look more like you're worrying."

Mac smiled. Like a book...

"Maybe I am." He smiled sincerely. "I have a lot to do, you know."

"Like…" Anaiya played along, propping herself up gingerly on some pillows.

"Like being a Stormbreaker, a bodyguard, a doctor, a nurse, a nanny…" Mac let the last perfectly placed word trail off as he waited for the expected reaction. Sure enough, a pillow came whizzing at his head. He let it hit him.

"Feeling better I see."

"A nanny?" Anaiya asked incredulously. Her blue eyes flashed with mirth as her shoulder length, blonde hair swung back and forth with the disapproving shake of her head. "Mackinsi Wrighton, if I was well, I'd teach you a thing or two about being a nanny!" Her effort expended, she lay back down with a sigh, a smile still on her face. "Thank you again for saving me," she murmured.

"Don't mention it," Mac replied. He rose and moved to the nightstand, retrieving the vial filled anew with the healing blue liquid.

The healing medicine had appeared anew each morning and each morning he gently gave it to Anaiya. It was working wonders. The wound on her stomach that had once been fatal was now closed and healing nicely. As he placed the empty vial back into the drawer in the nightstand, he once again read the label on it. "To Anaiya, from Michael. May it keep you safe."

The vial had been Anaiya's gift from Michael at the end of their training together. Mac was grateful for the gift … very grateful.

Anaiya gasped as the healing cold spread through her body. Mac let the medicine do its restoring work, and walked to look out the window. A grimy brick wall greeted him, the view broken only by the rusty fire escape attached to it. Anaiya's hideout was perfectly located. Glenn would have a hard time finding them.

**

Anaiya lay quietly on the bed. She could feel Michael's medicine restoring her body. The blue liquid felt like ice going down her throat but fire once inside her.

She took a deep breath and smiled. It was the first time she had done so without pain. Slowly, she pulled herself up on her pillow, taking care to keep herself covered.

Mackinsi had been wonderful. So many times he had held her as she cried tears of pain or frustration. She knew when the nightmares came he would be there to drive them away.

She glanced at the broad-shouldered man at the window, and felt the familiar feelings inside her. Excitement, mingled with fear, skipped about her heart like a nymph at play.

With great effort she swung her feet to the ground and, wrapping a sheet around her, she slowly stood. The blood rushed to her head and a wave of dizziness swept over her. She steadied herself and fought through it.

Mac felt her soft cheek lean against his shoulder and his arm immediately wrapped around her waist to support her.

"Talk to me when you're worried," Anaiya said quietly. "You helped me and I'd like to help you."

Mac felt the tension leave him. "Thank you," he said just as quietly.

The two of them looked into each other's eyes.

"I think its time for your shower," Mac said, breaking the silence.

"Is that a hint?" Anaiya asked.

Mac pretended to hold his nose and got a punch in the stomach for his trouble.

"Let's go, stinky," Mac said, leading her toward the bathroom and taking another savage punch.

With his eyes to the floor, Mac took the sheet from Anaiya and wrapped a towel around her.

"Will you be okay?"

She grinned. "If you hear a loud thud, it's me."

He gave a halfhearted chuckle as he left her in the bathroom. He would be standing outside the door until she came out. He was not about to lose her.

***

Anaiya let the warm water fall over her body and tilted her face back to let it run through her hair. As she closed her eyes, an image returned to her. She was surrounded by blackness, like a swirling mist. Green trails pierced the blackness in many places, trails left by a Stormbreaker's double markings. She knew she was once again seeing Mac's battle with the Reap. In her hundred years of life, she had only seen one other with such weapons prowess, and that was Michael himself. She remembered the blow from Mac's katana that severed the beast's tongue and saved her life. Where had he learned to fight like that? In her mind, she replayed the conclusion of the battle, remembered Mac's stoic expression as he walked out of the dissipated darkness. His eyes had been as hard as stone.

It was difficult to reconcile the image of that warrior with the quiet man she knew was standing just outside the bathroom door. There was a caring spirit inside Mackinsi that coexisted with the capability to utterly destroy evil.

Her thoughts drifted toward the prophecy Michael had spoken to her about the Stormbreaker who would defeat Destroyer. He had told her the one would be double-marked. Mac was the only Stormbreaker she had ever met who had the two crosses, one on each wrist. When she had first met him and Glenn, she had had her doubts, but after witnessing Mac's prowess in battle and observing the depth of his spirit, she believed what Michael had believed. Mackinsi Wrighton was the fulfillment of the prophecy. He was the one.

Wiping the water from her eyes, she smiled to herself. He was more to her than that.

***

Night fell quickly without a word from Michael. Mac could tell even Anaiya was beginning to grow concerned, yet all they could do was wait. He lay on his side holding Anaiya as she slept.

"Hold me tighter," Anaiya directed and Mackinsi pulled her closer. He felt her naked back against his bare chest and took great care where he placed his hands. She was not a conquest. She was a friend. Maybe someday she would be something more but now was not the time.

"Good night, Anaiya," Mac whispered.

Anaiya sighed contentedly.

"Good night."

Chapter 12: Twisted Dreams

An enormous shadow flew through the roof of Leviathan Headquarters, plummeting through insulation, structural supports, and wires to land directly upon the sleeping Man of Power sitting in the golden throne. The man sat up smiling; it was good to be home. He gently placed the black sphere onto the pedestal beside him, giving it the cursory pat. Destroyer had defeated Creator's top warrior and had not only destroyed his ancient foe, but had shattered and slaughtered his entire army in the process. No one could stand against him now. The Seventh Dimension was as good as his.

Normally, such a thought would have brought Destroyer some measure of happiness, but not today.

"What good are all the dimensions without the scroll?" he growled to the flickering candles on stands all about the room. Sometime before his conversion of Glenn Cross, Destroyer had felt a surge in the dimensional fabric.

The surge had been for the Power of Light and should have brought despair upon the Dark Lord, but quite the contrary had occurred. Destroyer was well versed in the prophecy. The surge of power could only mean one thing. The double-marked Stormbreaker truly lived!

At first Destroyer had been confused. The last of the bloodline had seemingly been destroyed. There were no records of a double-marked Stormbreaker walking the Seventh Dimension. With no Stormbreakers being born into the world, where had the power come from? As he had been pondering those thoughts, the answer had come to him. It had been so obvious! The second marking came at the Covering! He had come to that conclusion moments before one of his hunters had entered the throne room battered and bruised.

At that moment Destroyer had realized the truth. Somehow, the young Stormbreaker had received the double marking. It was the only explanation.

Destroyer had sent an army to the house to retrieve the Stormbreaker only to find him gone. They were left with a simple name. Mackinsi Wrighton.

The search had been an unrewarding one until the night he acquired his traitorous lackey. A similar spectacle had appeared before him that night. A beaten Glenn Cross had told him Mackinsi Wrighton had pulled a woman named Anaiya Lynn to safety. Glenn had claimed he killed her, but Destroyer knew better than that. He knew this woman and she had trained under Michael himself. She would not die that easily. Since then, Mackinsi and the woman had vanished. All of his hunters had been unable to locate them.

"Fools!" Destroyer screamed, hurling a fireball into a Dimlock attendant, utterly incinerating it instantly.

He had come to realize, through studying the prophecies, the Aquillian Scroll would only awaken to the Chosen One.

He needed that scroll for his final battle, to destroy Creator and form everything anew in his own image.

"Talon!" he cried. The hunter glided gracefully into the chamber answering to his name.

"It is time to stop chasing the boy!" Destroyer bellowed. "Raise the stakes. Bring him to us."

"The usual tactics?" the tall hunter asked, grinning wickedly.

"No," Destroyer sardonically stated. "Raise the stakes."

Destroyer let the words sink in then continued. "Bring Glenn to me."

A siren wailed as an ambulance rushed along the busy New York streets. Destroyer smiled. Somewhere one of his subjects had been at work. Soon enough the Seventh Dimension would fall. Victory was at hand. It was so close he could taste it.

Chapter 13: Raising the Stakes

Arty Jones wandered haphazardly down the sidewalks of Brooklyn. His sleep had been restless and full of nightmares. Ghastly monsters had assaulted him and tried to take control of him. He had awakened in a cold sweat. Eventually, Arty had drifted back to sleep, getting a few needed hours before he had to get up for work. He worked at First Savings and Loan, one of the only banks in the area, and had never been late in his thirty years of employ. Today would be no exception. Ten minutes early, Arty arrived at the large, wooden doors of First Savings and Loan. A minute later, he flopped down into the plush, red chair behind his desk. He enjoyed what he did. Helping people appealed to him.

He watched his co-worker Anna Morton slip into her chair as well and caught her eye. She winked suggestively at him and he smiled, remembering the last night of their casual relationship. Co-workers, parties and alcohol led to some wild things.

A movement in the corner of Arty's eye made him turn his head. His boss was moving toward the front doors, key in hand. It was time for another beautiful day. He turned back to send a wink Anna's way and froze. The rotted corpse, the monster from his nightmare stared back at him from her desk. He could feel its hateful yellow eyes burning into him. Trying to breathe, he turned to his boss. It was not his boss looking back at him, but another of the monsters beginning to come toward him.

"No!" he screamed. Arty pushed his wheeled chair back until he slammed into the desk behind him. He spun to see a monster reaching out toward him. It seemed to be saying something.

Screaming, Arty leapt from his chair and opened his bottom drawer. He pulled out a 45-caliber pistol and aimed it at the monster sitting at Anna's desk. He had been told he would need the gun in his dream and had found it by his front door. He was glad he had brought it to work the day before.

The monster shrieked and stood waving its arms, but Arty would not let it escape that easily. "Stop torturing me!" He put a bullet through its head and proceeded to do so to every monster the room. After killing the last monster, he heard laughter begin to echo in his head. The room flickered and blurred. An intense pain shot through him as the room came back into focus.

The gun dropped to the bloodstained carpet. Arty felt himself trembling as he gazed to where the first monster should have been. Anna lay sprawled across her desk, a gaping bullet wound in her forehead. Her eyes were frozen in a look of shock and confusion. Arty felt his insides churning. He scanned the room. There were no monsters … only dead and dying people.

The wail of a broken man split the early morning at First Savings and Loan.

***

Mac looked into the mirror. He was just getting used to the face staring back at him. Ruggedly handsome, with a slight layer of stubble on his square jaw, Mac looked a far cry from the gangly eighteen-year-old he had once been.

From what Anaiya told him, he was different from other Stormbreakers in three areas. The first was that he was the youngest person to ever receive the Covering. The lowest age before him had been a warrior in Asia who had received the covering at nineteen years old. The second difference between him and other Stormbreakers was the shift that had occurred in his appearance. At the time of the Covering, a person's aging process was halted. They would remain forever appearing as they did at the time of the Covering. Mac knew he was an exception to the rule. During his Covering, he had aged, physically and mentally, five to six years! Michael had told him it was because Creator could not wait any longer. He told Mac that Creator needed him now. That left Mac with more questions than answers, as did the third difference. All other Stormbreakers on Earth had the flickering, shimmering cross marking on their right wrist. It was the symbol of what they were and a conduit of their power. Mac had two markings; one on each wrist. When Michael had seen the second mark, which had come with the Covering, Mac had seen excitement flash across his stoic face. Anaiya too had reacted in similar fashion. Her reaction had sent his thoughts sailing back to his first meeting with Michael. He would never forget Michael's words. To Glenn's dismay, Michael had expressed the belief that Mac could be the one the prophecies spoke of— the one who would save the world.

Mac shuddered involuntarily at the thought. What if it was true? What if the fate of the world rested upon his shoulders? *I wasn't even able to defeat Glenn,* Mac thought somberly. *How could I ever defeat Destroyer? I'd rather leave that to Michael.*

Sighing, and feeling heavily burdened, Mac walked from the bathroom to the kitchen table, where Anaiya was busy studying the morning's paper.

Once again in her Stormbreaker garb, Anaiya looked stunning. Mac marveled at her recovery, but marveled more at her attitude. Through the last two months of her recovery, Anaiya's indomitable spirit had been a support to him, the one who was supposed to be supporting her.

"Another slaughter," she said quietly.

Mac felt the hair stand on the back of his neck. This would make the third story in the last week. Each tragedy contained similar elements, one lunatic killing several people they had close relationships with and claiming they had been trying to kill monsters instead.

The first had been a poor wretch who worked for a bank. He had killed his coworkers just before the bank was supposed to open. Sadly, the man killed himself a day after the incident while in police custody, leaving more questions than answers.

The second killing had moved the story to the front page because a pattern had emerged. A daycare worker had shot all 20 of the children in her nursery claiming they were demons. She maintained her claims even after confronted by the bloody corpses of the children.

Mac reluctantly scanned the front page of the day's paper and froze. A seven-year-old child had murdered his parents and sister with a kitchen knife as they slept. Tear marks splattered the page and he looked up to see Anaiya crying.

"He said he was killing monsters that had taken his family," Anaiya said quietly. "He can't even begin to comprehend what he's done."

"Dimlocks?" Mac asked, placing his arm around her shoulder.

She nodded in agreement and leaned into his chest.

"Let me see the other articles," he told her.

"I'll help you look," Anaiya said, regaining her composure, and wiping her eyes. "I think there is a pattern too."

Mac moved to the couch with the articles. "I wish Michael was here," he stated.

"Me too." Anaiya nodded. "Me too."

***

Several hours later, Mac and Anaiya began to formulate battle plans. Anaiya had healed enough to battle, and the slight pain in her stomach was nothing compared to the fires that burned in her eyes. She was determined that not another innocent soul would die!

The pattern of the previous attacks had been difficult to unravel, but Anaiya had proven to be extremely effective at it. Mac fingered the ivory-like hilt of his katana, the green crosses feeling smooth and slightly cold to the touch. Tomorrow, the monsters would meet the red edge of his blade. He thought of his victory over the Reap, of the righteousness that had overwhelmed him as he vanquished the darkness. "Nightsbane," he murmured, addressing his sword, "tomorrow you will battle the darkness once more."

***

Talon watched as the events before him began to unfold. Irwin Middle School was the perfect selection for the next phase of the hunt. His stone cold eyes watched the middle-aged bus driver prepare the buses for the arrival of the children. He knew the man was already under the control of a Dimlock.

Talon checked the magazine of his black Glock to make sure the 40-caliber hollow points were loaded correctly. Assured of the weapon's functionality, he slid it into his shoulder holster and straightened his long, black trench coat. His two short swords rested just underneath its folds. The hunter suspected that the Stormbreaker that Destroyer sought would have already figured out the pattern of the previous massacres. That had been the point, after all. That Stormbreaker had killed his partner when he received the Covering. Destroyer's orders or not, he had a score to settle.

***

The Dimlock controlled the bus driver like a marionette. At the moment, he had the driver walking back into the garage and toward his large tool cabinet. Of course, the fool was oblivious to the fact he was being controlled. His world was going to seem like a horror movie in a few short moments.

The man's eyes bulged yellow as the Dimlock peered about from within his body. A wave of junior high students would swarm to the buses in a matter of seconds as school ended. To the bus driver they would appear as a wave of monsters. Where was the key to the tool cabinet?

***

The bus driver felt a chill rush over him. Fear overwhelmed his reason as obscene screeches seemed to sound all around the bus garage. Quickly, he grabbed the key to the tool cabinet and flung the doors wide. His 12-gauge, pistol-gripped shotgun met his frantic eyes. The screeches around the garage grew louder. This scenario was not new to the middle-aged man. He ran a hand across his balding forehead, wiping the cold sweat onto his denim overalls. He recognized the wails. They had been in his nightmares for weeks, so he knew what was approaching.

This time the creatures would not hurt him. This time he was ready. He had smuggled the shotgun into the school several days earlier for just this type of emergency. Grabbing the shotgun and extra shells, he raced out of the garage toward the buses and the monsters he knew were rapidly approaching. He had to save the children!

***

The wave of monsters rounded the corner, coming from the direction of the classrooms. The driver's breaths were ragged as he put his back against the side of the yellow school bus. He knew he would not stand a chance unless he attacked by surprise. He looked to the three other bus drivers for assurance and support. They waited behind their buses as well, shotguns in hand. The four of them against the monsters was better odds. They would attack together!

***

The children rounded the corner and began to split off, heading to their prospective buses. With a nod, the four bus drivers moved to step out and confront the creatures … but they never made it.

Time flickered. The sudden shift in the fabric of time caught the Dimlocks by surprise and they fell in unison from their puppets' bodies, still clutching their firearms tightly. Panic and hate shone from their sunken visages as they overcame their shock and turned to confront the beings they knew had arrived.

**

Mac and Anaiya raced across the asphalt then raced in opposite directions. They had seen the shotguns and knew how dangerous this battle would be.

Anaiya dove headlong behind the nearest bus as a shotgun blast tore a gaping hole in the yellow metal where she had just been. Without stopping she leapt straight up, flipping backwards onto the roof of the bus. Swiftly and silently, she raced to the edge of the roof and dropped straight down onto the confused pursuer. Her bladed staff cut true, piercing through the Dimlock's heart and lungs then punching through its chest. She hefted the skewered Dimlock to the right and its body absorbed another shotgun blast.

Anaiya kicked the dead Dimlock from her blade and it slammed into the Dimlock in front of it, both tumbling to the oily pavement. Anaiya leapt sideways, evading another blast from the downed Dimlock. As the buckshot raced past her, only inches from her face, she saw an arrow pierce the attacker's throat. Mackinsi was somewhere close. A volley of whines and squeals washed over her and she spun in surprise. Dimlocks poured into the bus lot from every direction. Even as they streamed toward the buses, she saw them drop one by one, arrows protruding from chests and necks. She glanced up to see Mac on top of the bus garage raining arrows down onto the approaching mob. She spun and raced toward the garage, her red cloak billowing behind her. To win this battle they would have to stand united and strong. Despite the odds, Anaiya felt a grim satisfaction. The massacre had been prevented. They had not allowed another innocent to die.

***

One after another Mac drew and fired his bow and, because of Creator's blessing, as swiftly as the arrows left his quiver they reappeared. With each second an arrow rocketed down finding its intended target. Anaiya climbed the side of the garage to join him. As she appeared on the roof beside him he felt peace settle over him. He looked at her determined expression and felt the familiar flutter of his heart. She was an amazing woman.

"Keep them off the roof," he called to her and she responded by hacking the arm off of one of the Dimlocks who had managed to get a hold of the edge. The beast went careening off the wall, taking several of its companions with it.

"I've got you covered." Anaiya laughed. This was beginning to get fun. Like a carnival game, Anaiya chopped the heads off the Dimlocks that reached the top of the roof and, as the creatures moved back from the garage to see what was stopping them from gaining the roof, Mac's arrows blew through them.

Anaiya thrust her blade through a Dimlock's shoulder, sending it flying from the wall. As she rose, Mac saw two Dimlocks gain the roof behind her. One lunged at her with its claws extended. Mac loosed an arrow.

Anaiya spun to see Mac's arrow impact the first Dimlock's head and continue through it to blast through the second one as well. Both beasts slumped lifeless to the roof. Anaiya realized she was holding her breath and willed herself to breathe again. That shot had been inches from her head. That was twice Mac had saved her life. "Once again, I owe you."

The Dimlocks kept climbing and the Stormbreakers battled on.

***

"Excellent," Talon muttered under his breath in satisfaction. The two Stormbreakers were tiring. The Dimlocks were serving their purpose. Destroyer had long ago sent him to wipe out the last of the bloodline. He had found the woman in the hospital and had killed her and her baby boy.

The bloodline should have ceased to exist; yet, several months earlier, Talon and his partner had witnessed a Covering of the man now fighting on the roof a hundred yards in front of him. How could he still be alive? The realization hit the hunter like a sledgehammer to the face.

"Of course!" he bellowed, and began to walk swiftly toward the garage.

He did not agree with Destroyer's quest for the Aquillian scroll. Stormbreakers should never be spared for any purpose. They should all be destroyed ... especially the double-marked one. His existence could spell the end of them all.

***

Through the chaos of the battle, Mac's heightened senses alerted him to the approach of a powerful, black-shadowed figure. "Anaiya," he called, "can you handle yourself up here for a while?" She smiled and cracked the thin tip of her staff against a scrambling Dimlock's head. The creature fell lifeless and broken to the asphalt below. "Good enough," Mac said then leapt from the roof.

He landed gracefully, rolling to his feet, already in an all out sprint.

The hunter ran also, his hand under his coat. Mac slid Nightsbane from its scabbard, the ring echoing across the lot. Each step confirmed his suspicions. He had fought this attacker the night of his Covering.

Mac reacted faster than sight, dashing to the side. A hollow point whizzed by his shoulder. Another followed but the first had been enough warning. Mac felt the power pulse in both wrists and let it overwhelm his thoughts. Instinct controlled him perfectly. Nightsbane rose before him, splitting the next bullet in half. With a leap to the side and a flick of the wrist, a slender throwing knife embedded itself into the hunter's shoulder. If the knife did any damage the hunter didn't show it. He continued to run and fire at Mackinsi. As another bullet was narrowly avoided, the power within him flared again.

Time seemed to move even slower as Mackinsi dove into the air to the right. He pulled an arrow from his quiver and fired in one smooth motion, returning the bow to his back before landing softly and rolling to his feet. His arrow embedded itself into the barrel of the hunter's pistol, meeting a hollow point round attempting to go the other way.

The Glock exploded in a shower of sparks. The hunter's countenance never shifted at Mac's seemingly miraculous feat. He barreled into the Stormbreaker, his two short swords drawn and flashing.

***

Above the battle, Anaiya continued a battle of her own. Without Mac's arrows, the Dimlocks were able to get onto the roof. The battle had shifted from bashing the creatures that looked up over the edge of the roof to fighting against three at a time who had reached it. The Dimlocks should have had the advantage, but Anaiya had lived for one hundred years. Her bladed staff spun and flashed white as she moved in a dizzying pattern. As her blade pierced a Dimlock's spine she whirled to the left, catching another across the throat. She then flipped backwards over another. As she landed behind it, her blade cut its hamstrings then rose in an S-shaped arch to sever its head from its neck.

Another Dimlock cleared the roof and smiled as it saw the lone female. This would be too easy. It grinned and drool puddled on the roof as it saw the thin, white staff she held. It lifted a heavy broadsword. This would be much too easy. With a gurgling growl, the Dimlock rushed the woman in red, its sword raised for a downward stroke. It roared in victory as the woman raised her staff predictably in the horizontal overhead block the creature had hoped for. It would cut through the thin staff and split the woman's head. It was a pity the Dimlock did not stop to consider the scores of piled Dimlock bodies littering the roof. It was also a pity the creature did not know it was not the first to attempt this obvious tactic. Its sword thundered into Anaiya's raised staff. The white pole of Creator's forging accepted the force of the blow then instantly returned it. The broadsword shattered into dozens of pieces, falling to the ground and adding to the rubble of other shattered weapons. Anaiya's staff whipped like lightning across the startled Dimlock's face. The last thing it heard was the sickening crack of its own neck.

Anaiya spun around to find she was alone on the roof. No more Dimlocks crawled onto it. She walked to the edge and noticed there were none left around the base of the garage.

Sounds of metal upon metal rang out from Mac and a man in black. Anaiya knew a hunter when she saw one, and she recognized this one. "Talon," she whispered to herself. Suddenly, she feared for Mac's life. He had killed a hunter before but he had never had a chance to battle Talon, the leader of Destroyer's hunters.

Anaiya knew Mac was lost in concentration. She would not aid him by jumping into the fray and distracting him. If she did that, she might allow Talon to land a fatal blow. No, she had to watch and pray. "Creator, keep him safe," she whispered.

***

Talon's short swords were a blur as they pounded relentlessly against Nightsbane, seeking an opening. But Nightsbane seemed to have a life of its own in Mackinsi's hands. It was an extension of his soul … of his will. Each of Talon's strikes was calculated and planned, but Mac could move faster. Mac reacted as he had the night of his Covering.

The Power of Light raged within him and Nightsbane met its call. The double-marked, red-bladed katana rose, savagely connecting with the blade of one of Talon's short swords … then cutting right through. The stunned hunter stumbled backwards, now holding only one sword in his hand. It was time to play the ace. "Sarah Duncanson!" the hunter screamed at Mac.

The name pulled at the back of Mac's mind. It was as if a locked door bulged against its hinges, threatening to release the memories locked inside. The hunter took advantage of the effect his ace had upon the Stormbreaker and rushed at him, his single sword cutting deadly patterns in the air.

Mac pulled himself back from his contemplation just in time to save his life. Nightsbane parried the deadly blow and Mac's leg shot out for Talon's ankles. The hunter flipped backwards over the sweep. "Sarah Duncanson!" he yelled again.

This time the name unlocked the door. A wave of images and emotions washed over Mackinsi and he crumpled to his knees.

His mind raced back through the years, finally coming to an unsettled rest. The feeling of anticipation fell over him.

He was in a very warm place and someone else was with him. The warmth was wonderful, he was content and yet ... anxious. Harsh voices entered the quiet warmth in muffled tones. Loud sounds startled him and then a sliver of light appeared above. Gloved hands reached beside him, pulling the other person up through the sliver of light ... cold light. He saw someone holding the other person. Then his heart jumped as the dark man made a loud noise with a black object and the person he held stopped crying. He threw the person to the ground then aimed the black noisemaker at him ... no ... above him. His warm place shuddered as the loud explosion happened again. Then, after one more explosion, all was still. Mac knew something had changed because the place he was in began to lose its warmth. Gloved hands reached through the sliver of light and wrapped themselves around him, lifting him up and out into cold.

He realized he was screaming. He looked down to where he had come from to see a woman covered in red with a slit in her abdomen. The person carrying him was also covered in red with more spilling onto his white clothes every second. He staggered and fell to his knees. Holding Mac with one arm, he pulled himself along with his other. He pulled himself and Mac through a long, cold room and into another where a woman in white rushed up to them. "Sarah Duncanson," the person carrying him whispered to her then collapsed.

Talon watched as Mac struggled with his memories. His surprise had worked wonderfully. Mac had realized the truth, just as Talon had. On that day, eighteen years earlier, they had been duped. The doctor had pulled a child from Sarah Duncanson's womb, but had left another. The woman had been pregnant with twins! They had walked away from Rockefeller University Hospital, leaving the second Stormbreaker baby alive! Now he was the double-marked one! The irony caused Talon to chuckle as he moved in for the kill.

**

"Mac!" Anaiya screamed. Something was wrong with him. He wasn't moving and she knew she could never reach him in time.

***

Sarah Duncanson. Sarah Duncanson. Sarah Duncanson! The name pounded with every beat of Mac's heart. His mother! Sarah Duncanson. She had been shot by the man in black … the man who had killed his brother. The man in black! A hunter!

He heard Anaiya's voice break through his thoughts. The hunter! Mac's eyes flashed open locking onto the hunter in front of him. Within his eyes burned a bright white fire. Mac had discovered his past only to find that the Resident before him had taken it all away. With a scream of grief and rage, Mac rose, Nightsbane meeting Talon's deathblow.

But instead of impacting the falling blade, it sliced through the hunter's wrist. Talon's sword went spinning free with his hand still attached. Even as the shock registered on Talon's face, Mac's fatal blow hit him on his right collarbone. Nightsbane sliced through the hunter exiting his body at his left hip.

Anaiya staggered to a halt as the blow landed. Its intensity startled her. Picking up her pace, she raced to Mac's side.

The hunter attempted to inhale but could not make his lungs move. His shocked expression slowly turned into a death mask as his torso slid diagonally from his other half, falling like half a watermelon to the asphalt below.

Mac stumbled backward, breathing in deep, painful gasps. The truth of his family's demise was too much for him to handle. He sagged to his knees once again, his eyes filling with tears. Then Anaiya was there … holding his head against her … cradling his sobbing form in her arms. They sat there for what seemed like hours, each drawing their support from the other. It was not until hours later that Mac told Anaiya the entire story.

***

At the top of Leviathan's headquarters, Destroyer felt the wave of the Stormbreaker's power wash over him. Talon had done his job well, though Destroyer doubted he had survived the encounter. The double-marked one had come out of hiding. The Aquillian Scroll would soon be within his grasp!

Chapter 14: Anthony Ward

Several days passed as Anaiya and Mac scanned the papers. The wave of tragedies had come to a halt with the death of the hunter. The truth of his past both soothed and weighed upon Mackinsi. His questioning mind had found peace but a new void had been opened in his heart. He had a blood family, but he would never know them.

Anaiya sat at the table, her head lowered in thought. Mac had noticed the gleam slowly fade from her eyes since the day of the battle, replaced by a sad resignation. Mac knew what she was resigning herself to, and he feared it as well.

"You don't think he's coming back."

Anaiya glanced up thoughtfully and then looked back down again. Her blonde hair swayed gently with the subtle movement. "I know he is not coming back," she said quietly.

Her statement caught Mac off guard. "What do you mean?"

"Michael has never been this late before."
Anaiya stood up and walked to look out the window.
"You're important to him, Mac. There's only one
thing that would keep him away this long."

Mac felt a chill shoot up his spine. "You
think he's dead."

"I know he is," Anaiya answered and Mac
saw there were tears in her eyes. He felt his own
eyes fill and he went to Anaiya, wrapping her in a
tight embrace.

"I can't feel him anymore," she said softly.
"Look inside, Mac, you will see."

As they stood there in silence, Mac realized
Anaiya spoke the truth. He searched for the soft
warmth of reassurance he had felt when he had been
in Michael's presence. It was gone, replaced by an
anxious emptiness.

He looked into Anaiya's knowing eyes and
held her tighter. "What could kill Michael?"

"I believe that nothing in the Seven
Dimensions could defeat Michael except Destroyer
himself," she answered.

"But that means Destroyer would have had
to be in Los Angeles."

Anaiya pulled slowly away to gaze again through the window. "I pray he did not discover the Gathering. If he did, all may be lost." She paused thoughtfully then turned toward Mac, her eyes regaining some of their sparkle. "Well, perhaps not all."

Mac knew her meaning and wished he could have the same hope she and Michael had in him, but Mac knew his limitations. His fighting skills could not compare to Michael's. If Destroyer had defeated him, how could Mac hope to stand against him?

Anaiya seemed to read his mind. "Michael believed in you, Mackinsi. He would have given his life to protect you because he knew you were the key we have been waiting for." She turned his wrists over so his two cross markings shimmered up at him. "You must believe."

"I'll try," Mac answered quietly.

Anaiya nodded, sighing softly. "Thank you."

Mac realized he had been pacing across the room and stopped. "What do we do now?"

Anaiya sighed. "I was hoping you could tell me. I hoped Michael had left some plan with you. I have nothing."

Something tugged at the back of Mac's mind but slowly slipped away. "I wish he had too."

"With no plan, we can only do one thing. We pick up his torch."

"Fly to Los Angeles?" Mac asked.

"Unite the Stormbreakers," Anaiya answered. "Even though it's hard to say out loud, even with Michael gone, the storm is still coming. He would have wanted us to go on. He would have asked us to continue if he had suspected his death would come so soon."

Mac noted the break in Anaiya's voice and felt for her. What must it be like to lose someone you had known for 100 years? "Okay," Mac said in the most confident tone he could muster. "Let's pick up his torch ... our torch."

***

Mac drifted to sleep late in the night, finally able to separate himself from the sobs of the beautiful woman next to him. He had to let her grieve, but it tore him apart to see her in pain.

Suddenly, a great darkness settled over him and he spiraled downward. Farther and deeper he plummeted, mist rushing past his face. He expected to hit the ground each moment, but each moment only brought a blacker darkness and a longer fall. Suddenly, he landed on something smooth, knocking the wind from his body. Painfully, he pushed himself up to his feet. He had to maintain his balance as the ground shifted beneath him. A deep, rumbling laugh seemed to resonate all around him then a dim light filled the area with an eerie glow. Mac looked about him to realize he was standing on some sort of sphere. Looking deeper into the shadows, he started in surprise. A clawed hand held the giant sphere. Realization hit Mac hard and he spun to see a ghastly face emerge from the blackness. Its glowing eyes probed his mind and he felt a pull from within the sphere.

"Mackinsi Wrighton," Destroyer boomed. "It is so good to see you."

Mackinsi's pulse raced like a frightened rabbit as Destroyer continued.

"I have been searching for you for so long. It is nice to finally see you in person."

Mackinsi spun, sprinting toward the opposite edge of the sphere. He would not allow Destroyer to manipulate him. Better a dead savior than a powerful pawn. But Mac skidded to a halt as Destroyer's face appeared looming before him.

"You can't run, my powerful puppet. I have already found you. It took some sacrifices, but it was worth it."

Mac thought about the hunter and the massacres in the paper. Rage boiled inside him, flickering in his eyes. It had all been to find him? His hand flew for Nightsbane but hit only air. His bow too was missing. He stood straight and tall as Destroyer laughed.

"You will not find it so easy to destroy me, Mackinsi Wrighton. I have waited too long to find you only to fall to your pathetic weapons."

"So, you have come to kill me," Mac stated bluntly, his voice echoing off unseen walls.

"Fool! This is merely a dream. I have come as a messenger."

"Why?" The anger inside Mac bubbled still. He suspected he already knew the message.

"I wanted to be the first to inform you of Michael's demise, and that of every Stormbreaker at the Gathering!"

Mac felt the air rush into his lungs as he involuntarily gasped.

"It seems they met a tragic end. Creator's lackeys were always too trusting," Destroyer growled.

Mac regained his composure as he pondered the weight of Destroyer's words. Too trusting? The realization came swiftly. "Glenn! He led you to them!"

"Very good," Destroyer boomed. "It is good to see the double-marked Stormbreaker also possesses slight intelligence."

"I am destined to destroy you, you must know that," Mac stated evenly.

A sardonic grin spread across Destroyers' face. "We shall see who destroys whom."

Mac had heard enough. He had to wake up. He had to tell Anaiya of this meeting.

"Creator," he prayed, "guide me." A peace settled upon him and he decided his course of action, bursting into a sprint straight toward Destroyer. Before Destroyer could react, Mackinsi leapt from the sphere. The image of Destroyer shattered like glass as he passed through it, and then he was once again falling through darkness.

"Mackinsi Wrighton!" Another voice cut through the black. He thought he recognized it.

Ahead, he saw a pinpoint of light. It grew larger and brighter as he fell towards it.

"Mackinsi Wrighton!" This time Mac recognized the voice, his heart filled with hope.

"Michael!" he shouted. "You're alive?"

"Listen!" the voice commanded, and Mac grew silent. The light grew brighter and larger as Mac fell closer to it.

"Remember my words, Mackinsi Wrighton!" The light filled Mac's vision.

"When all seems lost!" The voice echoed, and then Mac plunged into the light and into consciousness.

"Michael!" Mac screamed, sitting up in bed.

Anaiya started awake to find Mackinsi soaked in sweat and breathing hard. She slid closer to him beneath the blankets, laying his head against her chest. "What is it?" she asked.

"I heard Michael's voice in my dreams," he replied. "He was trying to tell me something, and I saw Destroyer. He told me all the Stormbreakers at the Gathering—"

Anaiya's eyes were wide. "Whoa, settle down Mac... You're safe now. Start from the beginning and don't leave anything out."

***

The two friends talked into the early morning.

Anaiya did not doubt Destroyer's message about the fate of the Stormbreakers at the Gathering. If Mac was right about Glenn's role in it all, it would explain how Michael had been caught off guard. Michael's voice in the dream, on the other hand, confused her. She felt his death within her, but Mac claimed the voice had been his. She wondered what magic was at work.

Mac had focused on Michael's final sentence before he had awoken. "When all seems lost…" Mac knew it was supposed to help him remember what to do, but although he could sense the memory's presence in the back of his mind, he could not grasp hold of it. Anaiya wished he could remember.

"Mac," she called from the kitchen table, "we leave in two days for L.A. at noon."

"Sounds great," he replied from the bedroom.

"Should we take a taxi or drive the car and pay for parking?" she called to him.

There was silence from the other room.

"Park … the park!" Mac yelled. He rushed into the room Anaiya was in. "The park!" He ran over to her, cupped her head in his hands and kissed her cheek.

Anaiya flushed red. "What are you talking about?"

"Before he left, Michael told me that if all seems lost I should return to the park where we first met!"

"New York?" Anaiya asked, rubbing her cheek.

"Yes," Mac answered. "Walker Park!"

That night Anaiya had trouble sleeping for another reason. She could not stop thinking about Mac's kiss. Amidst her pain, she drifted into slumber, soaring on the clouds of hope.

***

The night drive was uneventful and, as Anaiya and Mac approached the park, they could hardly contain their excitement. They would pick up Michael's torch and whatever Michael had left for them at the park would surely help them do that.

It was well past midnight when they entered Walker Park. The fluorescent lamps lining the park stretched the pair's shadows across the sparse grass. Mac had no idea what to do now that they had reached the park. He had done as Michael had instructed, and only one idea presented itself to him. He would begin his search at the statue of General Walker.

The familiar characters roamed the edges of the park, and Anaiya watched them all.

"It's not safe here," she whispered to Mac. "I'll stay here and watch your back."

Mac nodded in agreement as they reached the statue. He began to scan the park in a spiraling fashion. He glanced at the blonde woman watching the area like a hawk and smiled. He couldn't have had a better protector. Slow minutes passed and he finally completed his search. "Nothing obvious," he muttered to himself. He turned again toward the center of the park to see Anaiya sprinting his way. Her red cloak billowed behind her and her face showed pure concentration. Mac spun 180 degrees and saw the target of her focus. Several dark shapes had entered Walker Park. As he watched, more and more appeared. By the time Anaiya reached his side, thirty trench coat clad men stood before them. Nightsbane whispered through the night air as Mac drew it, sending a ringing echo through the still night.

"Residents?"

"I don't think so," Anaiya answered.

Mac's wrists flashed and time flickered. The crosses on the hilt of Nightsbane flashed to green fire. That had never happened before. Slimy corpses oozed from the men, taking the black trench coats and Desert Eagles with them.

"Dimlocks!" Anaiya shouted.

Then, all at once, absolute chaos erupted in Walker Park.

Anaiya and Mac bolted in opposite directions, zigzagging as bullets ripped past their bodies. The blazing gunfire mingled with the bone chilling, wailing cries of the Dimlocks.

As Mac darted left, avoiding a wave of bullets, something caught his eye. A thin shaft of green light rose from the ground next to the statue in the center of the park.

Another bullet whizzed past his right ear, pulling him back to the task at hand. If they died here, all would be lost. Circling around the trunk of a convenient tree, Mac raced up and into its branches. He was glad someone had planted trees in Walker Park.

***

Anaiya dodged behind the trunk of a nearby tree. The wood shuddered as the 45-caliber slugs crashed into it. Wood chips exploded past her head as the density of the wood stopped the deadly projectiles, creating a momentary safe haven. Anaiya silently thanked Creator for the trees. A noise overhead caught her attention. She looked up to see a form that blended in with the trees land in the branches of the one she was taking cover behind. A barrage of arrows rained down, dropping three Dimlocks before the figure leapt to the next tree. Mac! Anaiya smiled in spite of her circumstances. He never ceased to amaze her.

***

Mac leapt from tree to tree with effortless grace, his tireless quiver sending arrow after arrow into the unwitting Dimlocks. He would follow the line of trees until he could drop into the midst of them. He knew getting close to the firearm wielding monsters was the only way to stop them. Nightsbane could work its magic once Mac drew close enough. The branches hardly moved as he swept toward the group.

The creatures were almost entirely focused on Anaiya though several fired into the tops of the trees hoping to hit the source of the arrows.

Three more bounds brought him directly above the mob. Mac dropped straight down, Nightsbane drawn and ready.

***

Anaiya had made it to safety behind another tree trunk when she noticed the sound of battle change. Risking a glance, she saw the mob was turned in upon itself. Mac had made it! Silently, she came out of hiding and sprinted toward the Dimlocks. Her white staff rested comfortably in her right hand, ready for battle.

***

Mac felt as if he had fallen into the center of a continuous explosion. The sounds of gunshots surrounded and deafened him as each of the remaining twenty-five Dimlocks attempted to shoot him. In such close quarters their efforts only served to shoot several of their own.

Mac darted and spun, Nightsbane an extension of his thoughts and will. The nearest Dimlock aimed his pistol at his head but Mac's reactions were faster than the creature's trigger pull. He shifted to the right and the bullet shot harmlessly by him. He followed his shift with a right cross-body slash, severing the Dimlock's shooting arm at the wrist. Immediately, he brought Nightsbane in a reverse arc, taking off the Dimlock's head. Without a moment to celebrate, Mac turned Nightsbane's blade backward and stepped back hard. He felt the blade bite into flesh and bone and continued driving Nightsbane into the ambushing Dimlock.

Even as he did, two more Dimlocks took aim at his chest. Without a moment to spare, Mac performed a layout backflip over the head of his still skewered adversary. As the guns went off, he used the dying Dimlock's body as a shield. It absorbed the rounds as Mac rushed toward the shooters. He hurled the body at one Dimlock, knocking it to the ground, and simultaneously executed a jump spin hook kick, breaking the other creature's neck.

His cloak jerked slightly, tugging at him, as several bullets smacked its edges. This would be a long battle, but Mac knew he had to win. Looking up, hope rose inside him. Anaiya had joined the fray.

***

Anaiya watched Mac's flourish of precise attacks with awe. It seemed as if he could see several seconds into the future, avoiding point blank shots moments before they would have killed him. Her thoughts shifted ahead of her as she saw several Dimlocks run out of ammunition, draw notched swords, and turn to face her. She remembered the years of training with Michael and smiled. This would be fun.

The Dimlocks saw her smile and hesitated and, in that moment, her staff went to work. She blocked the nearest Dimlock's lunge and swept the creature off of its feet and into the air with the bottom of her staff.

As it flipped backwards, her razor sharp blade found its heart, skewering it and keeping it suspended in the air. Anaiya's muscles strained with the effort of supporting the weight but her adrenaline gave her the needed push. She hurled the writhing body off of the end of her blade and into its companion. Even as the startled creature absorbed the heavy blow, Anaiya's blade silenced it forever.

A sickening crack and splatter resounded as she brought the thin, white shaft of her staff down on the head of a Dimlock firing at Mackinsi. Several more cracks filled the night as she waded into the midst of the chaos.

***

Three knives flew from Mac's hands as he sprinted sideways, each blade finding a Dimlock throat. His cross markings blazed brilliantly in the night and his skills grew sharper.

Unconsciously, Nightsbane rose, slashing to the left and right, slicing first one bullet then another out of the air before they could reach Mac's body.

Fifteen Dimlocks remained. The green shaft of light still beckoned from the center of the park, but he could not possibly get to it now. His green cloak hung in tatters, torn to shreds by near misses. He could see Anaiya was bleeding from her arm and mouth, but could not stop to help her. With fifteen semi-automatics firing at you, one misjudgment would surely bring death.

Mac pulled his bow from his back and into his left hand. He prayed it had been blessed with the resilience of Anaiya's staff. He dropped swiftly to his knees, savagely swinging the wood of the bow into a Dimlock's shins. They shattered and the Dimlock toppled over into Nightsbane's rising arc.

Mac moved through the crowd in lightning quick movements, alternating strikes between his bow and sword. Dimlocks fell left and right, but those not mortally wounded continued shooting at the pair of Stormbreakers.

Mac saw Anaiya losing ground. She was barely able to stay ahead of the bullets being fired at her, and, though she was inflicting damage on her opponents, their numbers were overwhelming her defenses.

Mac doubled his efforts, feeling the Power of Light blaze inside him. Nightsbane slashed and thrust true as his bow followed, cleaning up the remaining resistance of an opponent. Sweat covered his body, soaking through his clothing and matting his hair to his head. He knew he was tiring and he guessed the same was true of Anaiya. Panic whispered to him deep within his soul. *Anaiya could die here, be lost to you forever. If you fall … would the world then be doomed?* As the terrifying thoughts assaulted him, he noticed the Dimlocks had stopped fighting. With their weapons down they moved away from the pair. Not missing the opportunity, Anaiya and Mac trudged together, back to back. They both knew they were thinking the same thing. If this was the end, they would face it together. But the Dimlocks continued to keep their weapons at bay. Sneers rose on several ghastly Dimlock faces but they made no move toward Mac and Anaiya. The two Stormbreakers breathed heavily, waiting for the creatures to lift their weapons, waiting to fight what could be their last battle.

The chill night air swirled like an unseen river around them, injecting ice into their damp clothes. It came as a welcome relief to the tired warriors.

The ground trembled and the two pulled closer together, weapons extended. Again, the ground shook as if it had been hit by a tremendous hammer.

"What's happening?" Mac whispered to Anaiya.

Anaiya answered through labored breaths. "I would guess we are about to meet another fiend."

Mac thought back to the battle with the Reap and shuddered. He did not want to meet another fiend, especially being as tired as he was from the previous melee. He guessed that had been the point of the Dimlock attack.

A large shape moved in the darkness as the ground shook again, and then it appeared. Melting out of the darkness, the twelve-foot-tall beast emerged. Its black, volcanic skin shimmered in the low light and its eyes blazed red with an inner fire. It held a 6 foot long sword, which widened upward to end in a spiked, horizontally angled tip. The blade was matted with hair and blood.

"Tremorda," Anaiya stated grimly.

The beast's roar pounded Mac's eardrums, threatening to break right through them.

"It looks like a troll," he whispered to Anaiya.

"Yeah," she replied. "But you only wish these guys were slow and stupid."

In the blink of an eye Mac strung an arrow and let it fly. It blazed toward the creature, burying itself deep into its molten eye. The creature roared and stumbled, pulling the arrow from its head. No damage had been done to the eye, but the shaft of the arrow had been halfway incinerated.

"How do we hurt it?" Mac asked, replacing his bow and drawing Nightsbane.

"I don't know," replied Anaiya.

"Well, then let's find out!" Mac yelled and, with wrists blazing, rushed toward the charging fiend.

The ground trembled with each step the Tremorda took. Mac raced toward the fiend, his cloak trailing behind. Even as he ran his wrists glowed brighter and the tears in his cloak began to mend, caught up in the Stormbreaker's power, the power of Creator.

Anaiya moved to follow but the Dimlocks sprang into motion, drawing swords and falling between her and Mackinsi. She battled furiously but soon came to realize that, for now, Mackinsi was on his own.

Mac dove under the swing of the massive blade as the Tremorda fell upon him. Mac rolled to his feet, slashing a savage swipe across the beast's thick leg. His eyes widened as he gazed at the leg. Nightsbane had done no damage! The Tremorda's left hand grabbed at him but he rolled to the side, barely escaping the deadly grasp. As he rolled to his feet the giant's backhand caught him, blasting him head over heels into the trunk of a tree.

The Tremorda swung its massive blade at its fallen prey, but Mac dove behind the trunk of the tree. The huge blade drove halfway into the side of the tree and stopped fast, stuck by the pressure of the weight above it. The Tremorda bellowed as it realized its weapon was stuck. Mac took advantage of the delay to spring from behind the tree and stab Nightsbane downward into the beast's foot. This time Nightsbane's blessed edge pierced the monster's volcanic exoskeleton. A gout of molten stone spewed from the open wound as Mac darted away but, within several seconds, the wound closed as if it had never been made. The Tremorda howled in pain and slammed a great fist into the tree. The force of the blow blew the top of the tree off of its trunk and onto the wet grassy ground, freeing the creature's sword.

The beast spun with a roar and was hit by three throwing knives and two arrows before it could locate its attacker. The projectiles ricocheted off the creature's skin and Mac leapt to another tree just ahead of another tree-felling blow.

As Mac leapt from tree to tree, the Tremorda gained ground until he was finally directly behind him. Mac had anticipated what would come next and knew it was his last option. He waited at the top of the tree and, as the Tremorda blasted a fist into it, Mac leapt high into the air, flipping backward. His markings and those on his sword left green trails as he flipped high into the night air. The tree fell and Mac landed securely on the creature's shoulders.

Immediately, he put Nightsbane in motion, driving the sharp blade downward, piercing the Tremorda's thick skull again and again. Trails of molten stone rained down around Mac, but he paid them no heed. He was intent on the kill.

The Tremorda screamed in pain and shook its head violently, attempting to dislodge the attacker.

Mac continued his brutal attack, hoping with each thrust that it would be the fatal blow. With its attempts to dislodge Mac unsuccessful, the Tremorda dropped its sword. Magma flowed down its neck as it grabbed Mac tightly by the throat, pulling him off of its shoulders. A powerful right hook sent Mac sprawling across the grass.

***

Anaiya cried out as the punch landed squarely against Mac's temple. She watched him fly through the air and onto the grass where he lay still. Anaiya felt herself hyperventilating. "No!" she screamed. The Tremorda turned her way, covered in flowing molten rock. Its roar washed across her as the Dimlocks fighting her moved backwards rapidly, leaving her alone in the path of the charging monster. Her staff came up, parrying the Tremorda's first mighty blow. The sheer force of it sent her flying to her left. She rolled to her feet desperately looking for Mackinsi, but he had not moved. He was still lying motionless on the grass. Somewhere in the back of Anaiya's mind, it dawned on her that this battle could be her last. Mac could be dead, and she was no match for the fiend. Gritting her teeth, she drove those thoughts away. She would survive, and so would Mac! They had too much resting upon them to fail now.

She screamed into the still night as she leapt toward the beast. Her blade drove into the Tremorda's stony flesh, releasing flows of magma, but each wound sealed itself quickly, leaving the Tremorda unhurt and enraged. Anaiya leapt to the right as the Tremorda's fist whistled over her head. She rolled to the ground, attempting to come up and engage the fiend, but as she rolled to her feet, the Tremorda was already upon her. A blow fell heavily toward her head. Like lightning, Anaiya lifted her staff. The black fist of the Tremorda met her thin, white staff. Any other wood would have shattered upon the impact but her staff held. Despite its strength, Anaiya's hands could not meet the force of the blow. The staff flew down and out of her hands, flipping sideways to embed its blade into the ground. The Tremorda rushed over the weapon and Anaiya scrambled backwards across the grass. Each step of the heavy creature shook the ground, sending chills through Anaiya's spine. She was out of ideas and time. The Tremorda stood over her, a foot on either side of her body. She tried to squirm out of the trap of his legs, but each way she moved a huge, black fist blocked her way. Anaiya finally stopped struggling.

She stared defiantly up into the eyes of her killer and, as the Dimlocks watching jeered and mocked her, the Tremorda leaned forward, its enormous face inches from her own. She felt the heat from its eyes and smelled the sulfur on its breath.

With a menacing laugh, the Tremorda lifted its hand to crush her. Anaiya felt her muscles tensing for the strike, and willed her eyes to stay open. Michael trained her, she was a Stormbreaker, and she would remain one until the end. The Tremorda raised its fist then brought it down heavily. The impact of the blow shook the ground violently. The Dimlocks cheered wildly, but the Tremorda was not elated. A large blade hung from its back, and attached to it was the Stormbreaker it had left for dead. Fire burned in Mackinsi's eyes as he wrenched his sword downward, slicing a 3-foot-long gash in the fiend's back.

Anaiya's eyes had remained open. She noticed her chest was still rising and falling with breath. She wasn't dead. She turned her head to the right to see an enormous, black fist lodged into the ground only millimeters from her head. The bottom of a green cloak flowed into her vision as the person she desired to see alive more than anything in the world stabbed Nightsbane into the back of the Tremorda again and again. Mac had saved her life again. Moving her shoulders and hips in unison, she shimmied out from beneath the behemoth as it tried to pull its fist from the earth. Frantically, she rushed to her weapon and with a mighty tug she pulled it from the ground. As she turned to join Mac, she met another obstacle. The Dimlocks had swarmed between her and the raging battle. She screamed in frustration and leapt at the first Dimlock.

Mac breathed easier as he saw Anaiya escape the hold of the Tremorda. He had recovered just in time to distract the falling punch of the fiend. His head still swam from the tremendous blow the Tremorda had landed on him earlier but he was focused.

He had saved Anaiya and now he would kill the creature that had tried to kill them both! With a roar of rage, the Tremorda pulled his hand free of the ground and spun on his stubborn attacker. The fiend was fast, unlike the trolls of fiction, and used it to his advantage. With a feint to the right, he drew Mac's parry. Faster than Mac could blink, the Tremorda's right fist shot out, striking Nightsbane, and the sword flipped away. Mac tried to dive to the left but the Tremorda's right hand caught him around the neck. Its other hand closed around the other side of his throat and Mac felt himself lifted off of the ground, felt the burning heat of the Tremorda's skin.

***

Anaiya cried out as Mac was lifted high into the air by the monster. She could sense the crushing grip. She knew Mac could not escape. She dodged a thrust of a Dimlock sword. The Dimlocks attacking her would not let up. She would not be able to get to Mac in time.

***

Mac felt the stranglehold tighten. Death was only moments away and yet he felt no fear, only assurance. This was not the end. The grip of the Tremorda tightened and Mac noticed his vision beginning to blacken. As the world flickered from light to darkness, he heard a voice in his mind.

This is not the end, Mackinsi Wrighton! There is more power inside you! Awaken!

The pressure on Mac's neck increased as he reached deep inside and found a glowing spark.

Awaken!

A brilliant green light exploded from the markings on Mac's wrists as he wrapped his fingers around the monster's forearms. Power surged from his body and into the fiend.

Green-white lightning flowed up Mac's hands and radiated and blasted into the body of the enemy. The Tremorda shuddered, burning eyes locked onto Mac in disbelief. A sharp crackle split the night as cracks appeared in the fiend's exoskeleton.

Green light glittered beneath the surface of the monster, visible through each crack as it began to widen. As the rifts in the monster grew wider, beams of light poured out. The Tremorda was vibrating wildly as it dropped Mac, who rolled into a crouch a safe distance away, wrists still glowing brilliant green, bathing the night in emerald. The Tremorda watched its large hands crack then explode into powder leaving the stubs of its forearms shooting beams of emerald light. The fire in its eyes cooled to the same brilliant light and, with a gut-wrenching scream, the fiend exploded, volcanic rock showering across Walker Park.

The Dimlocks watched the event in disbelief then turned to attack. The sight before them stopped them dead in their tracks.

Out of the night and through the still falling shards of the shattered fiend came another Stormbreaker. The tall, blond man's white cloak billowed effortlessly behind him as he rushed straight into the indecisive monsters.

In two swift slashes of his dual katanas, three Dimlocks fell. Another aimed its pistol at the man from a distance. The stranger turned, just as the Dimlock fired twice. As the bullets moved toward him, the Stormbreaker flared his cloak, moving in a circular pattern. The bullets impacted the cloak halfway through the motion. The spinning motion absorbed the bullets' momentum. Completing his spin, and with a snap of his cloak, he sent the bullets straight back at the attacker, killing the startled Dimlock instantly. The man's katanas moved in a blur. Mac stared in wonder, his breath still coming as ragged gasps from his previous exertion. The man in white was very close to Michael's skill level with a blade. His heart rose as he stood to his feet. Perhaps the man had been trained by Michael. The spectacular battle continued as Mac and Anaiya stood speechless. Each movement was perfect. Within the span of ten moves, all of the remaining 16 Dimlocks were dead.

The white clad Stormbreaker wiped his blades on the garment of one of the Dimlocks, re-sheathed them and approached Mac and Anaiya.

"Hello Mackinsi, hello Anaiya."

The man's voice showed no strain from the swift battle he had just fought.

"I have been away a long time. My name is Anthony Ward. I was a friend of Michael's."

Chapter 15: The Torch

"That was an impressive show," Anthony said, brushing leaves from Mac's shoulders. "I've never seen someone channel Creator's power quite like that."

Ignoring the newcomer for a moment, Anaiya turned to Mac. Her eyes were wide. "What happened back there, Mackinsi?"

"What do you mean?"

"When the Tremorda exploded," she clarified, "what did you feel?"

Mac remembered the feeling well. "A voice guided me to a spark in my mind. When I found it, my wrists felt like they had burst into flames and I felt a raging river of power inside me." He paused in thought. "I channeled it through the fiend."

"A voice?" asked Anthony. "Whose voice did you hear?"

Mac reflected quietly. "I think it was Michael."

"Michael?" Anaiya glanced around hopefully. "He's alive?"

"No, Anaiya." Anthony's face fell as he delivered the grim news. "The Gathering was compromised. Michael was killed by Destroyer, as were most of the other Stormbreakers."

Mac felt despair begin to settle upon him. "How many survived?"

Anthony's expression hardened. "Very few, I'm afraid. I survived only because an oath took me from Michael's side before the battle's end."

Anaiya's eyes glittered with tears under the night sky. "What oath?"

"I promised Michael that I would find and protect the double-marked Stormbreaker and lead him to Los Angeles to continue Michael's work."

Mac nodded grimly, sliding an arm around Anaiya's shoulder and pulling her into a comforting embrace. "Did Michael know this was coming?"

Anthony nodded. "I believe Michael expected his death would come soon. With him, the Stormbreakers were a mighty army. Without him—" Anthony waved his right hand through the air, his cross mark shimmering in the dim light "—we shall see."

Anaiya stood tall.

"Michael maintained hope, even knowing he would die." She turned to Anthony. "Can we do any less?"

Anthony nodded solemnly. "Of course, you're right," he said. "The right side will win the day." His gaze drifted to the brilliant green beam shining into the sky.

Mac noticed and turned to look as well. He glanced at Anthony. "I can tell from your prowess with the blade that you were trained by Michael, as was Anaiya." Anthony nodded and Mac continued. "Because of that, Michael will never leave you. His training will be with you always, leading your reflexes and sharpening your mind. In a sense—" Mac smiled "—it will be as if Michael is still beside you, protecting you every moment of your life."

He looked to Anaiya to find her eyes filled with tears. Her face shone with the soft, green light of the beacon.

"Thank you, Mac."

***

The earth flew away under the three Stormbreakers' relentless hands. Mac had informed Anthony of the reason for the dig and Anthony had eagerly joined in. The hole became a foot deep, then two. Dirt flew and expectations heightened. At three feet, the green light winked out. Anaiya looked in confusion to Mac, but his confidence reassured her, as did his words. "We must be almost there."

Anthony cried out first as his fingers hit a flat, solid object. The three quickly doubled their efforts and soon a featureless rectangular box sat unearthed upon the grass.

"What is it?" asked Anaiya. She lifted the rectangular box to her eye level, examining it intently. "I don't see any way to open it."

Mac looked at it as well. He too saw no way to get inside. "There are no hinges or latches." He rubbed his hand across the flat surface of the box.

"Wait!" Anthony interjected. "Do that again."

Mac slid his hand across the flat surface a second time, this time watching the ends of the box as Anthony was instructing him to do. His heart raced as he saw the cause of Anthony's excitement. As he touched the box, two faint crosses appeared upon it: one on each end. They faded as his hand left the box's surface.

Anthony smiled. "There's our way in."

"What do you mean?" Mac asked.

"Touch your markings to the ends of the box."

Mac slowly did as Anthony instructed. The black box felt cold against his wrists. Nothing happened at first, and then he felt a tingling in his toes.

"Something's happening," he announced.

The others took a tentative step back from him as the tingling shifted upward through his legs and chest and then down into his wrists.

As the sensation reached his wrists, they flashed green once, accompanied by a loud click from the black box. A large rectangular square rose up from the center of the box and then all was still. Mac looked at it closely then, on a hunch, pushed it back into the box. It slid easily and, as it fell flush against the lid, a sound like tumblers spinning met his ears. The sound was followed by another pronounced click. A green line appeared around the box, separating the hidden lid from the rest of the box. Silently, the box opened. Inside rested a flat, triangular piece of stone.

Anaiya and Anthony moved back to look at the stone triangle Mac had lifted from the box.

"What is it?" asked Anaiya.

Mac studied it closely. "I don't know, but it is definitely old."

"I have an apartment around here," Anthony interjected, "it would be safer to continue this conversation there."

Mac looked to Anaiya who nodded in agreement.

"Lead the way."

The three made their way from Walker Park in single file, constantly watching their surroundings.

Mac held the box under his left arm. His mind spun with questions. The box had been designed to only open to a double-marked Stormbreaker. *No*, he thought, *not a double-marked Stormbreaker, THE double-marked Stormbreaker.* Michael had told him he was the only one. The box had been designed for him. He pulled it tighter against his side as he followed Anthony's flowing, white cloak.

***

The subway ride passed without incident and a short time later the three Stormbreakers were walking up the white stairs toward Anthony Ward's apartment.

Anthony casually opened the front door and Mac and Anaiya hurried in behind him. He led the two to the kitchen table.

Mac let the warmth of the room sink in. The kitchen table was finely polished oak and several glass cabinets lined the walls with fragile sculptures of Fantasy battles. Anthony Ward had an interesting taste in art.

He turned to face them, his white cloak flaring behind him. A smile returned to his face. "We are safe here," he said, beckoning to the box. "Let's see what Michael left us."

Mac touched his wrists to the ends of the box, and then pushed the protruding square down, opening the box once again. The triangle of stone felt heavy in his hand as he gently lifted it from the molded black velvet lining. He placed it onto the table and the three gathered closely around it.

"What are those markings?" Anaiya asked, peering closer.

Mac looked closer as well and was surprised to see the flat surface of the stone was indeed marked.

"An eagle, a spider and a snake," whispered Anthony, "each at one of the points of the triangle."

"What do they signify?" Mac asked.

Anthony paused a moment to run his fingers across its surface. "It could mean many things. Each creature is a predator, the ruler of all it surveys."

Anthony lifted his gaze to the two Stormbreakers staring at him. "If I'm correct about what this is, Michael may have left you with more than you can chew."

Mac straightened his back, standing taller. He had felt overwhelmed many times since the Covering, but he had faith in Michael, and he had Anaiya with him. "Michael believed I could handle this."

Mac noticed Anthony's eyes weighing him, probing into his.

"True enough," Anthony conceded. "I fear I must open a very dark door for you."

Anaiya leaned closer. "What door can be darker than the one we must walk through after Michael's death?"

Anthony responded immediately. "The door I must show to you is within the very door you speak of. Michael's death opened the way to it and this," he said, pointing to the stone, "is its key."

Mac sighed. He was becoming tired of riddles. "What door does this key open, Anthony?"

Anthony's face was solemn but the gleam remained in his eye. "It is the key that unlocks the door to the Aquillian Scroll."

Anaiya gasped despite herself, quickly regaining her composure. "Why in the seven dimensions have we dug it up?" she asked incredulously. "Destroyer seeks the Aquillian Scroll relentlessly! It is not wise to be simply walking around with the method he can use to get his hands on it!"

Anthony nodded. "I felt the same way when I first saw the key in the park," he said to Anaiya.

"Why would Michael have us dig it up?" Mac asked.

"That's simple," Anthony easily replied. "Destroyer seeks the scroll. If the Stormbreakers got to it first, it could be destroyed or hidden again where it would remain safe from him forever."

Mac looked with renewed amazement at the stone triangle resting harmlessly on the table.

"Why does Destroyer want the scroll so badly?" he asked.

Anthony began to reply but Anaiya cut him off. She spun her white oak staff in her right hand as she spoke. Mac guessed it was either due to nerves or excitement.

"The scroll gives the wielder the knowledge of all things. It was designed by Creator at the dawn of time as a gift to humankind." Anaiya paused in thought and then continued. "If Destroyer assimilates all dimensions, that is as far as he can go. He will rule the fused dimensions until the end of time. But if he gains the knowledge of the scroll, he gains the knowledge of Creation. With that understanding, Destroyer could create a new universe in his image. He would rise to become an equal of Creator." She stopped, letting it sink in.

"If that was his fear," Mac said, "why didn't Michael destroy the scroll already?"

Anthony lifted the key from the table, flipping it in the palm of his hand. "He couldn't bring himself to destroy Creator's greatest gift."

"Besides," Anaiya added, "Michael hoped the Aquillian Scroll would never again have to be disturbed. It was he, thousands of years ago, who moved it to the hidden location, forged the key and enchanted it. He hoped to defeat Destroyer without the scroll even coming into the picture."

Mac began to understand. "So he suspected the Gathering could be compromised."

"I don't think he expected it," Anthony replied, "but he prepared for it."

Anaiya continued before Anthony could. "Michael would have known that, if he fell, the scroll would be unprotected. That is why he left instructions for you to claim it."

Anthony nodded solemnly. "Mac, you'll notice the box only would open to you."

Mac nodded, he had definitely noticed.

"If Michael could not guard the scroll, he wanted you to do it," Anaiya finished. "You know he believed in you," she said a bit softer. "He wouldn't have trusted anyone else with the protection of the scroll. That is why he enchanted the key box to open only to you. The scroll is the same way. According to legend, it requires your touch to awaken."

Mac noticed he had begun to pace. He looked up to see the others looking at him.

"So... I now have the key that unlocks the most powerful weapon Destroyer can possess, and it's sitting here on a wooden table in New York?"

Anaiya nodded somberly.

"Well"—Mac's voice rose with the question—"what do I do with it now?"

He noticed Anaiya's lips lift in a faint grin before she quickly turned away. "We go to L.A. and pick up Michael's torch," she answered.

Anthony placed the stone back into the box, closed it and handed it back to Mackinsi.

"There is a remnant of Stormbreakers that are still alive," he stated firmly. "Marcus Stone survived and, as one of Michael's closest friends, I'm sure he will have more answers."

Sleep did not come easily for Mac that night. The familiar warmth of Anaiya's body next to him provided the only sense of security he felt. He gazed at the black box on the nightstand then picked it up and held it next to him. The fate of mankind rested on that small stone key, and that key was his responsibility. He prayed that Creator would guide his actions. He silently hoped a remnant had indeed survived the Gathering. Mac finally drifted off to sleep to thoughts of black, evil things. He did not sleep well.

Chapter 16: The Remnant

"Thanks," Grady Reynolds said quietly, accepting the white porcelain mug filled to the brim with black coffee. The waiter nodded then turned away, leaving the 60-year-old to his thoughts.

Grady slid his right wrist further out of the sleeve of his brown trench coat, examining the flickering cross. His emotions were still a jumble. He closed his eyes and tried to wipe the terrible images from his mind, without success. They flashed like an unstoppable slide show in his memory. He saw his fellow Stormbreakers being slaughtered, blood exploding all around him. He heard the inhuman shrieks of the Dimlocks as they rolled over his companions.

He opened his eyes quickly, drawing in the scene before him. He tried to slow his breathing. He was safe, he reminded himself. The memories were just those ... memories. He picked up the coffee mug downing a mouthful. The liquid felt like fire burning down his throat.

Michael! The slide show began again, its unstoppable procession leading him to the last place he wanted to go. He saw Michael walk through Destroyer's shield of fire. He saw each blow of the ensuing battle. Grady's breathing came faster and his heart raced as he saw Michael blasted across the warehouse. Destroyer lunged after him and released his blazing fire. Somewhere something shattered.

Pieces of porcelain were strewn about the table and Grady's shaking right hand was covered in hot coffee. He looked up quickly to see people staring in his direction, looking very confused. Glancing down at himself, he realized his trench coat had flowed back into his brown cloak. *Just as well,* he thought, leaving a tip and rising quickly.

The sidewalk rolled by as Grady walked the streets of Los Angeles, but his mind was in another world completely. Michael had been the strongest of them all. His death, in addition to all of the others, seemed to drive the fact home that all hope was lost.

Grady knew that the remnant of Stormbreakers would seek each other out and attempt to organize an attack upon Destroyer, they were honor bound to do so, but what chance would their small army—Grady guessed less than a hundred had survived—have of defeating a being as powerful as Destroyer?

Shaking his head, Grady kicked himself mentally. "Stupid old man," he muttered to himself, "always forgettin' faith." His heart lifted slightly as he reminded himself that Creator was still in control and that he was still more powerful than Destroyer. Looking up at the skyscrapers towering above him, he shut his mind to the morbid thoughts. "Creator will have the last say," he whispered to the sky, "don't you doubt."

Grady was an interesting Stormbreaker. His Covering had not come until his sixtieth year, when he had been car jacked. Well, when someone had attempted to car jack him. He had destroyed the Dimlock inside the young criminal and had then been found by Michael.

Years passed and Grady watched his children have children, and their children have children. This was all from a distance, of course. His 80-year-old great grandchildren would not understand why their great grandpa was still 60. They believed he had died in a car accident many years before.

Sometimes he felt his age, albeit for an extremely fit 60-year-old. His arms were layered with muscles and his white hair and thick, white mustache contrasted against his tanned and leathery skin. He was a stubborn man, refusing to accept defeat, and his years had made him wise. Grady Reynolds was nobody's fool.

His meandering walk eventually led him to the door of his apartment complex. As he opened the door of his modest apartment he noticed a letter lying on the floor. He picked it up, unfolding it. It was simply blank, white paper. He smiled grimly. This had been quicker than he had anticipated. He placed his marking against the paper and watched words melt into existence. Perhaps there was hope after all.

***

Her two short swords worked in perfect harmony as Celeste Kauffman glided through her sword dance. Her straight, shoulder length, black hair, combined with the gentle slant of her eyes, gave her a distinctly eastern appearance. She was fifty years old, but did not look a day over twenty-three. Her white halter-top covered what Celeste thought to be average sized breasts and her khaki pants were already damp with sweat. She had been practicing for an hour. Her right sword stabbed high as she executed a right, reverse sweep, rising with a left slash to the knee and a right reverse slash to the neck of her would-be opponent. Her violet cloak settled gently around her.

A knock sounded at her apartment door. A letter was slipped under it.

As Celeste opened the letter, she smiled, and then touched it with her wrist.

***

The light of St. Dominic's invitingly beckoned to the brown-cloaked Stormbreaker as he glided up the cathedral's white marble staircase.

Rows of stained wooden pews stretched out to his right and left as Grady Reynolds walked to the front of the cathedral, directly under the icon of the crucified Christ, and made a right. He entered the confessional and glanced quickly at his watch. Several minutes passed by and then he sensed a presence enter the confessional opposite him. He tensed every muscle. If the answer he expected did not come immediately, he would have to move extremely fast. He steeled himself. "I am a servant of the light."

He waited for the appropriate response. The one the person he was supposed to meet would know. Too Long! A dagger fell from each of his sleeves into his waiting hands, and his toe pressed hard against the floor of the confessional.

"The light will calm the storm," a low voice replied from the opposite booth.

Grady relaxed at once, his daggers slipping back into his sleeves. He ran his gnarled hand through his white hair. "Marcus." There was relief in his voice.

"Grady," Marcus replied, "I'm glad to see my message reached you."

"Me too," Grady replied. "You aren't trustin' puttin' what you got to say in the letters?"

"No," Marcus replied. "I trusted few before, and after the Gathering, I trust fewer. For the time being, I'm taking initiative to organize another meeting of the Stormbreakers."

"I like the way you're goin' about it," Grady replied.

"I can't take enough precautions," Marcus replied. "We can't afford to lose any more of our number."

"After Michael's sacrifice…" Marcus trailed off. Tense silence hung in the air for several seconds. Grady filled it. "You know it wasn't your fault." Silence stretched for a few seconds more.

"I know."

"He would be proud of you, you know," Grady added, his grandfather-like demeanor showing through.

"Thank you, Grady." Marcus sighed. "The meeting will be at 10:00 p.m. the day after tomorrow. It will be at the fallback shelter. Do you understand?"

"Loud and clear, boss," Grady replied. "I will see you and the rest of the remnant there." Rising rapidly, he passed silently out of the cathedral.

Marcus sat for several moments more, enjoying the silence. What would the meeting bring? What hope remained? As another person entered the confessional Marcus replied to the first part of the code. Celeste answered, her heart beating more rapidly as she heard the news.

Chapter 17: En Route

The ticket agent smiled at the three well-dressed people as she handed them their tickets. "Gate C," she said, smiling at Anthony and batting her eyelashes. Anthony smiled back and the three made their way toward the gate.

"Three first class tickets," Anthony said casually to Anaiya. "That's a lot to put on your credit card."

Anaiya flashed a smile Mac's way then looked toward Anthony. "It's not like we have a time limit on paying it off—" she laughed "—we do live forever."

Anthony smiled but didn't laugh. "You assume there will be a forever to live," he said without much mirth.

"We'll stop Destroyer," Mac interrupted. "Creator has foretold it in the prophecies." Hadn't he? His mind spun through the memories of what Michael had told him about the prophecies.

"I have no doubt what the prophecies say will come true," Anthony answered, "but they say only that the double-marked one will face Destroyer. They say nothing about who will be the victor." Noticing Mac's countenance drop, Anthony quickly added, "But not to worry, Mackinsi. Michael lived for several thousand years. He studied the prophecies more intently than almost anyone." He put his hand on Mac's shoulder. "Although the prophecies do not state directly who will prevail, Michael believed that all signs pointed to Destroyer's downfall." He sighed deeply. "I'm sorry, my young friends, I am ever the pragmatist. It is not my intent to discourage you."

"I understand," Mac said, lifting his chin and straightening his posture.

Anthony seemed to relax as Mac's mood warmed. Anaiya smiled at them both.

"Metal detectors," she stated.

She had briefed Mac earlier on their procedure for the airport. At her statement the nice clothes the Stormbreakers were wearing transformed back into their cloaks, shirts and pants. They walked to the left of the metal detectors, through the exiting crowd, and then jumped the divider filled with potted plants. When they were safely heading toward Gate C, three well-dressed people re-appeared as if they had simply moved into the crowd's field of view.

The 747 arrived and they took their seats, courtesy of Anaiya's credit card, in first class. The three sat side by side with Anaiya in the middle and Anthony by the window.

"Do you fly much?" Mac asked Anaiya, as he buckled his seatbelt.

"Not really," she answered, smiling at Mac. "I can tell you don't fly the friendly skies much either."

Mac laughed. "Is it that obvious?"

"Of course not..." She tried to maintain a straight face, but failed miserably.

"Okay," Mac said, "how can you tell?"

Anaiya let her smile surface. "Just a little thing called sheer terror I read all over your face."

Mac laughed. He was indeed nervous about the flight. It was the first time that he could remember being on a plane.

Anthony leaned forward as the 747 taxied onto the runway. "If nerves are getting to you, you can try my guaranteed nerve soother."

The plane rushed to takeoff speed then lifted smoothly into the air. Mac felt his stomach rise into his throat. "I'm ready for that nerve soother," he groaned.

Anthony laughed as he reclined his chair. "Follow my lead." With that, he closed his eyes.

Mac looked incredulously at Anaiya.

"Sleep?"

Anaiya shrugged. "If sleep eludes you, you always have me for company."

Mac felt his stomach settle slightly, permeated by the familiar warmth of Anaiya's presence. Somehow the thought of getting to spend hours with Anaiya made the flight more bearable.

An hour passed with Anaiya and Mac involved in a pleasant conversation. Anthony was fast asleep, his chest rising and falling with each deep breath.

"How does it feel to have those?" Anaiya asked, gesturing toward Mac's wrists. "I think it would be a pretty big burden."

Mac turned his wrists over, examining the flickering crosses thoughtfully. "It's pretty stressful," he admitted. "I try not to think about the prophecies too much because, when I do, I sometimes feel overwhelmed."

"Look at me, Anaiya." He laughed softly. "I'm the supposed super warrior, the Savior of the World and here I am freaking out about flying on an airplane."

Anaiya laughed too. "You didn't seem frightened when you jumped into the shadow of the Reap," she reminded him.

"That was different," Mac replied.

"How so?"

"You were…" Mac began. "A lot was at stake."

"I see," said Anaiya, a faint smile showing on her lips. "So, if a lot is at stake you find courage?"

"I guess so," said Mac.

"Then what have you got to worry about? The entire race of mankind is at stake!" Anaiya concluded cheerfully.

Mac slowly shook his head. "Thanks, that's really a load off of my shoulders."

"That's what I'm here for," she answered, taking Mac's sarcasm in stride.

Mac watched her smile, her lips curving up delicately.

"You know," he began, "if I were you, I'd be nervous hanging around me."

Anaiya put on a 'listening very intently' expression. "Why is that, Mac?"

"If I am the sole threat to Destroyer, he will spare no expense to kill me. People who are around or close to me might be caught in the crossfire."

"You're worried about me?" Anaiya asked with mock seriousness.

Mac laughed. "Well, I'll just say that you dying would not make my day."

"If they come after me, why should I be afraid?" she asked, her mouth turned up into a half smile. "I'm sure you'll protect me."

"How are you so sure I can?" Mac asked.

Anaiya leaned closer to him, her lips drawing extremely close to his. "A lot would be at stake."

"Excuse me," interrupted the tall flight attendant, "dinner will be served shortly, would you like chicken or steak?"

"Chicken," both Anaiya and Mac replied, pulling away from each other.

"What would your friend like?" the flight attendant asked.

"I don't know," Mac replied. "Would it be okay to bring it when he wakes up?"

"Yes sir," the flight attendant replied. He made a note then continued on his way.

"So do you think Anthony's a steak or chicken guy?" Anaiya asked Mac, as she looked at the sleeping Stormbreaker

"I'd guess steak," Mac said, sharing Anaiya's gaze. "While we're on the topic of Anthony," he whispered quietly, "what are your thoughts about him?"

Anaiya pondered his sleeping form for a few moments before responding.

"A Stormbreaker to be admired," she said in hushed tones. "He survived the Gathering and carried Michael's message to us in time to save both of our lives."

"How old do you think he is?" Mac asked.

"Definitely not as old as Michael, but I would guess many hundreds of years … maybe a thousand."

Mac's mind lingered over Anthony's stunning display of swordsmanship in Walker Park. "Do you think Michael trained him?"

"If he didn't, then there is another 2000-year-old sword teacher wandering around somewhere," Anaiya answered. "Unless he had Creator imbue mastery of those two swords he carries, Michael trained him."

"Did Michael ever mention him to you?" Mac pushed.

Anaiya looked at him quizzically. "Not that I remember but, Mac, I only knew him for a small fraction of his life. He trained hundreds of Stormbreakers."

"I guess you're right," Mac conceded. "Ever since Glenn, I'm just paranoid."

Anaiya nodded, placing her hand gently on his shoulder. "Trust takes some time to grow between people. Take us for example." She squeezed his shoulder a little tighter. "I remember when I first saw you in the alleyway. You didn't know me from Eve, but you trusted me."

Mac closed his eyes, remembering the feeling of that moment in time. "There was just something comfortable about you. I didn't have to work at it."

Anaiya accepted the compliment with a smile. "You won my trust when you saved me from the Reap. When that disgusting tongue wrapped around me, I thought it was over."

"I wasn't going to let that fiend take you," Mac said softly.

"I owe you my life."

"You would have done the same for me."

"Anthony did the same for both of us," Anaiya added. "We owe both of our lives to him."

"True enough," Mac agreed.

"If we can't have Michael with us," Mac said, "at least we can have one of his students."

"Hey!" Anaiya exclaimed. "Forgetting someone?"

"Two of his students," Mac corrected.

"Thank you," Anaiya teased.

The flight attendant pushed the cart up next to their seats handing them two steaming plates.

"Dinner is served."

***

An hour later, Mac sat staring absently at the cushioned headrest of the seat in front of him. Anaiya had drifted off to sleep ten minutes earlier, joining Anthony who had not awoken for dinner.

He glanced down at her. She looked so peaceful asleep against his shoulder ... so beautiful. *Get hold of yourself, Mac* thought. *She's your friend ... don't ruin it.* Despite his attempts to convince himself, he remained unsure. Before the flight attendant had interrupted them, he was sure Anaiya was going to kiss him. If he combined that moment with all the sideways glances and half smiles she threw his way, he came up with a pretty promising picture.

He was glad for her conversation and, in fact, had learned a few things about himself during the course of it. He learned that he was unprepared to take on the responsibility of saving the world. Sometimes he still felt like the gangly high school student, living his adventures by reading of adventure.

Everything had happened so fast and Mac was unsure if his head had stopped spinning. Nightsbane rested invisibly by his side. He felt like it was a part of him, a necessary part of him. He honestly could not remember life without it.

Anaiya had been right about his fear of flying. He realized that now as he looked out the window. He had battled evil incarnate to save her when he confronted the blackness of the Reap. He touched his finger to his neck and winced as he felt the circular burn left form the Tremorda's volcanic hands.

The power locked inside him had saved him once again that night when he had vanquished the fiend. After that, he and Anaiya had faced certain death, prevented only by the appearance of Anthony. In the light of these hair-raising events, what was a plane ride anyway? He silently thanked Anaiya for that wisdom as he looked out into the night sky. The speckle of city light met his eyes, and the fear he had felt was gone.

Mac slowly moved his left hand to his armrest, so as not to wake Anaiya. He looked at Anthony's glittering mark. It was true Anthony had saved both their lives, and had given them the answers to the questions about Michael's gift. He had been kind, if a bit blunt at times, and Mac felt a familiar connection to the white clad Stormbreaker that reminded him of Michael. All in all, he was grateful for Anthony's presence, not only because of his prowess with his blades, but because of his support. Mac leaned his head back against the soft cushion of his headrest. He enjoyed the warmth of Anaiya's soft cheek against his shoulder. *Yes,* he thought, *I will give Anthony Ward a chance. It is the least I can do for the memory of Michael.*

Chapter 18: Preparations

Hundreds of candles cast a bright but flickering glow across the master suite of Leviathan's top floor. Destroyer lounged comfortably in his ornate throne listening intently to a report from one of his Resident officials. Two Resident soldiers stood on either side of the large, wooden doors leading into the chamber. Their mission was simple—to kill anybody foolish enough to enter unannounced.

Destroyer was grinning wickedly, his dragon-like face a twisted image of hate and joy. His official brought incredible news. The infestation of evil had increased ten-fold. After his annihilation of the Gathering in Los Angeles, his Dimlocks had surged across the globe, possessing weak-willed people and prompting them to rape, kill and destroy. His wave of evil was having helpful repercussions as well. People not possessed by Dimlocks wanted vengeance for the rapes and murders and were committing murder themselves.

Destroyer laughed a deep, booming laugh. His world was such a beautiful place.

"Threl"—he addressed the Resident before him—"it is almost time; I can taste the scroll!" He leaned forward in his eagerness, his skin shining wetly in the flickering light. "All is falling into place. When I loose the storm upon the world, I will do so with the full support of the Aquillian Scroll."

Threl looked slightly bemused. His gaze drifted to Destroyer's flaming eyes then quickly fell back down to the floor. "Master," he began, "no one but the double-marked one can use the scroll. We have not been able to locate it yet, although we continue to search and..." He jumped at Destroyer's outburst of fury.

"Fool!" Destroyer cried, rising from the throne and towering over the official. "Arrogant Son of the Light!" he seethed. "Do you dare to believe that you know more than I, your master, Destroyer?"

The Resident shuffled backward several steps, his gaze riveted into the floor.

"Even as we speak, I know the location of the double-marked one, this Mackinsi Wrighton!" Destroyer spat onto the ground. "He is the key. He will bring me the scroll!"

"Yes, Master!" the Resident stammered, but Destroyer was not finished. With a mighty flap of his leathery wings, he was beside the Resident, grabbing him by the hair and lifting him into the air.

"If you ever question me again, I will slaughter you! I will watch your eyes dim as I tear out your black heart! Do you understand me?" Destroyer bellowed.

"Master," one of the guards interrupted from the door, "Glenn Cross is here as you requested."

Destroyer threw the Resident across the room. The warrior smashed heavily into the wall and crumpled to the ground. He quickly up-ended himself and made as graceful an exit as possible.

"Show him in," Destroyer purred, now utterly calm. He sat smoothly back upon his throne and, somewhere deep within him, a soft laughter sounded. He had been expecting Glenn earlier, but now would suffice.

When Glenn entered the chamber, Destroyer knew why he had been delayed. Two scantily clad women walked in with him. They giggled and the woman with the blonde hair rubbed his chest softly. The brunette licked her lips and began running her hand over the blonde's arm. Glenn just basked in the attention, grinning up at the Master of Evil.

"Sorry I'm late, Master." Sarcasm dripped from his statement. He obviously was not sorry in the least.

"Do I scare you, Glenn Cross?" Destroyer asked, his voice low and grating. His red eyes seemed to bore into the dark Stormbreaker as he waited for an answer.

Glenn looked from one woman to the other and then back up at Destroyer. Despite his effort, he couldn't keep his eyes from drifting over the Heartstone on the pedestal beside the throne. He felt himself begin to salivate. The power the stone contained was too much for him to take. He wanted it … he needed it.

He was startled back to reality by a flash of light and searing heat directly to his left. Startled, he turned to see his blonde lover engulfed in blue fire. She screamed frantically, reaching for him, but he backed away, horrified. The blonde's clothes burned away, leaving her naked body bubbling. She staggered after Glenn, still wailing at him to save her. The brunette fainted dead away and Glenn stumbled, trying to escape the horror before him. All sanity gone from the blonde, she cried in terror, flopping all about on the ground, then finally became still. The flames continued their barrage until she was nothing more than an ashy pile of charred, reeking flesh. Glenn felt dizzy and the room swayed in his vision. He turned and emptied his stomach onto the unfortunate brunette, who had fainted at his feet. Gaining control of his heaving body, he turned accusing eyes to Destroyer. Destroyer sat comfortably in his chair, admiring a small, blue flame hovering over each fingertip. "When I ask a question, I expect an answer."

"You killed her!" Glenn accused, tears welling in his eyes despite his efforts to stop them. "She was innocent!"

"Oh, I'm sure she was anything but that, Glenn," Destroyer mocked. "I question your loyalty."

Glenn felt a chill run along his spine. Could Destroyer read his mind? Did he know of Glenn's desire for the Heartstone? Glenn stifled the panic welling within him and hurriedly stepped away from the ashes on the floor.

"I am loyal!" Glenn said through clenched teeth.

"Really?" Destroyer chided. "I heard you were planning on killing Mackinsi Wrighton and that whore he travels with."

"Anaiya," Glenn growled.

"That is it, yes, Anaiya Lynn," Destroyer replied.

The rage inside Glenn gave him courage. How dare Destroyer humiliate him! "So what if I am?" he growled defiantly.

"You confirm my doubts. If you killed Wrighton before he gave me the scroll," Destroyer stated evenly, "you would die slowly. I would stretch your torment out for thousands of years."

He still stared into Glenn's eyes, weighing, searching, and promising he would do as he said.

Glenn glanced at the cold eyes of the Residents in the room and his shoulders slumped in defeat. "What do you want from me?"

Destroyer grinned once again. "Only this, Glenn… Continue to rally the Dimlocks. They know to take your orders. Lead them into creating the coming storm."

"What of Mac and Anaiya?" Glenn asked softly.

"Leave them to me. When I have finished with them, you may do with them what you will."

Glenn knew he was walking on eggshells and had to be extremely careful now if he valued his life. "That sounds reasonable," he lied.

"Good," Destroyer crooned.

Glenn helped the brunette stand and the two began to walk from the chamber. The two Residents quickly drew their 45 caliber Desert Eagles and blocked their path.

"One more thing, Glenn," Destroyer stated, "one more test of loyalty. Listen well and act quickly. This is the only way you are walking out of the room alive."

Several moments later, Glenn emerged from the large, wooden doors alone. He wiped the blood from his scimitar and slid it back into its sheath. Destroyer had seemed pleased when he had left the room. Glenn hoped he had gained his trust. It would be necessary someday. He would use it to steal the Heartstone and kill the abomination. It would be he, Glenn Cross, who would rule the assimilated dimensions. When he got to his room, he picked up the telephone. He needed more women.

Chapter 19: Stepping Forward

The 747 touched down a bit roughly at LAX. The terminal was awash in lights due to the growing lateness of the night.

Anthony and Anaiya had awoken during landing and the three Stormbreakers now moved rapidly through the terminal toward the exit.

"Anyone have a plan on how to begin to gather the Stormbreakers?" Anaiya asked.

"It is possible they were not left leaderless after the Gathering," Anthony replied. "If that were the case, the remnant may already be gathering."

Anaiya had to walk quickly to keep up with the men's long strides. The trio passed through the exit.

"Do you have any ideas, Mac?" Anaiya began, and then stopped as she noticed he was not next to her anymore. She and Anthony turned to find him staring into the distance.

"What is it?" she asked, hurrying back to his side.

"Can't you see that?" Mac asked her, pointing up toward the distant skyline. She turned to look in the direction he was indicating. Anthony turned as well, but quickly turned a curious look back in Mac's direction. Anaiya stared for several seconds then looked back at Mac, angling herself in an attempt to look exactly at the angle Mac was staring. All that met her scrupulous gaze was the hazy night sky of Los Angeles.

"What's going on, Mackinsi?" Anthony asked, moving back to stand beside the two.

"I know where to find the remnant," Mac said quietly. He turned his wrists over revealing his cross markings shining against the darkness.

Mac saw more than the L.A. sky as he exited the terminal ... much more; and what he saw had stopped him in his tracks. A brilliant beam of green light blazed from somewhere in the city, streaking into the night sky and rising upward until it disappeared from Mac's view. He quickly explained the sight to Anthony and Anaiya.

Anthony looked at Mac's wrists and then nodded. "I sense a surge of the Power of Light as well. I can't see anything, but I believe you. It is most likely a beacon of some sort."

"Can you lead us there?" Anaiya asked, still looking hopefully into the distance.

"I think so." Mac nodded. They turned to find a cab waiting beside them with Anthony already inside. "Come on you two," he called from inside. "We have no time to lose."

The two jumped in beside the pragmatic Stormbreaker and, with Mac guiding the cab driver, they hurried off into the Los Angeles night.

***

"Thank you all for coming and for maintaining the secrecy of this meeting." Marcus Stone's voice was amplified by the Power of Light and each Stormbreaker heard him as if he were standing directly before him. One hundred Stormbreakers were in attendance. They had all survived the Gathering. Some had their arms in slings and several others' heads were decorated with bandages.

It was true they had survived the massacre, but some of their wounds would have them out of the battle for a long, long time. The gathered Stormbreakers resembled battered soldiers coming home from a brutal war. Only a few seemed to be unharmed.

Grady stood somberly amidst the small crowd. He was anxious to hear what Marcus had to say. He imagined that most of the people around him were anxious for the same thing. They had scattered after Destroyer's attack on the Gathering, each attempting to stay undercover, under the radar of Destroyer and his minions. In that time, he imagined many had lost hope. He had struggled with the same overwhelming feelings, but had come to an uplifting conclusion. Despite the loss of Michael, Creator was still in control.

Several Stormbreakers next to him began to mutter together. When Grady heard them scoff at Marcus' notion that Destroyer could still be defeated, he decided he had heard enough. It was enough that they were so few in number, but when people began to undermine the already shaky foundation their potential success rested upon, he boiled over.

"Shut your yaps!" he snapped at the sling-armed man who was muttering with a bandaged-headed woman. "Ain't it enough we are so few in number without you rotting us away from the inside out?"

The two looked shocked as people began to stare their way; however, Grady was not finished … by any means.

"Destroyer killed a lot of us," Grady conceded, "but not all of us! And that is where he made his mistake. We're Stormbreakers," he stated, looking not only at the two mutterers but also at the people turning to watch. "We stand for something more than ourselves. We fight for something more than ourselves! No matter the cost. No matter the odds!"

All eyes had turned to Grady now and Marcus stood at the podium silent and smiling.

"We are Creator's weapon against Destroyer!"

He raised his arms in a pleading manner and a piece of white hair slipped out of place to curl on his forehead. "I've gone through the same turmoil of feelings ya'll are goin' through, but I found somethin' there. I found my faith! Michael believed the prophecy was being fulfilled, and so do I. We are not lost," Grady said, winding down. He felt a hand on his shoulder and turned to see Celeste standing beside him.

"I too believe the prophecy is being fulfilled, and I too plead with you to have faith," she shouted to the crowd. "Wait on Creator! He will not let the last dimension fall!"

Grady smiled, tears filling his old eyes. Celeste was like a daughter to him. They had met several years before and had formed a fast friendship. He was grateful for her support.

"Thank you, Grady." Marcus' voice boomed throughout the small, bare warehouse. "I could not have said it better myself." All eyes turned back to the platform. The two mutterers stopped muttering. Both had turned crimson red and had taken up the hobby of gazing at the floor.

Marcus stood tall, confidence brimming from his deep voice. "Michael died saving my life and many of yours as well. If he had not battled Destroyer for the amount of time he did, we would all have fallen to his fire. We owe our lives to Michael." Marcus paused, looking into each person's eyes. "What does that simple statement mean? Well, it means we owe it to Michael to never give up. It means we must take up where he left off. Michael believed the double-marked one had appeared despite Destroyer's seemingly successful attempt to destroy our bloodline. The stories he told me of the young Stormbreaker convinced me as well. None but the double marked could have done the feats he accomplished on the night of his covering.

"This brings us to a critical point. His existence means two things for the Stormbreakers. Michael made these two things very clear to me. The first is that there is hope. The prophecies tell of the battle between the Chosen One and Destroyer. The second thing is that the Aquillian Scroll must now be recovered. We are sure Destroyer knows the double-marked one is his key to the scroll."

Marcus paused for a breath then came to the conclusion he had been leading up to. "We now have a specific mission. We must find the double-marked one and keep him safe while attempting to find a way to get to the scroll before Destroyer does. I am sad to say that Michael was the only one who possessed the key to its whereabouts. When he died, this knowledge died with him." Mutters began about the room but Marcus silenced them. "The double-marked one will be found, as will Michael's key. They must! Our future and the future of the world depend upon it." Marcus froze as a tingle shot up his spine, like a wave sliding onto the shore. It appeared the tingle affected everyone because they all appeared startled, glancing nervously in every direction. Some put their hands upon their weapons, easing them in their scabbards.

Marcus, on the other hand, waited in anticipation, staring at the door to the warehouse. He was not surprised to see the man in green enter silently, flanked by a woman in red and a man in white.

"Welcome, Mackinsi Wrighton!" Marcus said in his strong, clear voice. All heads snapped toward the entrance, taking in the newcomers. "I introduce you to what remains of our forces.

"Fellow Stormbreakers," he addressed the hundred, "I introduce you to our new leader, the one who is double marked!"

Many things happened at once as Marcus stated Mackinsi was the new leader of the Stormbreakers. Cries of protest erupted about the warehouse, mixing with them were shouts of support.

Mac heard Marcus' words but they didn't register at first. As the cries erupted around him, the weight of the large man's statement settled upon him. "No!" he yelled, "I didn't come to take control!" but his voice was drowned out by the shouts of the crowd. Panic began to grip him, and then he felt a familiar hand on his shoulder.

"Let it happen, Mac," Anaiya whispered into his ear. "It feels right."

Mac started to respond, to tell her that he wasn't ready to lead, that he wasn't capable of taking on so much responsibility, but the words wouldn't leave his mouth. There was truth behind her words. He had realized it on the plane. Although he didn't desire to lead, it did feel right. With this realization he grew silent, listening to the pandemonium erupt around him.

"Why should he lead?" a large man shouted from the edge of the crowd.

"Michael will always be our leader!" shouted another.

"What qualifies him to lead us?" an older man near the front asked loudly. "He's just a child!" Muttered arguments rippled around the room.

Mac could understand the Stormbreakers' dismay. He felt some of the same sentiments himself. He was young and unqualified. He could not even compare to a leader like Michael. Maybe the crowd was right.

Mac was still thinking this and was surprised to see Anaiya take the platform next to the man leading the meeting. He had not seen her leave his side.

Grady and Celeste had remained silent throughout the commotion. They watched and contemplated the happening around them. Both could clearly see the double crosses shining brilliantly from the young Stormbreaker Marcus had introduced as Mackinsi Wrighton. When Anaiya moved onto the platform, they were all ears.

After a brief discussion with Marcus, Anaiya turned to face the crowd. She opened her mouth and her words leapt out to every ear in the same way Marcus' had. Marcus looked at her with a new respect.

"My fellow Stormbreakers! I am Anaiya Lynn, a student of Michael's and a friend of Mackinsi Wrighton. I beg of you to hear me out before making any decision regarding him." The crowd remained silent, drawn to the eloquent blonde before them. "As Mackinsi's friend, I have witnessed what he is capable of. Believe me when I tell you that Michael was right to believe in him."

The crowd shifted slightly at the mention of Michael's name, but could not deny the fact that Michael had always been excited about the prophecies of Creator.

Anaiya paused for impact then continued. "In the time I have known him, Mackinsi has done things no Stormbreaker has ever dreamed of, all the while keeping a humble attitude and an uplifting spirit. How many of you killed a hunter on the night of your Covering? Mackinsi did!"

The crowd began murmuring again, but this time amazement edged their voices. "He defeated a second hunter at a junior high school, preventing the slaughter of innocent children. His sword, Nightsbane, has tasted the blood of hundreds of Dimlocks, and even the black blood of a Reap!" Several gasped as Anaiya named the fiend. "Recently, a Tremorda fell to the blazing power within him. How many of you can make such claims, even after living hundreds of years? He is truly the Chosen One the prophecy speaks of. He is the only one qualified to lead us after the loss of Michael! If Michael were alive, he would give his title to Mackinsi, and serve as his first in command."

The crowd erupted at this. Hostility rippled across the room as Stormbreakers milled about, some waving Anaiya off the stage, others clapping encouragement.

Mac watched the tumultuous events unfolding around him as Anaiya attempted to regain the crowd's attention. He noticed tears in his eyes and casually wiped them away. He would thank Anaiya later. During her speech he had made up his mind. It was time to leave the child he had been behind and step fully into the shoes of the double-marked Stormbreaker he had become. It was time.

He opened the black box he had been holding at his side. Gently, he lifted the key out of its black velvet casing. The key felt different somehow as he gripped it tightly, closing the box once again. It tingled faintly in his palm.

Mac took one step toward the stage and ten stopped as the key grew hot in his hand. Suddenly, he was away from the warehouse, flying through a day lit sky. He flew across the country then down through Florida and out into the open sea. Onward he soared. He felt the wind whipping through his hair. He began to pass over several islands.

He finally slowed to a stop, hovering over a specific small island. In a flash, his vantage point shifted. He was no loner directly above the island but was miles above it staring down at one of the islands of the Caribbean, an island he somehow knew held the way to the Aquillian Scroll! He felt himself being pulled backwards across the sea, and the country, into the warehouse. The heat vanished and the stone key returned to its cool temperature. Somehow it had connected to him, had shown him where to find the scroll. The center of the key now flashed with a soft, green light. Mac silently held the glowing triangle aloft and waited. One by one, Stormbreakers around him saw his double marking pulsing along with the glow of the stone triangle. Word spread quickly and soon the room had again fallen silent.

When Mac spoke, it was twice as loud as Marcus and Anaiya combined. He felt his heart grow strong as words flowed, unprepared but perfectly formed, to the listening crowd.

"Why do you bicker amongst yourselves? You are the Stormbreakers of Creator, the last line of defense between the people of the Seventh Dimension and utter annihilation! The storm is coming rapidly and all you can do is stand and argue? Where is your courage? I know you are wounded. Your spirits are broken as well as your bones, but remember who you are. Remember your heritage. Remember the Stormbreakers who have given their lives to save yours. You owe it to them and to yourselves to fight the coming storm, and, in order to do that, you must first defeat the conflict eating at your hearts, sapping your courage. Anaiya spoke the truth when she told of my adventures. It is true I am young, but, as Michael believed … and despite my lack of experience, I am the Chosen One!

"I do not ask to be your leader. I am merely walking the path Creator unfolds before me. Sometimes it terrifies me, but I press on. Sometimes I feel like I'm completely alone, but I know I am never alone because I have other Stormbreakers beside me. Destroyer has hundreds of thousands of soldiers while we have a mere hundred, and yet the odds are still weighed in our favor.

We have the skills bestowed upon us by the Covering—the strength, agility, and speed. More than that, we have each other. Creator uses each of us for a purpose he has designed. Michael lived to touch all of our lives in his unique way and then to save you from destruction at the Gathering. I live not to replace him, but for another unique purpose. I am destined to confront Destroyer, and, with Creator guiding me, to destroy him! In my hand I hold the first step to this end. I hold the key to the Aquillian Scroll!"

The crowd murmured in amazement at this revelation and continued to listen intently as Mackinsi continued.

"I know its location and will begin my journey tomorrow morning to recover it. I will succeed because Creator has given me friends. Anaiya and Anthony will walk beside me. I will stand beside you as we defeat the coming storm! And if you choose to elect me your leader, I will lead you to the light!"

As Mac finished speaking, he lowered the key to his side. His tongue was dry and his heart raced. He knew Creator had inspired the words he had spoken. Despite his nerves, he held his head high, meeting the wide stares of the people around him.

Complete silence stretched for several seconds, but to Mac it felt like hours, then, one by one, several Stormbreakers pulled their heels together and pulled their right fists to their chests. Some of them had tears running down their cheeks. The soft sound of a few Stormbreakers' fists soon became a roar as every Stormbreaker in the warehouse saluted Mackinsi Wrighton.

He looked around in amazement and, gradually, a smile rose to his face. Anaiya had been correct. Everything felt right. With a nod, Mac pulled his fist to his chest, saluting the crowd, then, after Marcus beckoned him, he approached the platform. He had done it. He had left the child behind. Mackinsi Wrighton was now the leader of the Stormbreakers.

The air was one of excited anticipation for the rest of the night. Mac explained the location the key had shown him. Anaiya beamed from the side of the platform, her eyes never leaving Mackinsi. Marcus took the floor when Mac finished. He restated the importance of claiming the scroll for the light; stated the danger but also the necessity of getting to it before Destroyer. By the time both men had finished, the room was united in a common focus.

"The prophecy speaks of five who will seek the scroll," Marcus told Mac with the Stormbreakers listening in. "Who stands with you?"

Anaiya immediately stepped forward, her jaw set. Her red cloak flowed behind her as she gracefully glided to his side. "I stand beside him," she stated solemnly.

"As do I," a voice sounded from the back of the room. Anthony walked smoothly through the crowd, his white cloak flowing behind him. He stepped onto the platform. "I didn't save these two to let them die hunting the scroll." He smiled and stood by Anaiya.

Marcus waited... "That makes three..."

"I accept any two other Stormbreakers who desire to come," Mac stated, looking over the crowd. Several moments later, a brown-cloaked man stepped forward, followed by a violet clad young woman.

"Grady Reynolds at your service," the cloaked man addressed Mac. "I may look old, but, as Marcus will attest, my knives and I can handle ourselves." As he said this, daggers flashed into his hands and back into his sleeves.

Celeste patted the old man lovingly on the shoulder. "I am Celeste Kauffman. I go where he goes." She laughed. "If his daggers fail him, which is highly unlikely," she quickly added, catching a stern look from Grady, "he can always defeat enemies with his temper." She laughed again.

Grady did not laugh, but his bushy mustache twitched back and forth rapidly.

Marcus smiled at Mac. "If you accept the aid of these two, you will be a wise man indeed."

Grady's moustache stopped twitching and he beamed up at Mac.

"I do accept their help and I am grateful for it," Mac said. He helped them up onto the platform, and they moved to stand by Anthony and Anaiya. Mac nodded to Marcus and to his four companions. "We leave in the morning."

Chapter 20: Dark Musings

The room was still dark as Glenn Cross slipped quietly out from under the covers. He walked casually, not caring whether he woke the two prostitutes asleep in his bed. He didn't bother to turn on the light in the bathroom. The darkness better fit his black mood.

The water of the steaming shower washed over his body, but the heat of the water was like ice when compared to the boiling cauldron of rage burning in Glenn's heart and mind.

Fool! Glenn's thoughts raged. He pounded his fist against the wall, imagining it was Destroyer's face. He was tired of suffering humiliation at the monster's hands.

It was true he had accepted the Dark Covering from Destroyer, pulling him into a binding agreement, but he had fulfilled his end of the bargain.

He had led Destroyer to the Gathering as they had agreed. He had proven himself and yet he was still being treated as a slave. He had been given command of the Dimlocks, but that paled in comparison to Destroyer's original promise.

What happened to ruling Creation at his right hand? Glenn thought bitterly. He was just a lackey, a stooge for Destroyer's dark designs. That did not settle well. Why did Destroyer get the privilege of running the show? Why not he, Glenn Cross? Even as he thought the question, he knew the answer. Destroyer had the power to get whatever he wanted. Glenn couldn't begin to compare with that dark power. No, he reminded himself, there was one way, but to take that road would be to risk everything. He remembered the horrific death of his blonde bed companion by Destroyer's hand and took a deep breath. He knew his plan was dangerous, but he also knew it was foolproof. He would avoid her fate. He would bring Destroyer to his knees! And after that, Mac and his whore would die. The water slid off the angular features of Glenn's crazed face as he grinned into the darkness.

"You think I'm cowed?" he whispered into the black room. His laughter was too rapid. His eyes burned with a fevered light. Soon the world would respect and fear Glenn Cross, the dark Stormbreaker thought to himself. After months of planning, today was the day. His dark musings would become action. Destroyer was out of town. It was now or never and Glenn would settle only for now.

***

Seeka sat stoically at the large desk on the top floor of the Leviathan building. The desk was the first place news from the Resident captains went before being directed to its intended commander. If there was information to be found, she knew it, but Seeka could keep a secret.

She smiled in surprise that afternoon when Glenn Cross walked into her office. He was so graceful, so deadly. He reminded her of her former lover. Glenn truly looked like Talon. And although he had been a Stormbreaker instead of a Resident, she felt a strong attraction to the tall, blond man in black.

Glenn had made several comments that prompted Seeka to think he felt the same way. It was not common for a Resident such as Seeka to seek a sexual relationship with a human.

She was beautiful, with long, dark hair and dark eyes. Her long legs led upward to her other curvaceous attributes. Residents did not attach themselves to only one partner for moral reasons. They chose one lover to be paired with based on how powerful they were. Talon had been the best. Seeka's eyes noticeably roamed Glenn's body. He was so fit, so beautiful, so dangerous. All these thoughts passed through Seeka's mind as Glenn approached her. But he was also crossing the line.

"Seeka." Glenn smiled. He noticed her body language. The beautiful Resident had always been business before pleasure and she maintained her reputation by crossing her arms over her breasts and staring fixedly at Glenn.

"You are out of bounds, Glenn. You know you must be invited here to even step onto this floor."

Glenn smiled confidently. He knew the great hunter, Talon, had been Seeka's lover, and, despite her bravado, he knew she desired him now that Talon was no more. He was Glenn Cross. He considered it part of his job to read women.

"Who says I wasn't invited?" he crooned, gliding a step closer to Seeka, who stood defiantly behind her desk.

Seeka smirked at the arrogance of the young man, but she liked his attitude. Perhaps she would let Glenn have her, but not yet ... not without some fun first. "Well, I certainly didn't invite you and Destroyer isn't in."

Glenn feigned confusion, stepping forward to the desk opposite Seeka. "So you're telling me that there's no one here but us?" His smile, intimate and alluring, slid through Seeka's defenses.

What would it hurt? thought Seeka. The guards inside the throne room wouldn't hear, and there were no meetings on the other small side rooms of the floor. Without another thought, she climbed onto the desk. "I'm inviting you," she whispered.

Glenn smiled and fell on top of her, tearing at her clothing as she tore at his. He had never before bedded a Resident, and was happy his plan was going so flawlessly. Seeka writhed silently on the desk. She smiled as she compared Glenn to Talon. Glenn was more powerful and a much better choice for a lover.

This thought sent her mind reeling to the hundreds of lustful possibilities this young man offered. As her mind wandered, it suddenly ran into something different, strange. Numbness spread through her body, like a hot liquid flowing through her veins.

She struggled savagely, but could not move. She needed to get free! She had been poisoned! Yet, even as she struggled, her mind relaxed, and suddenly it didn't matter that she couldn't move. All that mattered was answering Glenn's questions. He stood shirtless before her prone and beautiful form, grinning evilly. "Seeka," he stated evenly, "what must I do to unlock the Heartstone?"

Seeka smiled wanly up at her lover. Why did she feel such peace? Oh well, it did not matter. What mattered was his question. Without any hesitation she opened her mouth, revealing the darkest secret of all.

Glenn smiled sadly and ended her life with a swift slash of a scimitar. Her eyes remained locked lovingly on him as her blood poured out of her neck. *What a waste,* he thought, *there were several good hours left in her.* Inside his dark heart, Glenn glowed with pride. His newly discovered weapon had proven useful.

He had been developing the new talent on the women he brought into his room for the last several weeks, and was becoming quite proficient at mind control. Who knew what other gifts the Dark Covering would bring? With a curt chuckle, Glenn wiped his blade and moved toward the large, wooden doors. Yes, all was falling into place.

***

The Residents guarding the throne room were bored. They had been given the tedious task of standing for hours in a dimly lit room. Destroyer had left some time ago and the room had been as silent as the grave. The first Resident glanced over, not to the golden throne but to the empty pedestal beside it. When Destroyer was there, the Heartstone sat on top of it. His master must have the stone hidden in a portal of some sort when he was away.

"When do you think the master will be back?" the second guard asked.

The first leaned his weight on his drawn sword. "Soon—" he grinned "—the storm is almost here."

Both grinned now, visions of slaughter dancing in their heads. When the door burst open, they hesitated one second too long.

Bloodletter cut cleanly through the first Resident's right elbow, sending his sword clattering to the floor. His cry of agony rang in time with the sickening gushing sound as Glenn drew his flaming blade through the other Resident's throat. It dropped, kicking to the floor, its blood pooling about its head.

The first Resident drew his pistol to fire at the black-cloaked specter before him, but hit only air. He realized too late that the murderer was behind him and felt the fatal bite of Bloodletter.

Glenn laughed shrilly as the last Resident slumped to the ground. "The mighty Residents," he scoffed. "Destroyer put too much faith in you." The firelight flickered in Glenn's eyes, reflecting the gleam of madness. The pedestal loomed before him. It was forbidding yet he found it more attractive than all of the women he had ever known. It would give him the power he yearned for. He would become the most powerful being on Earth.

Glenn stopped before the pedestal. He re-sheathed the now cold and spotless Bloodletter. The blood had been burned away, leaving its curved, razor edge shining like new. He licked his dry lips and braced himself. The moment was finally here— the moment he would gain the strength to annihilate Mackinsi Wrighton. He smirked at the thought, and then focused on the pedestal.

The secret words he had learned from Seeka rang out loud and strong from his mouth and instantly a tear appeared in the very fabric of space directly above the pedestal. The baseball sized sphere materialized and the tear evaporated into nothingness.

Glenn realized he had been holding his breath and released it rapidly, stretching his hand forward to clasp the shiny, black stone tightly. He lifted it from the pedestal and reveled at how cold it felt against his skin.

He felt the change within him immediately. Its subtlety surprised him. Waves of power did not wash over him. He felt no burning sensation explode within. The change that occurred was simply a sensation of warmth at the core of his being, a new glow behind his eyes. The power the Heartstone contained, on the other hand, staggered him. It seemed somehow familiar, yet above anything he could have imagined.

As Glenn held the stone up before his face, seeing his reflection staring back at him, he realized how the weapon functioned. It channeled its power through its user. The warmth inside him was the channel it would use. So he began to channel the power of the Heartstone, letting its fire wash through him. His eyes blazed like lightning and his mind spun, giddy with power. He would now wait patiently. Destroyer would come to him!

Chapter 21: Domination

The dark shape rocketed through the night sky. It was a fleeting shadow to the nightlife of New York so many hundred feet below it. The shadow dipped below the clouds, its red eyes flashing, and then it rose upward again. The shadow's black, leathery wings beat the air, propelling it forward. Its claws reached forward, stretching, wishing he was already there. He felt the power unleashed before him. Someone had the Heartstone in their possession! How could it be? He had hidden it outside of the Seventh Dimension, through a dimensional door.

Destroyer ground his sharp teeth in frustration and rage. "Who could have the knowledge to open the portal?" The miles rushed by in a blur as he picked up speed. "No matter," he tried to assure himself. "The thief couldn't possibly know how to use the stone's powers … could they?"

His mind spun through the possibilities of who could have pulled the stone from its dimensional safe. He tried futilely to reach the minds of his guards, receiving only silence in reply. Someone was waiting for him in the throne room.

New York met his hungry eyes as he spiraled downward toward the Leviathan building. As he neared the building, he could feel the power being channeled inside. He cursed loudly. The thief was able to use the power of the stone! Destroyer flared his wings, coming to rest on the roof of the skyscraper. He stalked to the edge of the building, waiting ... sensing. Then, slowly, a smile slid slowly across Destroyer's grim countenance. It was true the power of his beloved stone was being channeled, but in very small amounts compared to its potential. He paced several steps backwards and melted through the dimensional hole built into the roof. It allowed him to come and go from his throne room without using the main door. If the thief thought he would use the power of the stone against him, he was in for a big surprise.

***

The throne room had filled with a thick mist that pooled several feet thick upon the floor, swirling with each air current. Glenn sat upon the throne, his eyes blazing. The Heartstone rested in his left hand, his blazing scimitar in his right. Glenn had felt Destroyer's presence growing stronger each second he flew nearer to New York. He was surprised how little time Destroyer's flight had taken him. He had a long way to come. As Glenn dwelled upon this, the candles suddenly dimmed, their light barely enough to see across the room. A shadow fell from the ceiling and the mist swirled franticly, disturbed by a large object's passing. Two red eyes towered above the mist, watching the imp sitting in the stolen throne.

Glenn leaned back in the throne, crossing his legs nonchalantly. His voice was pure confidence.

"What kept you?" he asked the shadow. He smiled as the two large eyes narrowed. He could feel the hate washing over him; smell the rage swirling through the mist. Yes, Glenn smiled to himself, it would be a pleasure to kill the foul beast.

"Your hiding place for the stone was very clever, if a bit too easy to access," Glenn teased, "just another example of your incompetence. Another reason I am the Heartstone's new master." He laughed madly, and the inferno in his eyes flickered and danced. He uncrossed his legs, tense and waiting for Destroyer's rage to explode for the inevitable attack. But the shadow remained silent and still. Glenn thought he could hear a quiet laughter swirling on the mist. No! It had to be his imagination. His mind was swirling with power and was simply playing tricks on him. But tricks or not, it was time to end this dialogue. It was time for his destiny to be realized. He deserved no less!

He stood swiftly and the shadow slipped backward, the mist obscuring it from view. But that did not matter, because Glenn could still feel where his former master was. He drew on the power of the Heartstone deeply until the blood in his veins seared his flesh, until his eyes bulged from his head.

The power grew like a hurricane inside him, threatening to destroy him, but he would be its master. Then, he focused all of the power, all of the hate and fire into one thought, one willed action—to annihilate Destroyer. A split second before he released the power, he hesitated. Another's laughter drifted through his mind, a familiar voice broke through his concentration. Michael's voice whispered in his head! "Glenn Cross!"

"No!" Glenn screamed, and with his cry exploded the power within him. A wave of pure white-hot light exploded from his position across the room, followed by a wall of fire so intense that the candles melted instantly in its path, falling into sizzling puddles. The large wooden doors fell to ashes and washed over the charred throne room.

The Heartstone again felt cool in his grasp as Glenn stared into the inky blackness around him. His sword's fiery glow barely penetrated the smoke now swirling with the ghostly mist. He could no longer feel Destroyer's presence. He smiled more confidently. Nothing could have survived that blast. He was therefore surprised when the large shadow emerged from the swirling haze.

Destroyer lifted his razor clawed hand and the Heartstone flew from Glenn's white knuckled grasp into its waiting embrace. With the Heartstone back in his possession, Destroyer emerged completely from the shadows. Glenn's flaming sword cast wild shadows across the ridges of bony armor that made up Destroyers' body.

Glenn cowered in the golden throne, his mind franticly attempting to find a way out of the hopeless situation. "How did … I mean, how did you…" His voice faltered at Destroyer's grave laughter.

"Did you really believe that you, a mere human, could wield the power of the Heartstone against its creator?" His laughter stopped abruptly. "Did you actually believe you could use fire to destroy the Lord of Fire?" His tone was cold and his eyes burned with a murderous glee. Destroyer raised his other hand and Glenn felt the power he had taken from the Heartstone torn violently from his body. He fell whimpering onto the floor before the throne at Destroyer's feet.

His body was racked by waves of pain, from the abrupt tearing of the power. Tears poured from his eyes. Glenn opened his mouth to speak, to beg Destroyer to spare him, but before he could get a word in, he was launched by a powerful kick across the room. He slammed into the wall and sagged to the floor. He gagged trying to breathe but found the wind had been knocked out of him. Destroyer stalked after him, darkness following him like a cloak. Glenn felt his tunic gripped by large claws and then was lifted from the ground. He closed his eyes tightly, expecting a painful death. His legs dangled futilely below him. After several moments of silence, he slowly opened his eyes. His face was inches from Destroyer's own. He felt the hot sulfur of Destroyer's breath; saw the razor fangs of his mouth and the cold burning of his blood red eyes. Terror and despair washed over his soul.

Destroyer spoke, each word blasting reeking fumes into Glenn's nostrils. "Tell me why I should not kill you right now."

Glenn's mind spun as he sought for a reason, a salvation to his assured death. Suddenly, he remembered the voice in his mind. "I heard Michael's voice," he began, but Destroyer interrupted him with a mighty backhand. "Silence!" he bellowed, as Glenn flew across the room. "Never mention his name in my presence!" Glenn trembled before the raging monster, completely at a loss. He was going to die. Nothing he could say would change it.

"No—" Destroyer abruptly chuckled "—I am not going to kill you. I am going to give you a well deserved gift, an insurance policy."

Destroyer lifted the Heartstone and Glenn tensed, but no fire fell upon him. His heart was not torn to pieces. His face tingled slightly but, apart from that, he was alive.

"Rise, Glenn Cross, and gaze on my mercy!" Destroyer roared, a mirror appearing before Glenn's bruised and battered form. Glenn obeyed shakily. His arm barely supported him as he pushed himself to his feet. Slowly, he turned to the mirror. As his eyes locked with those of his reflection, a horrified scream erupted from the core of his being.

Destroyer laughed harshly. "I will return your face when I assimilate this dimension. In return, you will continue to lead my army and give me unconditional loyalty."

Glenn nodded, tears falling heavily to the charred floor below him.

He looked once more into the terrible mirror, hoping against hope he had not seen the truth, hoping it was some game Destroyer was playing with his mind, but the same gruesome, distorted face stared back at him. He slowly lifted his trembling hands and slid his fingers over the slimy, wrinkled surface of his once flawless countenance.

Destroyer spent several more moments listening to Glenn plead for forgiveness and then, when it was obviously not coming, pledge to follow him. Destroyer trusted he could use the dark Stormbreaker's vanity to gain his loyalty. He dismissed the sniveling imp, and then replaced the Heartstone, locking the portal with a different word.

Glenn slipped through the wooden doors, wiping the tears from his wrinkled face. The doors to his chamber welcomed him and he hurriedly opened then closed them behind him. He desperately needed to clear his mind. He picked up the phone and dialed the familiar number. A woman would ease his mind. The darkness of the bathroom called to him, he knew the mirror waited inside. *NO!* He snarled to himself. He refused to acknowledge the change he had undergone. Several minutes later, a knock snapped him out of his denial and he rose hurriedly to the door. He opened it, smiling at the beautiful blonde in the hall. But her reaction wiped the smile from his face. Her mouth opened in a silent scream, which finally pierced the air as she backpedaled, hitting the wall hard. Before Glenn could say a word she was around the corner and gone. "Son of the Light!" he screamed, slamming the door. Against his desires, he forced himself into the bathroom and in front of the terrible mirror. He looked into his yellow eyes flecked with red. In the hall, outside his room, a passing Resident started at the sound of breaking glass.

Chapter 22: Preparations

Glenn sat quietly at the large, rectangular table in the Throne Room and listened to the Resident leaders' report to Destroyer. An hour earlier, Destroyer had appeared at his room and had finally offered the position he had promised from the beginning. Now Glenn sat at his right hand. Glenn looked toward the raised platform, to the golden throne and the empty pedestal. For a moment, the hunger for the power of the Heartstone again flared within him. *NO!* He pushed the urge deep inside his mind. *I must bide my time, wait until my face has been restored.* The words made sense in his mind, but they ran contrary to the other thoughts swirling within him; the thought that if he controlled the Heartstone again, he would not make the same mistake as before. The desire for the stone sat smoldering where he had pushed it in his mind, but it would never go out.

"All is in place, Master," a Resident finished from the end of the table.

"Excellent," Destroyer crooned. "The scroll will be in my possession soon and then the storm will hit the Seventh Dimension." He rose from his chair, towering above all those seated at the table. His voice was supremely confident, and supremely evil.

A large Resident could no longer contain himself. He resented the Dimlock-faced human sitting at Destroyer's right. A position of honor such as that belonged to a Resident. They had battled through the dimensions for him. They had died in his name. What had this human done to deserve such honor? He rose recklessly from his chair, interrupting Destroyer's speech.

"Why does a human sit at your right hand?" he barked a bit more harshly than he intended.

Destroyer's eyes flashed, but he did not retaliate. Instead he spoke calmly, his voice like ice. "Glenn leads the Dimlocks. His mind is already linked with theirs. He will lead them at the front of the coming storm."

The discovery of the power Destroyer had given the human staggered and enraged the Resident. He knew he was on dangerous ground but his rage prevailed against his caution. "What right does a mere human have to sit at your side?" the Resident shouted. The others cringed back in their chairs, wishing they were anywhere else. "He is small and weak—" the Resident paused to look meaningfully at the pedestal "—and he has already proven he cannot be trusted!"

A smirk slid onto Destroyer's dragon-like face. "Are you having trouble trusting my judgment?" he asked innocently, almost sweetly. "We can't have that. No ... no ... we can't have that at all."

The Residents looked at each other warily. This was not the reaction they had expected from their master. The defiant Resident smiled victoriously. It seemed he had convinced his master of the truth of his words.

Glenn still sat silently. When Destroyer had come to his quarters, he had reassured him of the restoration of his face. This had been enough to pull Glenn out of his deepening depression, but had not quenched his rage toward the beast. Perhaps sensing this, Destroyer had amplified one of his original gifts from his Covering. Glenn could now hear the minds of the millions of Dimlocks. He could organize them all and reply to them with his own mind. He truly was the General of the Dimlock forces. Already they were poised in position. With a single thought they would fall upon the Seventh Dimension. He smiled at the thought. Now he watched Destroyer in eager anticipation. He eased Bloodletter in its scabbard. It would feast soon enough.

"Glenn," Destroyer continued sweetly, "can we have a subject of mine feeling so torn, so confused?"

Glenn understood and smiled, his corpse-like face twisting obscenely. "No, Master." He rose slowly. "Allow me to shed some light on the subject." Bloodletter flew silently from his scabbard and burst into flame. The other Residents pulled even further back into their chairs, shocked and wary. But one did not shrink back. The Resident who had questioned Destroyer stood stiffly. His face was a mask of panic. Slight twitches in the muscles around his mouth were all that hinted he was struggling to reach his own weapon, even to move at all. But Glenn would not allow him to. With the amplified powers Destroyer had given him, he controlled the Resident's mind. It was the same as with Seeka, but this Resident's mind was much stronger, much more resistant. Glenn knew that without Destroyer's gift, his attempt to control him would have failed.

He stepped onto the table, his black cloak flowing behind him. The Resident was the only one still standing. His eyes bulged, looking pleadingly at Destroyer across the long table. Destroyer grinned wickedly, but remained silent.

Bloodletter flared brightly at Glenn's side. He held it horizontally to the right, letting its majesty shine for all around the table to see, as he walked smoothly and determinedly down the table.

The Resident twitched as Glenn neared him. A small sound, like a whimper, rose from his mouth. Glenn leaned toward the imprisoned Resident. "You dare to question me?" he whispered. In one swift move, Glenn brought Bloodletter down into the top of the Resident's skull. The enchanted blade hewed through the unfortunate Resident's head and neck, coming to rest against the top of his sternum.

Glenn lifted his enchantment and the Resident's body slumped, supported only by his burning blade. The room was silent as all listened morbidly to the sizzling sound of burning flesh.

In one fluid movement, Glenn slid Bloodletter free and brought it slashing through the dead Resident's neck, sending his head flying away in two pieces.

All were silent as Glenn walked back across the long, wooden table.

An inhuman smile slid across his torn face.

Destroyer addressed them all. "If anyone else wants to question my judgment, by all means do so now."

No one did, but Glenn met every eye with the same challenging stare.

"I am leaving now," Destroyer continued, "but I will return soon and with the key that will release the storm. Be wary that you aren't in its path."

He let the threat hang in the air as he rose through the roof and rocketed into the night. Glenn remained seated at the table until each Resident had filed past him. His yellow eyes narrowed with mirth. His face was gone, but it could be restored. Destroyer had given him much more power. He could feel it pulsing in his veins. What could he do with so much power? What were its limits? If he had taken the Heartstone now, would the outcome have been different? He guessed it would, but his moment had passed. He was finally allowed to be alone in the throne room and he had no idea how to access the stone.

But Glenn had gained a new patience along with his power. He could wait until the moment presented itself, and, when it did, he would be ready. A Dimlock barked questions in his mind and he gave the desired orders with a single thought.

He had a lot of planning to do. The Dimlocks had to be ready for war.

Chapter 23: Deckside

Grady stood at the railing of the large ship Mackinsi and Anthony had secured passage on the day before, and enjoyed the view of the water sliding by. He could see nothing but ocean in all directions and the sight calmed him. It had been a long time since he had been away from the city. The ship they had booked passage on seemed as old as the ocean itself. Grady imagined it would have been at home fighting the pirates of old. Its sails were square and white and its cannons were a polished iron. The captain stood behind a large, wooden wheel near the stern of the sip, shouting orders and truly looking the part of an old sea dog. Grady felt akin to the man. He often felt like an old dog himself. "Shiver me timbers," he chuckled under his breath.

The five companions had booked passage out of Florida, and Grady guessed it had been Anthony who had finally convinced the captain to take the assignment.

A lot of money had changed hands, as well it should've. Mac could lead them to the island they were headed to, but he didn't know its name or coordinates. It had taken a lot of the white-cloaked Stormbreaker's money to persuade the captain and crew to embark on a voyage in which they did not know the destination. Grady looked to the stern to see Mac still standing beside the captain, softly instructing the old sea dog on the direction to steer the ship. Grady was not worried about their destination. He had discovered he trusted Mackinsi Wrighton completely. Perhaps it was because Michael had spoken so highly of him. Grady paused in thought as the spray of the ocean misted across his face, clinging to his thick, white moustache. Perhaps it was because Mackinsi reminded him of his son, Peter. He sighed and turned away from the railing and the memories of his past. He knew that all Stormbreakers struggled with leaving their old lives behind, but he doubted any of them had raised a large family before they had to.

Celeste was talking to Anthony again. It seemed like the two had not separated since their meeting in Los Angeles. Celeste caught his eyes and smiled. *She's beautiful,* Grady thought and smiled back. Celeste had filled the role of a daughter in his life, and he had filled her need for a father. In the world of Stormbreakers, she was the nearest thing to family he had. "Durn girl," Grady muttered under his breath. "Focused on those perty eyes o' his wile she should be preparin' for the fight that's comin' soon." In truth, Grady couldn't blame her for falling for Anthony. He was tall, good looking, and polite. From Mac and Anaiya's stories, he was also incredibly proficient with his two katanas. But that was not enough for Grady to trust the man. *I may be old fashioned,* Grady thought, *but my trust's gotta be earned.* He turned his gaze back to the endless ocean. Several strange birds caught his eye. They were black and white with long bills. Every so often, one would disappear under the waves and reemerge smacking its bill and swallowing a small fish. As he continued to watch, fascinated, he saw two birds attack each other as they both moved to dive. They dipped, squirming and writhing beneath the water. Grady waited but the two never surfaced again.

"Strange isn't it?" Anthony's voice from beside Grady startled him. "When one pulls the other under the water, they both drown." Anthony turned to face Grady. The expected scowl was already on the old man's face. "As you know, I very much like Celeste. She trusts me and I her. Mackinsi and Anaiya also enjoy my company, yet from you I get the feeling you would like to find me missing one morning … perhaps lost at sea?"

Grady stared into Anthony's crystal blue eyes. "I never said I wanted ya dead, but my trust's gotta be earned. My daughter," he emphasized the title, "may trust you, but you have a ways to go."

Anthony shrugged slightly, an amused glimmer in his eyes. "I guess saving Mac and Anaiya's lives at Walker Park isn't a good enough reason and that would mean that respecting your daughter enough to sleep alone every night doesn't qualify either."

Grady repressed the sudden urge to stab the man in the stomach. He hated being patronized. "If you want my trust and my blessin', Mr. Ward, you best be provin' yerself to me in the flesh. Times'll come when I've gotta lean on you, when Celeste's life'll depend on you. It's in those moments trust can be built. When we come through those moments livin', we'll jist see about my blessin'." Grady slid the daggers back into his sleeves. How had they come out in the first place?

Anthony sighed and nodded. "Understood," he said softly. "While I desire to win your trust and blessing, I pray we do not soon find ourselves in the situations it seems are required for me to do so." He turned to walk away then paused, glancing over his shoulder. "Just remember the birds." Grady realized the daggers were back in his hands.

As Anthony glided away, Celeste cast a curious look in Grady's direction and, receiving only a scowl, followed Anthony below deck.

Grady sighed but kept his daggers in his hands. He knew he was giving Anthony a hard road to walk, but he would not allow anything to hurt Celeste … his daughter.

**

Mac watched the entire scene unfold before him and shook his head. He didn't understand what Grady had against Anthony, but it had been there since the two had met in Los Angeles. Anthony had been nothing but a support to him and Anaiya, and he hoped Grady would give him a chance. He felt the pull of the island again in his mind and knew it came from the power of the scroll. He quietly conveyed the slight course change to the grizzled captain next to him then looked to the crow's nest and smiled.

Anaiya stood facing the bow, her hands gripping the edge, her golden hair flying in the wind. The crow's nest had been one of her favorite locations since the beginning of the voyage and Mac had enjoyed watching her breathe in the beauty around her.

She looked down and caught his eye. Her smile made his heart soar. He constantly re-lived the moment in the plane when he and Anaiya's lips had almost met. He wished they could have another like that, but none had arisen.

He wondered if Anaiya still felt the same way toward him. Did she regret that moment? Looking up at her smile, he felt nothing but sincerity. He waved and she turned back to the stretching blue expanse around her. Maybe they could talk about it tonight.

***

Anaiya turned back to the amazing view and felt butterflies dance in her stomach. Mac was such a good man. She could not deny the attraction she felt toward him, and she was beginning to understand that her feelings ran much deeper. That is what scared her. She had never been in love, except perhaps with Michael. She had never told him, of course, and had only just begun to understand it herself. At first she had believed she was attracted to Mackinsi because she saw qualities of Michael in him. Only recently she had discovered that her feelings went much deeper for the young Stormbreaker than they had for her mentor.

Mackinsi had qualities she had never seen in another human being and, whether or not she was ready, Mackinsi was pulling her in. Truth be known, she rather liked it but at the same time she was terrified. It took a brave person to open her heart up to another. She snuck a glance at Mac as he stared into the horizon. She was sure he was. "Just let it happen," she quietly chided herself. She had always let her mind control her actions, silencing her heart. Perhaps it was time for a change. Her heart felt safe when she was with Mac. She let the butterflies have control, surrendering to the dream. She would let the moment occur again this night. She knew she loved Mackinsi Wrighton. It was about time to let her heart lead the way.

***

Nightfall fell swiftly over the ocean and the ship anchored for several hours for Mac to get some much needed rest. Mackinsi went below deck to the quarters that he shared with Anaiya to find her already in bed. With a thought he shifted his casual clothing back to his cloak, tunic and breeches.

Anaiya rolled over so she was facing him. "Mac, I'm glad we met."

He smiled, draping his cloak across the chair by the bed. "Me too," he said, smiling, "although I've gotten into a lot more trouble since we last met."

"You brought it with you, Mackinsi Wrighton," she scolded.

Mac laughed with her. He supposed that could very well be true. His double markings flashed up at him, carrying more responsibility now than ever. The Aquillian Scroll weighed heavily on his mind each second, and mirth was welcome, especially from Anaiya Lynn.

Mac climbed into the warm bed and snuggled next to his friend. They both stared quietly at the ceiling, weighing their thoughts.

Anaiya broke the comfortable silence first. "Mac, I know you have the world on your shoulders. I want you to know you don't have to carry it on your own. Since the day I met you, you have been earning my trust. I have come to trust you with my life."

"As I have come to trust you," Mac replied.

"But there's more … a lot more." Anaiya fought the panic welling within her. *Trust your heart,* she whispered inside herself.

Mac felt his stomach jump and his heart miss a beat. Where was this going? Before he could inquire further, Anaiya took a deep breath and continued.

"Since the plane, I've noticed a tension between us. Have you felt it?"

"Yeah," Mac admitted. Suddenly he felt awkward.

Anaiya nodded. "Well, I have been doing a lot of thinking and I believe I know the source."

Mac rolled to face her. He was all ears.

"It's me," Anaiya said softly.

Mac blinked in surprise.

"I have been avoiding any situation that could lead to that kiss that was interrupted in the plane. I've been afraid to follow my heart, because my mind is terrified." She paused for breath. This much was out; she might as well say the rest. "I'm not afraid anymore... I love you."

Mac's jaw wouldn't close and coherent words failed to come to his lips. The warmth inside him blazed and his spirit soared.

He began to tell her he felt the same way, and that he had ever since he had seen her accost Glenn in the alleyway, but Anaiya hurried on.

"That interrupted kiss made me think about so many things. I didn't want to project my feelings for Michael on to you. That night, I realized how much responsibility rests on your shoulders, Mac. You are the Chosen One, the leader of the Stormbreakers. The fate of the world, in essence, rests in your hands. I felt selfish to seek to add another complication to your life and I didn't know if I was even ready to ... or if you'd even want me in that way." She hesitantly lifted her eyes to meet Mac's. The tears in her eyes reflected the soft lighting of the room. Mac gazed into those eyes intently, completely taken by surprise, but also completely certain of his feelings.

"Silly girl," he whispered, cupping her cheek with his hand. "You are the only thing on Earth that takes my mind from those complications and burdens. You are the only one I love."

The tears ran freely down Anaiya's cheeks, but her quivering smile lit up her eyes. Slowly, the two moved closer and rested their foreheads against each other's. Mac looked into his love's eyes and she returned the intensity of his gaze. He began to move in, to finish the kiss they had been denied earlier, but a small sound pulled at his mind, a gurgling from the floor behind him. He pulled back, tilting his head. Anaiya looked at him, confusion slipping across her face, and then she heard it too. The sheer terror Mac saw in her eyes was all the warning he received.

He rolled out of bed and to his feet, gripping and unsheathing Nightsbane in one fluid movement. A dagger slashed across his shoulder, ricocheting off and sticking into a wooden plank on the wall. Mac cried out as the pain exploded through his senses, but brought his blade whipping in an arc in front of his face, and not a moment too soon.

Nightsbane's arc slapped a second blade out of the air, sending it clattering to the floor. It was then Mac focused on the attacker. A small, dirty man clothed in many layers of brown, woolen material stood by the wall.

He wore a torn, wide brimmed hat with a spotless white feather in the band. He sniggered as Mac stalked closer, Nightsbane held before him. Faster than Anaiya could blink, Mac thrust his blade forward. He hit nothing but air. Franticly, Mac looked from side to side but the man was gone. He thought he could hear a faint gurgling sound all around him. Was it coming from the floor or the walls? He heard Anaiya cry out and turned to discover a terrifying sight. The man was halfway out of the wall, his hands locked around Anaiya's throat. He had opened his mouth wide revealing razor white fangs. As Anaiya struggled to break the creature's grip, its body squeezed in and out of a hairline crack in the wooden wall. Each time it slid back an inch or two it made a gurgling sound. As Mac moved to help her, the gurgling intensified behind him.

He spun, Nightsbane cutting a smooth, horizontal swath. The blade hewed right through the small man behind him. The upper torso fell to the floor, laughing hysterically as the legs remained standing stock still. Mac turned to see Anaiya bring the blade of her staff through her attacker's wrists.

With a shriek the man slid, wrist-less back through the seam in the wall. His hands let go of Anaiya's throat. She gasped, gulping in air. Mac could see bruises already darkening her slender neck. He felt a tug on his leg followed by a sharp pain. The upper half of his attacker had grabbed Mac's ankle and sunk his teeth into him. Mac felt something cold enter his blood. With a strong kick, he sent the half man flying. As it passed the lower half of its body, its hand caught its leg. The upper half quickly climbed the lower and the two fused together once again. Still laughing, the small man sank into the floor.

Anaiya hurried to Mac. "Edgelings!" she croaked, putting a hand to her injured throat. "I have heard they can't be killed!"

"What are they?" Mac scanned the room warily.

"They're fiends ... assassins hired by some evil force to hunt a specific target or perform a certain task."

"One of them bit me." Mac winced as he felt the cold slide deeper into his body.

Anaiya looked stricken. "You're poisoned," she said quickly. "We have to get you to a more open area and I will see what I can do."

Mac nodded and he and Anaiya slowly inched toward the door.

As they moved closer, the severed hands rose onto their fingers and scurried off into a crack in the wall. Anaiya shuddered. She had hoped never to meet an Edgeling.

The door burst open and Anthony stalked in, dual katanas drawn. "How many are in here?" he barked.

"We've seen two," Anaiya answered.

Anthony grinned strangely. "Good." He put his swords away and stepped forward, almost casually. "Don't say a word … no matter what you see!" His voice was like cool iron.

From behind him, the gurgling intensified and, slowly, like a drop of putrid water, the Edgeling slid from the ceiling. Its teeth were bared, a dagger in each hand. Its tattered clothing made no sound as it brushed against itself.

Its wet hat hung on its head, its white feather standing stiff and spotless. The creature slid down, hanging behind Anthony, and pulled its dagger backwards in preparation for a fatal thrust. Mac and Anaiya remained silent. They would trust Anthony … they had no other choice.

In the split second between the thrust of the Edgeling and the contact of its daggers, Anthony made his move. His katanas flashed out as he spun to his left. He parried the dagger thrust with his left blade and brought his right slicing through the stiff, white feather in the Edgeling's hat. The creature's eyes bulged as Anthony hewed the feather in two then the creature dropped from the ceiling. It lay twitching, and then dissolved into a fine, grey mist.

"The feather contains their life force. If you destroy it, you destroy the Edgeling," Anthony said. "Now that you know how to kill the foul creatures, you might want to save Celeste and Grady." The gurgling grew louder behind them and Anthony stepped past them. "I'll handle the second beast."

Mac and Anaiya rushed down the hall below deck, deciding to split up. Anaiya would go to Celeste's aid and Mac to Grady's. With one last glance into each other's eyes, they parted. Anaiya rushed through the door to Celeste's quarters, hoping the poison in Mac was slow acting. The scene she found was one of complete chaos. Celeste was backed into a corner. Her two swords were moving in circular arcs. Blood trickled down her face and, from what was occurring around her, she had been fighting for some time. Pieces of Edgeling writhed and squirmed on the floor. Several hands crawled like spiders, attempting to find their bodies. Torsos pulled their bloodless frames to reunite them with severed heads.

Anaiya realized that Celeste must have fought two of the creatures. Her eyes were becoming glazed as more of her lifeblood leaked out of her. There was not a moment to lose! Anaiya's voice cut through the horror and delirium reflected in Celeste's eyes. "Celeste!" The Stormbreaker's eyes saw Anaiya for the first time and hope flickered there. "They're demons!" Celeste called desperately. "I can't kill them!"

Anaiya nodded and shouted back over the slipping, gurgling cacophony. "Sever the white feather in the creatures' hats!" The Edgeling body parts reacted to her statement and began to scramble more rapidly to get back together. Celeste saw a severed head rolling toward a torso in front of her and brought her right sword slashing through the feather in its soggy hat. She was rewarded with grey mist in place of each piece of the Edgeling. Anaiya's razor sharp blade finished the last Edgeling off and she rushed toward Celeste.

Celeste saw her new friend move her way, but could not respond. The world spun and everything went black.

Mac was slowing down. The ice was everywhere inside him now. His lungs felt squeezed. He struggled for each breath and Nightsbane felt heavy in his hands. The thought of Grady in peril helped drive him forward. As he reached the door to the old Stormbreaker's quarters he heard the scrape of metal, like a long sword being re-sheathed, but when he pushed the door open, he found Grady sitting on the edge of his bed, breathing heavily.

Mist evaporated into nothingness all around him. "Durn fiends!" he griped. "An old man can't ever get any rest." He looked up at his would-be savior. "A little late, boy, but yer 'preciated none the less."

Mac felt the ice reach his heart. *The poison must be potent,* he thought dreamily. Distantly, he felt Nightsbane drop from his grasp and stick point first in the wooden floor. Grady was immediately at his side. He looked into the old man's worried eyes and smiled faintly. His vision blurred and he lost all feeling in his body. So, he thought sadly, this was how his story ended.

The prophecy had been a lie. He would never meet Destroyer in combat ... the world was doomed. *Creator!* he asked inside his mind. *What happens now?* He heard no answer. He began to spiral down a black well, sinking deeper into the blackness. The world faded from his view and he felt his heart beat sporadically, once ... twice ... and then it stopped altogether.

Grady Reynolds cried for help as Mackinsi Wrighton died.

***

The crew was rushing about frantically on deck. The old sea dog looked down sadly at the prostrate form of the young leader of his strange employers. The crew had been awoken by yelling and had rushed out of bed to discover the young man dead and his friends looking incredibly forlorn. The young lady, Anaiya, had not left his side, talking to the poor lad and crying on his chest. The large man in white had been pacing the ship's railing, glaring at the ocean waves, silent and contemplative. The old man sat beside Anaiya, along with the Asian woman.

The captain could see they were trying unsuccessfully to console her. He wondered about the suddenness of the death. Could the young man have had a weak heart? He couldn't explain the blood on several of the young people, but expected there was more to the story than he had been told.

***

Deep beneath the ocean's surface, an Edgeling kept pace with the ship. His clothes flowed with the swirl of the ocean's undercurrents, but remained bone dry, as did the Edgeling himself. He needed no oxygen so he was perfectly content under the dark waters. Well, not perfectly content. He should not have bitten the boy.

"Fool!" Glenn's voice roared in his mind. The Edgeling cringed. "You killed him! You out of control Son of the Light!" The Edgeling felt the insult keenly, but still had some excuses left.

"The Massster told me nothing about thisss." The Edgeling hissed its thoughts.

The intensity of the next thought nearly fried the creature's mind. "You were put in my control… You were my responsibility! You disobeyed my orders!"

"I am not your puppet!" the Edgeling snapped back. The silence in his mind unnerved him, but when Glenn's final thought hit him he knew the meaning of terror.

The thought was a primal growl. "On that we agree. You are not my puppet—anymore!" A bolt of searing violence burned into the Edgeling's brain, turning it to vapor. For a moment, the Edgeling drifted listlessly, and then its body disintegrated as well.

***

Light was all around him. He could see no walls, and no floor, only pure, white light. He felt a peaceful warmth ripple across each pore of his body, like a perfect wind had passed him by.

"Mackinsi." The voice was strong, yet peaceful. It flowed across his ears like a symphony, each chord in perfect harmony.

He turned to find a man before him. His hair was like the sun, brilliant and flowing. His robes were white and spotless, comprised of a seamless material that flowed like water. "I have waited for this moment since the dawn of time."

Mac felt completely safe, as if he had somehow left every worry behind. He heard his voice before he realized he was speaking. "Creator?"

The man smiled, it was like the first bloom of spring. "I have watched you, Mackinsi. I have heard Michael's prayer."

"Prayer?" Mackinsi blinked, trying to take in the situation he was in. Everything seemed surreal. He realized there was no hurry for his answer. Time seemed somehow slower here. "What did Michael ask of you?"

"To keep you and Anaiya safe was his request, Mackinsi."

Mac thought for a moment. "But, Creator, am I not dead?"

Creator smiled again, releasing joy into Mac's soul. "What is death, Mackinsi? What is life? Merely two phases of a created existence."

Mac looked down at his wrists. They were blazing a brilliant green. He had never before seen them brighter. "But if I am dead won't Destroyer defeat the Stormbreakers? Won't all be lost?"

"It would be, Mackinsi. Destroyer would assimilate my Seventh Dimension and control the world I created. But with your death, he would never create."

"I don't understand," Mac admitted.

"You are my chosen one, the Stormbreaker who is destined to confront the enemy of mankind itself. You alone can unlock the Aquillian Scroll. Destroyer knows this and will use you in an attempt to do so. Once he has the scroll, he will have the knowledge of creation itself. Because you are dead, he will never be able to unlock the scroll, thus the worst outcome that could happen is Destroyer will rule a hellish world but never be able to create beings in his own image."

"It is your will that I die?"

"Quite the contrary." Creator laughed loudly, a sound like wind chimes being caressed by a morning breeze. "You must live! I am not content to give Destroyer control of my beautiful Creation."

"So, you will bring me back to life?" Somehow the thought brought a little sadness.

"That I cannot do. Your body is poisoned. If I brought you back, it would be to another death sentence."

Mac tried to deduce the answer Creator was hinting at.

Creator's smile stole his thoughts. "I have someone who holds the answer, someone you know well. If you are ready I will whisper the answer to her."

Mac thought for a second. He was in the presence of Creator. He had died and now could ask the Maker of the Universe anything he wanted.

"Can I see Michael?"

A cloud passed over Creator's face, replaced immediately by a strange gleam. "I wish you could, Mackinsi, but he is not here, nor will he be for some time."

Mac did not know what to say. He had always imagined Michael would be with Creator since he had died, watching he and Anaiya on Earth.

"I cannot tell you more, but, rest assured, you will see Michael again. Now rest. I will whisper and you will wake."

Mac found himself alone again surrounded by pure, white light. He rested and waited … waited for Creator's whisper … waited to return from the dead.

***

Grady had his hand on Anaiya's shoulder. "Dear girl, he's gone. There's nuthin' we can do now. We gotta think of what our next move'll be without 'im." Grady grieved with the poor girl, but they were in a terrible situation. With the Chosen One gone, the future looked incredibly bleak. They needed to regroup … reform. Grady sighed. Life could be cruel sometimes.

Celeste watched Anthony with worried eyes. He looked as if despair would overwhelm him. He had been at the railing since he had found out that Mac had died, pacing, brooding. Celeste could relate. What hope did they have now? The prophecy was clear that the Chosen One must face Destroyer, but Mac was dead!

"Grady, I'm going to talk to Anthony." The scowl on Grady's face was the answer she expected. She got up quickly, and hurried to Anthony. He accepted her embrace and the two stood silently, leaving Grady grumbling and Anaiya silently caressing Mac's face.

As she brushed her fingers across the stubble on Mac's square jaw for the hundredth time, another tear slipped quietly down to fall onto his chest. "Creator," she prayed, "give him back. I've already lost Michael. Please don't take him too."

"Anaiya Lynn." The whisper made her jump, but it was with surprise, not fear. Warmth filled her, soothing her aching heart. "Anaiya." This time she was listening. Her heart fluttered as an image materialized in her mind. For a moment she was confused, but then it all made sense. The image was of a blue vial. "Thank you!" she screamed to the night sky. She rushed below deck leaving Grady gawking.

Anaiya ran full speed through the hall and into the room she had shared with Mac. "Creator be praised!" she shouted. Grabbing a small, blue vial from her overnight, she rushed back to the deck.

When she arrived by Mac's side once again, the others had gathered around his body.

"What the blaze is goin' on?" Grady asked her.

She produced the blue vial, her heart beating rapidly. "Mac used this once to save my life, and with Creator's blessing it will restore his."

Anthony looked skeptical. "A life cannot be regained with a vial of liquid."

"Michael told me to keep this close to me. He told me it was a gift from Creator himself," Anaiya whispered. She leaned forward and emptied the entire vial into Mac's mouth.

***

From within the light, Mac felt a tug. Suddenly he was falling upward. Ice was in his blood and he was dying again, or felt like he was. The black well engulfed him and he knew no more.

***

Nothing happened.

Anthony sighed heavily. "All is lost. What hope is there now?"

Celeste patted his shoulder sympathetically, but Grady turned angry eyes his way. "You durn fool! Give the drink some time!"

Anaiya heard none of the commotion around her. She did not feel the breath in her lungs or the beating of her heart. She was focused solely on the face of her love.

Another minute passed and the captain came down, curious about the commotion over the boy who was clearly deceased. Throughout his time at sea, the sea dog had seen many dead men. Keeping them around only brought more problems. There was nothing more they could do for the lad. The closer he got to the huddled group, though, the stranger he felt. They were all staring at the dead man, waiting for something. The captain inched closer, his curiosity drawing him in. It was then, in that moment, that the captain's notion of reality and physical laws was shattered. It was then that the story of Mackinsi Wrighton would find its way into the whispered legends of the human race. The captain's eyes went wide and his heart froze in his chest as he saw the lad's fingers move.

***

Mac was careening out of the well. He could feel the air rushing across his face. A light beckoned to him at the top of the well. Somehow, he knew Anaiya waited on the other side. Anaiya! He was a hundred yards from the light ... then thirty. The light engulfed him like a pool of frigid water.

***

The Stormbreakers waited, tense and hoping, as another minute ticked by. Anaiya felt despair creeping into her soul. It had to work! It just had to! The world needed Mac! Her attention was pulled away by a gasp from behind her. She turned quickly, seeking the source, to see the grizzled old sea dog struggling forward. His eyes were wide and he was pointing frantically. Anaiya turned back to Mac's still form and inhaled sharply. His fingers were moving! Then, like a wave had washed over him, Mackinsi Wrighton was back in his body. Anaiya would forever remember that moment as the happiest in her entire life.

Mac opened his eyes to find all of his friends gathered around him, as well as the captain of the ship and several crew. He glanced from one to another taking it all in.

Anthony seemed as if a feather would knock him over. He was standing and swaying ever so slightly. A shocked grin was painted across his face. "Our hope returns," Mac heard him whisper to himself. Celeste stood with a hand on Anthony's shoulder. The Stormbreaker was a mystery to Mackinsi. She did not reveal much of herself, but her feelings for Anthony Ward were blatantly obvious. He hoped to get to know her better. The captain and crew members were staring at him in disbelief, unable to form words. The same could not be said of Grady. "You durn fool!" he half-heartedly chided. "You nearly scared me an' Anaiya to death, dyin' on us like that!" A single tear glistened in the old man's eyes. It escaped, despite his efforts, and slid quietly down his cheek and into his thick, white moustache. As he was trying to prevent others from following in the first tear's path, Mac heard him quietly begin to pray. The only words he could decipher were the constant repetition of, "Creator, be praised."

Finally, Mac turned his eyes to Anaiya. If Grady was a rainstorm, Anaiya was a flood. Glistening streaks lined her face from the hundreds of tears she had cried. More were drifting down her cheeks, but they did not follow the lines of the first. Her smile caused them to create different pathways. Mac saw the empty blue vial still clutched tightly in her hand and remembered. Creator had whispered. He felt his eyes fill as he looked at Anaiya again. She had never looked more beautiful than in that moment. With a strength fueled by Creator's restoration, he sat up swiftly. No one would interrupt this moment! Placing one hand behind Anaiya's head and another softly on her cheek, he gently pulled her toward him. He felt her press her cheek into his hand, as if to convince herself he was really there. Her eyes caught his and held them as he drew her close. The rest of the spectators were silent as Mac's lips met Anaiya's. The two Stormbreakers seemed to melt into each other. Anaiya reached around his back, placing one hand on his broad shoulder and sliding her delicate fingers into his hair. She pulled him closer and he could feel her heart beating against his chest. Passion ignited inside of them and for several minutes the two lost track of the entire world. They alone existed. Their love was the only thing in the entire universe.

After what seemed like days to Mackinsi, the world slowly faded back into his consciousness. He kissed Anaiya one more time, softly, and then pulled back to gaze into her beautiful eyes. Mac realized he was grinning from ear to ear. He glanced around the circle of friends to see they had watched the entire thing. Their smiles matched his. Grady chuckled softly. "Well, you younguns, I have to say that was the best kiss I ever did see." Anaiya covered her face, blushing a deep crimson, but her smile remained. Mac pulled her into a tight embrace. "I love you, Anaiya Lynn," he whispered.

She clutched him tighter and whispered back. "I love you too. Thank you for not leaving me." Mac was aware someone had started to cry again. It was several minutes before he realized that it was him.

There was air in his lungs and his heart beat steadily. The ice was no longer in his veins. It had been replaced by the warmth he had experienced in Creator's presence. Creator had given him back his life and his love. "Thank you," he whispered, the emotion thick in his voice. "Thank you."

***

The remainder of the trip passed without incident. There were no more attacks and the captain and crew did as Mac commanded without question. Since his resurrection, they had shown a reverence toward him. Mac hoped it was not out of fear. The old sea dog had given their money back to them, saying the miracle had more than paid for passage. Mac enjoyed the company of the grizzled man. Sometimes when Mac stood beside the sailor he saw the hint of a smile on his scraggly face. Perhaps the man had found something to believe in.

Mac felt like a new person. His cuts and bruises had vanished, and the aches evaporated as well. His double markings burned hotter every day, as did his determination to free the world and the seven dimensions from Destroyer's foul taint.

Each night, he journeyed back again to his meeting with Creator. Every dream brought the same feeling of peace and warmth, reassuring him. With Creator beside him, no one could stand against him.

His confidence was infectious. Each Stormbreaker had seemingly risen with him from the dark well. Anthony was all smiles. He exuded excitement and anticipation. As usual, Celeste was at his side. To Grady's dismay, Celeste had disappeared from her room the previous night. The smile on her face and the wonder in her eyes was all the evidence Grady needed to know what was going on.

"Mangy ol' cur," he grumbled to himself. "If he breaks her heart, he'll be answerin' to me blades." He fingered the daggers in his sleeves longingly. One glance at Anaiya lightened his spirits. She was once again in the crow's nest, the wind streaming through her hair. She had transformed her clothing this morning to a thin, white dress embroidered with yellow and blue flowers. The wind whipped it about her slim figure, showing her delicate curves.

Her beauty was not what caused Grady's heart to soar, nor was it the near transparent nature of her dress. It was the gleam in her eyes. Since meeting Anaiya, Grady had been struck by the strength of her heart. When she had spoken on Mac's behalf at the meeting of the Stormbreakers, she had shone with dynamic confidence, with a courage not many possessed in such abundant quantities. When the poison of the vile Edgeling had pulled Mackinsi to the grave, Grady had watched the gleam fade from Anaiya's eyes. He had watched her heart begin to die. Now she stood like the very image of a goddess. Her beauty was undeniable, but the thing that brought the large grin to Grady's face was that brilliant gleam. He knew it heralded the revival of her heart. Blatantly ignoring Anthony, Grady watched the small mass of land appear on the horizon. The Aquillian Scroll would soon be in their hands.

Chapter 24: Veritas

The ship docked in the only harbor of the small Caribbean island as darkness fell. Despite his attempts, the captain had not been able to locate the island on his map. Mac smiled inwardly. He had expected the island to be uncharted. How else could the Aquillian Scroll have remained unclaimed for so long? Mac looked at the small island in his mind. It was walled in by small mountains. The harbor was the only access to the island for any sea-going vessel. It was an excellent hiding place for something as important as the scroll.

The crystal blue water faded to black along with the sky; the stars reflected on its calm surface. As Mac walked down the gangplank, he took in his surroundings. The exit of the harbor led into a small village. In truth, he had not expected a larger community on such a small island and, from the look of it, he guessed someone could walk around the entire island in 3 hours … if they went around the mountains.

The lights of the small village flickered warmly, beckoning the Stormbreakers and the crew to enter.

Anthony stood bartering with the harbormaster, a short, fat man wearing faded brow breeches and a shirt that was much too tight. Anthony paid the harbormaster for docking the ship, and motioned for the others to join him.

"This island is called Veritas." Anthony pointed to the village lights. "I asked him where we could hear any rumors of the island, and he told me that Veritas comes alive at sundown. The Barnacle is the town pub and the harbor master says the gossip is free, although the beer is not." He laughed, but stopped when he noticed he was the only one.

"Why are we interested in rumors?" Celeste asked.

Grady had to agree with Anthony here. "Most rumors are based on fact, child. In a town that ain't talkin', sometimes rumors are the only way to be findin' the truth."

"How do we know they won't talk?" Anaiya asked Grady. "They could be very helpful."

"Yeah—" Grady chuckled "—and I'm a boy band."

In fact, the villagers were most unhelpful. The Stormbreakers received suspicious stares everywhere they went. The people were not used to having visitors. Anthony repeatedly asked Mac if he could help, but, to Mac's disappointment, the compass in his mind had winked out as soon as they stepped on land.

The Barnacle sat in the center of the village and was the hub of activity. As the five Stormbreakers moved towards the pub, the sound of singing and dancing drifted on the smoke through the open door.

Anthony did not miss the irony of the pub's name. When the tide was out, nothing could shut up tighter than a barnacle. He hoped the tide was with them.

The Stormbreakers entered into a spacious, smoke-filled common room. Nearly 40 people were already inside and, as the strangers walked in, the dancing stopped, followed closely by the music.

Wary eyes stared accusingly at the group of friends and, one by one, the patrons turned to carry on huddled conversation. Several continued to stare and one particularly large man stood swaying awkwardly at the end of the bar. He took an unsteady step toward the Stormbreakers.

"Belligerent drunk at one o'clock," Anthony muttered.

Mac stepped away from the group, meeting the man halfway. "We don't want any trouble," Mac began politely to the 270-pound drunkard.

"Shut your hole, tourist!" The man spat his words through an unsure mouth. His words slurred together. "You ain't welcome in The Barnacle … now get!"

Mac tried again. "We are not trying to intrude; we're merely seeking any information about the Aq—" He was interrupted as the hulk swung his arm, aiming a massive fist at his head. Without a thought, Mac stepped slightly to the right. The drunkard's punch hit nothing but air and, because he had put all of his weight behind it, he lost his balance.

With a heavy crash the man fell onto a table, breaking it in half, then crumbled unconscious to the floor.

Mac sighed and looked around. The people had pretended not to notice. The private conversations were still going on and not a soul would make eye contact with him, except the strange man sitting in the corner. He called out to the Stormbreakers, startling his fellow villagers.

"You're quick of feet, my strange friend, but it is your wits you will need to sharpen to survive in this sink hole."

The pub seemed to grow quieter as Mac and the Stormbreakers moved closer to the stranger. The villagers may have closed their mouths but their ears were wide open.

"You will find my wits sharper than my blade, good sir," Mac replied. "You seem out of place in this pub. Would you care to accompany my travel weary friends and me outside? I'm sure that the chill the night might bring and the constant stare of the stars would be far more hospitable than the stares in this room."

The strange man nodded. "Perchance you're right, but I do believe I'm comfortable where I sit." He looked slyly at Mackinsi.

Mac laughed at the man and finally took a good look at him. Mac guessed his age at around 45. He had scraggly blond hair, uncombed but clean. His ruddy complexion spoke of many days under the Caribbean sun. His shirt was missing all of its buttons and hung open, revealing a hairy, tan chest riddled with scars. The man's cut off jeans and tattered sandals spoke volumes to Mac. This man would make a valuable friend.

"Comfort is in abundance here, but I hear that outside it is raining gold," Mac said casually as he turned to walk away.

"That would be a sight to behold," the man replied, standing. "I'm Dali, Keeper of the Secrets." Mac smiled, turning to shake Dali's offered hand.

Introductions were made as the group left the common room. The night had settled warmly and the sound of the animals of the night surrounded Dali and the Stormbreakers as they made their way to the docks.

It nearly rained gold. Dali demanded a high price for the secrets he claimed to keep. But the Stormbreakers purses ran deep as well. Soon the six were sitting on the docks, swinging their legs from the dock and talking of Veritas.

"My father was the Keeper of the Secrets on Veritas, and his father before him." Dali leaned back casually on his elbows, gazing up at the stars. "Since I can remember, I've kept the secrets as well."

Anthony sat brooding. He had not been happy with Dali's price. "Now that you have your ransom, will you perchance be sharing some of those secrets with us?"

If Anthony's tone offended him, Dali showed no sign. "Some secrets I will share and some cannot be bought. Those I give freely to someone who wins my trust."

"And how many have won your trust in the past?" Anaiya asked.

Dali grinned mischievously. "You would be the first, my dear."

Anaiya nodded. She had expected as much. Celeste turned to Dali. "How does one win your trust?"

"Well, dear lady, that is for the winner to discover."

Anthony's brows furrowed. "We do not have time for riddles."

"You will have to make time," the man replied, "the level of confidence I must entrust requires this caution. I will know to whom the truth belongs."

"Dali, why are the people of the village so paranoid?" Celeste had wondered about this since they had arrived.

Dali laughed. "It is an interesting relationship the people of this village have with the secrets of Veritas. They do not know them but they know of them. This lack of knowledge causes them to guard the secrets tightly. If an outsider were to discover the secrets of the island, they would learn more than the villagers themselves. Their pride could not cope with that. They will live up to the name of the pub where they spend their time in order to protect that pride. I alone hold the secrets of the isle. Soon I will father a son and he will in turn take the secrets to heart."

Mac put a hand on Dali's shoulder. "I thank you for guarding the scroll, Dali, but the time for secrets is over. Destroyer is coming for the scroll, and I have brought these Stormbreakers to help me spirit the scroll out from within his grasp."

The others gasped as Mac spoke so frankly to a human, but quickly realized, as Mackinsi had already, that the man knew about everything Mac had mentioned.

"I will keep the secrets, Stormbreaker!" Dali snapped. "Who are you to tell me otherwise?"

Mac pulled up his sleeves revealing his double marks. "I am Creator's chosen one."

Dali's face was a mask as he looked intently at Mac's wrists and then to his face. "You may truly be who you claim and you may not. Regardless, you have not yet earned my trust."

"So be it," Mac replied. "I hope trust will be quickly earned. My respect you have already attained."

Dali nodded solemnly. "Thank you, Mackinsi Wrighton. My respect you have earned this night as well."

Grady chuckled. Dali was a man after his own heart … stubborn to a fault.

Mac felt Anaiya's hand on his shoulder. She glanced toward the moon and started at the sight. It was low in the sky. Had they been talking that long?

"I have one more favor to ask of you, Dali," he said quickly.

The floor of Dali's small house felt wonderful to Mac as he drifted into dreams. Anaiya breathed heavily, pressed against his back … she was so special to him. He had enjoyed recreating the moment on deck with her again and again. He thought about how his lips tingled pleasantly each time he kissed her. Thoughts of kissing her filled his dreams.

***

A noise woke him in the night, or maybe it was the lack of one. Grady's snoring had stopped. Mac's eyes blinked open. He heard Anaiya's deep breathing behind him.

She was still in a deep sleep. His eyes adjusted quickly to the dim light in Dali's living room. The darkness left like a stubborn guest. It seemed deeper and heavier than the night before. Mac felt a chill slide down his spine. He knew the feeling all too well. His wrists were glowing a faint green, which cast a soft glow on his bedroll. He had felt the chill before every battle. It was the feeling that accompanied evil. Something had found them in Veritas.

Was the danger already there? Mac felt a cold sweat break out all over his body. His hand gripped Nightsbane tightly. A shadow slipped across the room as silent as the darkness. Mac tensed every muscle. Fight or flight was redefined for a Stormbreaker. There was only fight. When a Stormbreaker ran, they usually lost their life. It was not wise to turn your back on evil, especially if that evil was a fiend. A rustle caused Mac to pivot his head rapidly. Anthony rolled over, mumbling in his sleep.

I'm just getting jumpy, Mac chastised himself. *I'm supposed to be the leader of the Stormbreakers and I jump at every shadow…* A shadow slipped through the doorway, interrupting Mac mid-thought. Instantly he reacted. A roll brought him to his feet and brought up the blade of Nightsbane to touch the throat of the intruder.

"Whoa there, Mac." The voice was unmistakable. "Don't be killin' ol' Grady."

Mac relaxed, dropping Nightsbane to his side. Grady chuckled. "Keep bein' jumpy, boy … it'll save your life."

The others had stirred and Anaiya looked in confusion at Grady and Mac with sleepy eyes.

"I could have killed you!" Mac said, appalled.

"No harm done. Odds are my grizzled ol' neck would've stopped that nice blade of yours anyway."

Mac frowned thoughtfully, scanning the room. "I felt an evil presence."

Grady laughed loudly, his moustache twitching. If any of the Stormbreakers had remained asleep, they were awake now. "I've been following that thing all night."

"What is it?" Anthony asked, climbing out of his bedroll.

The sleep was gone from Anaiya's eyes, now replaced with her normal gleam. She stood, warily looking about the room, her hand on her bladed staff.

"Don't rightly know what it is," Grady said, glancing carefully at each Stormbreaker. He paused to shoot a glare at Anthony then continued. "Something's lurkin' in the night, killin' folks in the street. I tailed it here."

Celeste looked stricken. "Killing people? Who has it killed?"

"An elderly man died near the pub and that drunkard Mac made friends with won't be tasting a drop from now on."

Mac kept a grip on Nightsbane. He was still tense and battle ready. If Grady had followed the evil to Dali's house, it could still be there. The chill had not left him. Moments passed slowly but nothing more happened.

Grady sat through the entire night, his eyes locked on the door, his hands swirling his daggers. Whatever he had followed had spooked him greatly. Mac found no sleep either. Every time his eyes closed he imagined a dark shape falling upon Anaiya and slaying her. Anthony was the only one who drifted off. Mac couldn't blame him. He had seen the man fight. Even waking from dead sleep he imagined the white Stormbreaker could still dispatch any foe.

Morning came much too soon and all of the Stormbreakers awoke to the smell of bacon and eggs. One by one, they drifted into Dali's kitchen to find the Secret Keeper hard at work.

"Long night?" he asked them as they filed in.

"Incredibly," Mac replied, yawning.

Grady stumbled into the kitchen, his moustache twitching grumpily. The sight of bacon slightly brightened his mood. The smell of brewing coffee did even more. "Thanks be to Creator," he mumbled sleepily.

Dali turned the bacon over in the skillet, filling the kitchen with a pleasant sizzling sound. "I thought a good breakfast might help you get some strength for the road ahead. I know I need it."

Grady took a swig of his black coffee and sighed. The warm liquid reminded him of so many years. He took another drink before voicing what had been troubling him all night. "Saw you were not here last night."

Dali didn't pause for a moment. "I was out last night, it's true."

"Might I inquire where?" Grady took another sip.

"You may inquire, but expect no answer. You have not yet earned the trust of the Keeper of the Secrets."

"You ain't earned my trust neither." Grady's voice was low, almost a growl. "I followed somethin' back here last night and, whatever it was, it was not to be trusted."

Dali slid the bacon onto a plate and tossed some more to sizzle on the skillet. "I assure you, sir, I was not the shadow you were chasing."

"We'll see about that, now won't we?" Grady mumbled, leaving the room. Mac thought he saw the flash of a dagger. Seconds later, Anthony and Celeste entered the kitchen.

Mac was relived that Grady had chosen to leave before the two had arrived. The tension between Grady and Anthony was palpable, and Mac believed it all hinged around Celeste. Mac understood Grady's feelings. Celeste was like a daughter to him. Mac knew if he had a daughter he would be protective of her as well. He just wished the aged Stormbreaker would give Anthony a chance. If he would look past their personal differences it was possible Grady might find Celeste had made a good choice indeed.

Breakfast ended without incident and the Stormbreakers split up to accomplish different tasks. Mac gave the instructions then went to talk with Dali. The Secret Keeper told him he was making headway in the trust department, and he wanted to continue that progress.

Something inside Mac told him that the key to the Aquillian Scrolls rested with Dali. He wished the man would tell him their secret, but his best convincing could not convince Dali to disclose it. Dali told him the secret would be told only when the trust had been built.

Mac feared he did not have the time to wait. Because of this, he had sent Celeste and Anaiya to scout the island. He figured the women could scout the island in a day, and he hoped they would find a cave or other entrance that would lead them to the scroll. At the least, he hoped they would find some evidence of it. Grady and Anthony had been sent to sniff out other rumors that could potentially aid them in their quest. Of course, they were sent separately so they wouldn't cut each other to bits.

Mac found it hard to concentrate on his task. He had never been in love before. He found Anaiya was filling his thoughts, and hoped it was the same for her. *Later,* he thought harshly. *There is time for this after we stop the storm!* The weight of the coming storm weighed heavily on him.

They had to find the scroll so he could get back to Los Angeles. Marcus would know how to brace the world for the storm. Mac knew inside that it was a lost battle if he did not find and kill Destroyer. It was possible the dark army would crumble at Destroyer's demise. In fact, Mac was counting on it. How could the small group of Stormbreakers in L.A. hope to face Destroyer's millions? Mac knew he could not let it come to that. He had to preemptively strike Destroyer. It was the only way.

Dali began to chat about his youth and Mac's thoughts were pulled back to the present. Time was slipping away.

***

"Celeste!" Anaiya called out excitedly. She knelt on a cliff overlooking a short pathway to the beach below. It was solid, grey stone, covered in years of dirt and growth. Celeste rounded the corner of the path, her eyes filled with curiosity.

"Look at this," Anaiya said excitedly. She wiped the dirt from a patch of ground revealing smooth stone with a small groove carved into it.

Celeste knelt next to her and helped her clear the ground. Slowly, the two Stormbreakers uncovered a large, flat stone platform at the edge of the small cliff. The sun began to set as they finished their task and the fading light cast the women's shadows across the stone, which almost matched the gleam in their eyes.

"You recognize those symbols, don't you?" Celeste asked breathlessly.

"They are the same markings that are on Michael's key."

***

Darkness fell swiftly upon Veritas, carrying the same feelings of foreboding Grady had felt the night before. Shadows flitted around the buildings and Grady knew somewhere within them was something much darker. The old Stormbreaker had donned his tunic, breeches, and cloak, and he glided across the dirt street unnoticed by the hostile villagers. A small sound caught his attention. A shadow slid across the alleyway next to the Barnacle. Grady eased his daggers in his hands and raced toward the shadows. He would not let the fiend escape again this night.

The alleyway was unlit and the inky blackness swallowed Grady whole. For a moment, he saw nothing but the veil of darkness. His eyes adjusted quickly and soon he could see a single form propped against the alley wall.

As silent as the night breeze, Grady approached the dark form. He relaxed each muscle in his body simultaneously. He would flow like water. To relax was far more helpful in a dangerous situation than to approach the danger with muscles tensed. Water could take the shape of anything it was poured into. Given time, water would tear down stone. With enough time, water would overpower anything. Michael had taught him well.

His approach was fluid and swift, but as he neared the slumped form he felt a chill shoot through him. A dead man sat against the wall. His eyes were bulging and his neck bore dark bruises. *Just like the others,* Grady thought. The man's skin was still warm to the touch. *I'm close.*

Grady closed the man's eyes as he scanned the rest of the alleyway. So close. Something caught his attention. With steady hands and a racing heart, he lifted the white thread from the dead man's shoulder. His lips pressed together in a thin line as he rose from the ground. Suddenly, he understood it all. There was no fiend. It was much, much worse.

***

"You are a good man, Mackinsi. It is no wonder you lead the Stormbreakers." Dali and Mac sat gazing at the stars as they blinked into existence one by one. "I believe you have accomplished the task."

Mac felt his heart lift. Would the Secret Keeper finally reveal the location of the scroll? Mac knew that he and his companions had spent too much time on the island, but he respected Dali. Mac had played the game his way and now it seemed he would reap the fruits of his labor. The scroll would be in his grasp and then, ready or not, he would find and face Destroyer. A trickle of ice slid down his spine at the thought, but his wrists glowed hungrily.

"I wish Michael were here." Mac started at the sound of his own voice. He had not meant to speak audibly.

Dali nodded. "He was a good man." He turned to take a good look at Mac. "I can see him in you."

Mac smiled sadly. "I am nowhere near his caliber."

Dali laughed. "Always the humble one, aren't you? I can see him in the way you lead."

Mac felt the warmth of the compliment flood his soul. "I hope to live up to his shadow."

"Your deeds will show your worth, Mackinsi Wrighton. I believe they will sing of you until the world's end."

Mac laughed quietly. He longed for Dali's words to come true. *Creator, guide me.*

"He will," Dali answered, seeming to read Mac's mind. Mac found he did that often. He was the only human Mac had ever met who knew of the Stormbreakers, but Mac suspected he had some sort of secret power. He knew too much.

"In the morning, you shall have your answers," Dali said. "I have kept these secrets for so long; tonight I will walk under the stars and thank Creator for the opportunity he has given me." He patted Mac on the back and with that he was gone. *Until the morning, my friend,* Mac thought. *Then the future will begin.*

As Mac rose to head back to Dali's house, familiar warmth filled him. *Anaiya!* He turned happily to find her and Celeste walking out of the darkness. Each woman had an aura of excitement swirling around her.

Anaiya met Mac with a tight embrace, which he returned two-fold. Every time they separated Mac wondered if he would see her again. He wished the war would end so he and Anaiya could get on with their lives. The memory of Glenn thrusting his fiery blade into Anaiya's stomach flashed in his mind and he shuddered. Somehow he knew he had not seen the last of his former friend.

"Whoa there, hot stuff. Are you going to squeeze me to death?"

Anaiya's voice startled him and he realized he was still holding her and very tightly at that. He let go immediately, turning red. He hoped the night hid it from the ladies.

"We found something, Mac," Anaiya said excitedly. "We found a stone with the same engravings as your key on the far side of the island."

That was good news. "Good work," he said, smiling at the two ladies. "Dali says he is going to tell me his secret tomorrow. I'll bet it has something to do with your find today."

Celeste looked around. "Where are Grady and Anthony?"

"They're out there somewhere," Mac said, gesturing at the darkness surrounding the village, "rumor hunting. They'll be happy to hear they can have a good night's sleep tomorrow."

The three Stormbreakers fell into a comfortable silence, staring up at the multitude of stars. Each contemplated what would come on the morrow. What would Dali's secret bring?

***

Dali strolled quietly through the streets of Veritas. *They say the truth will set you free,* thought Dali, and he believed it to the very core of his being. In the morning, he would tell Mac the truth, the deepest of his secrets. He guessed the Stormbreakers had already found the gate stone, but without his information, it would remain only that—a cold, flat rock. Dali smiled. The morning would bring the end of secrets and the start of his new life. Maybe a vacation was in order. He had heard the high country was beautiful, and he had always wanted to see falling snow. Dali felt as if the stars were smiling down on him as he walked past the Barnacle. He trusted Mac completely. Creator had selected the right man to be double marked.

As his mind wandered, Dali turned down an alleyway between two dark buildings. A white flash moved in the corner of his eye and then he was lifted into the air. The breath blasted from his lungs as he was slammed against the grimy brick wall.

His hat flew from his head and froze halfway to the ground. As he gasped for air, a large figure stepped in front of him. Dali tried to lift his arm, to push the stranger away, but he couldn't move a muscle. All he could move was his eyes. He coughed slightly, testing his voice. At least he could talk. Shadows surrounded the stranger, masking his face in darkness. His voice was cold.

"Where is the Aquillian Grotto, Secret Keeper?"

Dali buried his fear deep inside himself and forced a laugh. "I have no idea what you are talking about."

"That may have worked on the boy, but you will find me much less patient."

Iron hands locked around Dali's throat. He felt them tightening, squeezing his life away. His heart raced in his chest. He could not die yet, Mac had to know the secret. Dali knew he had to stall.

"Who are you?" he gurgled.

"I'm hurt, Dali, I thought you would know me."

Dali strained to see the stranger's face. The voice was familiar.

"Where is the entrance?"

Dali felt the grip tighten. The world spun slowly and he knew he only had seconds until he lost consciousness. "Creator, protect the boy," he gasped.

A flicker of movement at the end of the alleyway caught his eyes and he summoned his last reserves of strength. "Help me!" His cry startled the stranger who turned to stare at the mouth of the alley.

Grady glided toward them. The aged Stormbreaker's brown cloak flowed gracefully behind him and his eyes glittered fiercely. "Anthony, let him go."

The white Stormbreaker smiled innocently. "Anything you say, Grady." With an inhuman burst of strength he hurled Dali across the alleyway to slam hard against the brick wall. Dali slumped to the damp ground and was still. Blood flowed freely from a wound somewhere under his hair.

Grady growled and approached Anthony warily. His twin daggers glistened in his hands.

Anthony turned to face him. The moonlight reflected eerily off of his pure white garb, giving him a ghostly appearance. "When did you know?"

"I knew you're slimy the moment I laid eyes on ya." Grady took several measured steps toward Anthony. "Still don't understand though. Why're you helpin' Destroyer?"

A sadistic smile spread across Anthony's perfectly featured face. "You pitiful old man." He laughed coldly. "You truly do not see. I am not helping Destroyer!" Anthony spread his arms wide. "I am Destroyer!"

Anthony, the Man of Power, lifted his face toward the night sky. His body seemed to ripple, as if the air around it was distorted by an intense heat. Grady took several quick steps backward. Slowly, an immense black shape stretched skyward from Anthony's body. Its leathery wings unfolded, unable to open completely because of the confinement of the alleyway.

Two blood red eyes bored into Grady's above a maw filled with razor fangs. The terrible beast began to laugh, then, as quickly as it had risen, it melted back into the Man of Power.

Anthony's eyes flickered with fire, but his voice was as calm as the grave. "What now, old man?"

Terror erupted inside Grady, but he gave Destroyer only the satisfaction of a single raised eyebrow. "Now ain't that surprisin'?" he drawled casually. As he spoke, he switched one dagger from his right hand to his left. His empty hand slid under his cloak and grasped the handle of a palm-sized crossbow. He had to be perfect. *Get your old bones movin'*, he thought fiercely.

In a blur that caught Anthony off guard, Grady hurled the two daggers in his left hand at the Man of Power's chest while raising the crossbow toward the moon. Anthony's twin katanas batted the flying blades aside, but his parry gave Grady the time he needed. He fired the crossbow and watched his sparkling, white-tipped quarrel arch into the sky. *Thanks for the crossbow, Michael.*

At the pinnacle of its arch, the quarrel exploded in a brilliant display of shimmering white particles. Unlike fireworks, the particles did not fade. Instead, they hung directly over the alley, blazing for all of Veritas to see.

A look of anger flashed across Anthony's face and then was gone. "A soulburst quarrel … how interesting." He circled to Grady's right, causing the old man to move in the opposite direction. "I thought the knowledge of their creation had been lost centuries ago."

"Michael thought otherwise." Grady smiled, despite his fear. "We'll soon be havin' company." He forced his body to relax. He would soon fight the Dark Lord himself. *Be like water*, he reminded himself grimly.

Anthony continued to circle slowly, like a lion cornering its prey. "It seems you have lost your daggers." He smiled in mock sympathy. "That's too bad. I wanted this to be entertaining."

"You underestimate an old man," Grady said, sliding another dagger into his left hand. With his right he reached behind his neck and grasped something hidden there.

He pulled his hand up and a long, slender katana slid free of its scabbard. Its blade glittered like opals and the shining soulburst reflected in its perfection.

"This is Evenin' Song. I had a hundred years to spare so Michael decided to train me with it."

Anthony frowned. Would Michael never stop plaguing him? He had killed him at the Gathering, had watched him fall into ashes, and yet still, from beyond the grave, he tormented him! No matter. He would kill this old man and, once Mackinsi was gone, the world would forget the tall Stormbreaker forever. "They say the student pales in comparison with the master. I killed the master and now I will finish you."

Grady smiled coolly and forced his mind to calm. *Like water.* "We'll see."

And under the light of the sparkling beacon, the battle began.

***

"Soulburst!" Anaiya said sharply as the white explosion lit up the night.

Celeste's face paled. "Grady."

With that, the three Stormbreakers were sprinting, heading toward the point beneath the burning white light. Mac ran behind the two women.

He had never heard of a soulburst but he knew from the reactions of the women that it signaled something very, very dark.

***

Evening Song moved effortlessly in the old man's hands, its colors shifting and dancing. Grady matched Anthony stroke for stroke. The old Stormbreaker's footwork matched the quality of his perfect blade as he twirled and shuffled fluidly. He was the water that battled the fire that was Destroyer.

The soulburst burned brightly as the two enemies clashed. Anthony's blades fell relentlessly, their patterns of impact constantly shifting, probing for a weak spot in Grady's defenses. He cursed as Grady parried another deathblow. Each time he thought he had caught the old man off guard his wicked blade had appeared to parry Anthony's strike at the last possible second. It was as if he was fighting his nemesis again. Michael's training was obvious in Grady Reynolds.

"Afraid, beastie?" Grady asked as he bent sideways, avoiding another deadly thrust. "Your time's comin'. If I don't kill ya, that youngin Mackinsi will put a blade through your belly." Grady deftly turned Anthony's right blade aside and brought Evening Song back across the impostor's shoulder. Anthony howled as the blade sunk deeply into his flesh. He staggered backward, regained his balance and tried to attack, but his left arm was sluggish.

Come on, Mac, come on. Grady rushed at Anthony again, opal blade twirling. The metal ring of their blades echoed across the town of Veritas. Again and again the two warriors clashed, trying to find an opening that would end the fight.

Grady saw the left strike coming slowly at his head, and as he moved Evening Song to block it he felt the right slip below his guard.

Destroyer's katana punched through his ribs and out of his back, startling him. Grady let out a startled breath. The metal felt cold inside him, like the silent toll of death.

"Just an old man after all." Anthony laughed and twisted his blade in Grady. "Thank you for taking care of Celeste. She is a tiger in the bedroom."

Grady moved his left hand before Anthony could react, plunging the dagger deeply into the imposter's stomach. The Man of Power gasped and stumbled backward, pulling his blade free. He clutched his stomach franticly, trying to stop the bleeding.

Grady's long life paraded before his eyes like drifting snow. He saw his family and the long years he lived without them. He saw Mackinsi and smiled. He would save them all. As blackness swirled around the edges of his vision, he thought of Celeste. She was the closest thing to family he had. A tear slid down his face as the darkness closed in around him. *Like water.* His last thought faded as his life slipped away. The last thing he saw was a large, black stone.

Anthony bent painfully and wiped his katana on Grady's cloak. He knew the knife had struck deeply. He had underestimated the old man. He was truly a student of Michael. He staggered backwards as the pain wracked his body, and sunk down to the damp ground. From the end of the alley, he heard the Secret Keeper take a ragged breath. He knew the man was a loose end, but he could not rise to do anything about it. He did not have time to find another body that would suit him. He could not afford to die now. He chuckled mirthlessly as the blood flowed from him, despite the pressure he was applying to his stomach. The old man might have actually killed him. It would be an ironic way to go. Fury exploded inside him. *No!* he roared inside. *The world is mine!*

He vaguely noticed the three Stormbreakers rush into the alley. They stopped at Grady's fallen form, and he heard Celeste wail in despair. Suddenly Anaiya was by his side. He felt her pry his lips open and pour a blue fluid down his throat.

It felt like fire going down, but the results were instant. He felt his wound mending, the heat of reforming skin where Grady had stabbed him, overwhelmed him, and for several seconds he was in another world of agony. Then the heat was gone. He stood to his feet slowly, testing his wound gingerly. It was almost completely healed and the blood had stopped flowing. He laughed inside. He had now seen true irony, the final insult to his enemy. Michael's gift had saved him. *Well, I better play the part.* He thanked Anaiya and rushed to Celeste's side. He wrapped his arm around her and she sobbed.

After seeing that Anaiya had taken care of Anthony, Mac saw Dali slumped at the far end of the alley. Grady was gone, but perhaps they could save Dali. He ran and knelt beside him. Blood dribbled from the Secret Keeper's mouth and his breathing was strained and shallow. When he saw Mac, the glaze left his eyes.

"Mackinsi." His voice was no more than a gurgling whisper. "I guess the secret can't wait until morning."

Mac felt the hot tears filling his eyes. The man was amazing. From the way he was laying, Mac knew the man's back was broken, and yet Dali was still focused on the greater good. Mac hoped he would be as valiant when his time came. "Tell me."

"On the west side of the island, you will find a flat stone overlooking the ocean. Do you have Michael's key?"

Mac nodded.

"The stone will have the same engravings as the key. You must be on the stone when the setting sun meets the horizon." He tried to take a breath but his chest would not rise. "Creator will do the rest."

With a smile halfway formed on his face, Dali's eyes glazed over. Mac placed a finger on his throat to feel his pulse, but the Secret Keeper was gone. Mac bowed his head as a tear slipped from his eye to the dirt beneath him. *Michael left such a trail of good in this world and all I leave is pain and death.* He felt a hand on his shoulder and turned to see Anaiya looking down at him, tears glistening softly in her own eyes.

"Dali?" she asked softly.

Mac shook his head and looked away.

"Grady too," she said quietly. "Anthony would not have survived if we had not arrived when we did. He lost a lot of blood."

"What happened here?"

Anaiya sighed and helped Mac to his feet. "Evidently, Grady found the fiend he was searching for. Anthony found him in this alley attempting to protect Dali from it. Anthony did not know what it was, but it was obviously more powerful than anything we have encountered before."

"Dali told me the secret," Mac said quietly.

"Good." Anaiya pulled him close and hugged him tightly. "Let's get our friends back to the house and bury them properly. The secret can wait until tomorrow."

Mac nodded and, together with the grieving Celeste and the wounded white Stormbreaker, they carried Grady and Dali out of the alley.

As they passed under the soulburst, Anthony smiled inside. That had worked out better than he had hoped. Unknowingly, the old fool had given him the perfect alibi. Mackinsi still trusted him and he guessed that Celeste would need some extra comforting that night. *The scroll will soon be mine.* He let his thoughts fly over the ocean and the hundreds of miles to New York City, to the mind of Glenn Cross.

His mental order rang in Glenn's mind. *It is time. Unleash the storm!*

Chapter 25: A Storm Unleashed

Lightning crackled like veins of fire over New York City. The roar of the thunder almost drowned out the relentless pounding of the falling rain.

In the streets of the city, gasoline fires burned out of control. Glass lay strewn about the street like spilled puzzle pieces as hundreds of people looted the city. A television shattered as it hit the ground. A small man pulled a knife out of the looter who had dropped it and bent to the ground, removing his hundred dollar shoes.

Through it all, Glenn Cross walked slowly. His black cloak billowed behind him, buffeted by the gale-force wind. The rain fell all around him but seemed to miss the dark Stormbreaker completely. A rotted sneer twisted his face at an obscene angle and each lightning flash reflected hauntingly in his fanatical yellow and red-flecked eyes.

He watched as his Dimlocks did their work. A lady looked warily out of her window and jerked as a Dimlock leapt into her body. A flicker of yellow appeared in her eyes and for a moment she disappeared back into her house. She emerged with a 12-gauge shotgun and stepped into the street. The rain instantly soaked through her nightgown as she joined in the slaughter.

His Dimlocks were doing well. He had given the order several hours before and had been pleased with the response of his army. The Dimlocks had swarmed into the city, possessing each person they came across. The possessed population had swarmed into the streets committing murder and rape and then looting the city. The police responded only to be possessed themselves.

Glenn could hear the voices of his army in his mind. New York was not the only city in peril. He could hear the evil boiling in every city around the world. And it made him very happy. *Soon my face will be healed, and I will have my reward!*

He stopped in front of an electronics store and took a moment to watch the breaking news on the only remaining television in the broken window. He smiled as the wide-eyed reporter shouted about the violence sweeping the globe.

Destroyer almost had the scroll, which meant he would be returning soon. Glenn's chance was coming. All he had to do was wait patiently and go through the motions. His wave of evil would soon turn the tide for the Dark Lord. When Destroyer returned with the knowledge of creation, his precious dimension would be ripe for the taking.

A line of worry creased Glenn's deformed forehead, and he lifted a hand to his mutilated face. He would not make the same mistake twice. He felt the power Destroyer had given him swirling inside of his mind. With it had come a new understanding of the power of the Heartstone. He would wait until the last moment and take control. *If the Aquillian Scroll doesn't tell him all of this already.* Glenn slid his hand over the handle of Bloodletter to give him confidence. He doubted the scroll would allow Destroyer the power of precognition, but he would have to be on his guard.

A man stumbled into his path, carrying a stereo system. In a swift movement, Glenn sent Bloodletter slicing through the unfortunate man's neck. The stereo fell from the man's stiff fingers and, as his headless body hit the asphalt, a Dimlock boiled out of him snarling. "Find another," Glenn commanded. "That kill was mine."

Chapter 26: The Way Downward

The sun dipped low in the sky on the west side of Veritas, casting long shadows over the island. The Stormbreakers stood silently on the western cliff, each lost in their own thoughts—the memories of friends lost and the mysteries of the future.

Anthony stood behind the others with an arm around Celeste. Every so often, Celeste would wipe a tear from her eye. Every time a small sob rocked her, Anthony pulled her closer, held her tighter. It was necessary for him to keep up appearances until the scroll was in his grasp. Celeste whimpered again and, for the hundredth time, Anthony fantasized about slitting her throat. *Wait,* the Dark Lord told himself. *Soon, all will be yours.*

Celeste stood straighter at Anthony's comforting squeezes. She knew that the fate of the world rested in their hands but all she could think about was the mounds of dirt beside Dali's house marking the graves of him and Grady.

Mac had given her the honor of making Evening Song Grady's headstone. She had stabbed the opalescent blade into the ground with all of her strength, muttering the few words every Stormbreaker knew but dreaded. The few syllables locked the sword into the ground for all time. Only the hand of its owner could remove it. Grady would be remembered forever.

She felt a shudder go through her body then relaxed as Anthony pulled her closer. She had given so much to the man, and was glad for his support. *He loves me,* she thought, and the thought stirred a distant happiness in her soul. *He loves me.*

Anaiya stood behind Mackinsi, watching the way the wind played with his brown hair and ruffled his cloak. He was such a strong leader. He had held them all together after Grady's death, kept them focused on what Grady would have wanted them to do. She felt the wind flowing through her fine hair and inhaled deeply. Whatever mysteries awaited her, she would not fear. As she watched Mackinsi standing upon the flat, carved stone, facing the unknown, she realized she had never loved him more.

On the outside, Mac appeared calm and collected, but inside he was a tornado of emotions. He grieved for his friends. *If I had been with them, it would have turned out different,* he told himself repeatedly. Dali had become a close friend, and Grady had been a rock he could lean on. *Destroyer will pay for their blood,* he thought gravely.

Despite the depth of his grief, there was another problem that weighed on Mackinsi. The night before, he had felt a darkness fall upon him, like a clawed hand ripping at his heart. He knew the storm had fallen upon the world. That night, he had lain awake, feeling powerless. Now he stood waiting impatiently for the sun to set. He needed to get to the scroll as soon as possible and make it back to the mainland. The hand of foreboding was closing on his heart, and he knew the dimension was rapidly slipping into position for assimilation.

The ocean below him was calm, save for the soft breaking of the waves upon the shore. Its peaceful sound calmed him, reminding him of Anaiya.

He could feel her gaze upon him and the love that came with it. Her strength in the midst of this chaotic time inspired him. She was an amazing woman, his solid rock in a shifting tide.

The sun dipped lower, and Mackinsi's thoughts sauntered back to an easier time. It seemed so long ago that he had been a gangly boy at Lathim High. So much had changed since then. *Am I still Mackinsi Wrighton?* he wondered, *or am I someone else? When I see my parents again, will they know me?* The weight of the world rested on him now, and he felt its burden heavily. Somewhere, deep inside, beneath the pain and grief he felt already, Mac grieved for the mother and brother he had never known.

As the sun met the blue horizon, he held his breath and heard the others do the same. For several seconds nothing happened. The sun dipped lower and the light faded. Just as Mac began to feel his hope slipping away, he felt the heat in his wrists.

It began slowly, like a warm sunbeam resting upon the two emerald crosses, then increased gradually. The sun slid lower and, as it did, the heat intensified. The wind began to grow stronger as well. Mac's cloak blew out straight behind him and he had to squint against the sudden gale. Below him, Mac saw the calm of the sea being broken. The wind did its work and the resulting white caps reminded Mac of snowdrifts sitting upon a blue-green world.

The heat in his wrists blazed into fire and Mac gritted his teeth against the pain. He felt the flames fly through his veins and into his body. His blood was like napalm as it boiled and surged its way through him. Never before had the power caused him physical pain, but, then again, he had never before attempted to open the path to Creator's greatest gift. With each beat of his heart, the burning power coursed through him, faster and stronger.

The wind roared against the Stormbreakers, threatening to topple them. Mac braced himself and, as his hair whipped back and forth, the fire burned fiercely within him. The wind turned to emerald-green mist before his eyes, as if it had become the breathing spray of the ocean.

The ocean raged and boiled as if it was alive. Waves of thirty feet crashed and frothed, and the green wind drove them to even greater heights. Through it all, the power gained momentum within Mackinsi.

The pain inside him was excruciating, overwhelming his rational capabilities. *I can't bear this,* he thought in dismay. His vision faded in and out as he teetered on the edge of unconsciousness. His heart beat once … twice … and then the power exploded.

The emerald flash from his wrists was brighter than the sun and the Stormbreakers shielded their eyes against its blinding purity. The concussion from the blast deafened them and seemed to change the storm. The wind pulled away from the group and hovered over the ocean for several seconds in a swirling tornado of sparkling green.

Then, as Mac's eyes widened, the sparkling tornado flew toward him, melting into his body.

Anaiya inhaled sharply but, aside from that, all was silent. The wind had vanished completely, leaving an unsettling calm. Mac took inventory of his body. He inhaled slowly. The only way to describe how he felt was saturated. He was saturated with power. The silence seemed to last forever, but in truth was mere seconds. In a sudden compulsion, Mac lifted his palms toward the sea below. He was a conduit of Creator's power.

The shimmering green exploded from his palms, sending a shockwave from his body. He knew he should have been knocked off of his feet but he felt as if he was rooted to the ground. Thick, swirling columns of emerald wind spiraled from each hand to the ocean below. Where the wind touched the water, the liquid pulled apart, sliding back upon itself and leaving dry ground where water once had been. Deeper and deeper the emerald air cut into the ocean and, slowly, a pathway was formed leading into its depths. The water formed a wall on either side of the path, refusing to collapse in upon itself but undulating fluidly nonetheless.

Mac focused all of his will into staying conscious. The exertion drained him greatly. For seven minutes he stood in a wide stance, allowing the power to pour from him to the ocean below.

As the gale stopped, he let his arms fall. Despite his fatigue he and the Stormbreakers gazed in astonishment at what they beheld.

The wind had done its work, and in its wake was a path, seemingly cut into the ocean itself. Beginning at the shore, dry ground, six spans across, stretched into the sea. To each side was a wall of shimmering water. Somehow the water did not fall back upon itself.

"By Creator," Celeste exclaimed with a gasp. Her eyes were dry and her mouth hung open.

Destroyer smiled. "The scroll is hidden beneath the ocean's depths."

Mac tottered to his left, but Anaiya's arms wrapped around him, steadying him. He turned to see her face. She seemed gaunt. Her eyes were rimmed with concern.

"We're almost there," Mac said weakly.

"Rest," she replied. Then she kissed him and he fell into blackness.

Twenty minutes later, he awoke to the first stars and the faces of the others. Anthony stood staring at the pathway into the dark depths. "How do you feel?"

Mac took inventory of himself and realized he was surprisingly refreshed. "I'm ready," he replied, rising.

He placed a hand on Anaiya's shoulder and she nodded.

Celeste nodded as well. "Into the deep."

***

The pathway into the ocean was a black tunnel. Anaiya took the lead. "This will help," she said to Mac. With a flick of her fingers she produced an orb of white light that hovered above her left hand. In single file the Stormbreakers followed her. The farther they walked, the higher the walls of water rose toward the stars. Eventually, there was blackness both behind and ahead. The water rose like slabs of cold, rippling stone to either side as the mist from each fell down upon the group like a light drizzle.

Anthony touched the wall with his index finger. It melted through and, when he pulled it out, it was wet with seawater. His face was also wet from the constant drizzle. "How long do you think these walls will hold?" he asked, looking behind the Stormbreakers and into the darkness.

Celeste replied without hesitation, "As long as Creator is willing."

For a moment Anthony's eyes became ice, but they thawed just as quickly. "Let's hope Creator is willing then."

The group continued silently for another hour. Anaiya and her glowing orb led the way, followed by Mac then Celeste then Anthony. Each held their cloaks tightly about them and pulled their hoods low to shunt off the incessant drizzle.

Anthony looked backwards into the darkness several times, finally turning with a satisfied expression.

"What's going on?" Celeste asked him.

Anthony smiled. "We're not being followed."

Mac listened to their footsteps against the damp earth. Each step took them deeper into the depths and closer to the scroll. He looked up to see the stars, but saw only blackness. The globe of light had taken his night vision or they had walked far enough for the water walls to block the stars from view.

It still boggled Mac's mind that he had done something of this magnitude. He wondered if Moses had felt the same way. He fingered the triangular key in his pocket.

The water wall to Mac's right seemed to ripple and he felt the hairs rise on the back of his neck. He watched Anaiya lean toward the movement. He opened his mouth to shout a warning but, before he could, everything happened in an instant.

A blotchy tentacle, two inches around, exploded from the water knocking Anaiya to the floor. Her globe of light winked out as she hit the ground and the group was plunged into darkness.

Anaiya felt a tentacle wrap around her throat and another encircle her waist, and then she was being lifted up into the darkness and toward the water. She knew she would surely die if she was pulled into the water. With all of her concentration, she summoned another ball of light.

Mac saw her as the ball of light appeared in her hand. Fear was evident on her face, but so too was an intensity he had seen several times. Anaiya had an incredibly strong will to live. She struggled at the tentacles as Mac pulled his bow from his back. As he nocked an arrow, Anaiya's light penetrated the wall, and what he saw sent a chill into his soul. Two three-story red eyes stared out of the darkness above a giant maw filled with ten-foot-long fangs. The creature had the body of a catfish and from the sides of its maw came the two large tentacles. Without hesitation, Mac released an arrow. It pierced the water wall and hit the creature's eye. He followed his first shot quickly, pulling and firing an arrow into the other eye.

The eyes exploded in billows of red blood and an otherworldly scream echoed through the surrounding water. Celeste's short swords severed the tentacles and Anaiya fell, rolling to her feet. With a wave of her hand, she freed the ball of light to float before her. Instead of light she filled her hands with the comfortable feel of her thin, bladed staff.

As the fiend's blood spread, more dark shapes moved within the water walls. Ripples appeared down the dark corridor and, in some places, tentacles probed searchingly. The large eyes of hundreds of creatures peered out from the darkness, only inches away from the wall of water.

Mac drew another arrow, nocking and firing it in one fluid movement. Another red eye exploded, adding to the foul stench permeating the path.

Amidst the fiend's death cries, Mac heard Anthony's yell. "These creatures are Harpers and will not stop attacking! We must run!"

Mac saw the truth of the statement as more red eyes appeared at the wall. "Run!" he shouted. The tentacles exploded from the walls like hundreds of writhing snakes as the Stormbreakers took flight.

The spray of salt water filled Anaiya's mouth as a tentacle wrapped around her arm. Her bladed staff quickly sliced it in two and she picked up her speed. Her globe of white light flew before her creating a water hallway of twisting shadows. Anthony ran unscathed. The servants would never harm the master, which would cast a suspicious light on their dear friend Anthony, and much too soon. *Attack me!* he commanded harshly. His minions would obey and did. Tentacles flew at him to find his flying katanas. *That's more like it,* he thought.

Mac's arrows flew like bullets, slamming into tentacles as soon as they broke the water wall. His hands moved in blurs as he drew and fired, drew and fired. Arrows flew in a stinging rain from his bow, each striking its target. Despite this volley, his quiver remained full.

The tentacles grew too thick for arrows and Mac drew Nightsbane. The tentacles fell effortlessly to the katana's razor edge. Mac leapt and danced over grasping tentacles. Nightsbane was always flowing and cutting in time with his movements. Around him, he saw the others doing the same.

Anaiya's blade cut swiftly as her white staff spun in blurs around her body. Celeste and Anthony fought side by side; each manipulated their double weapons deftly, cutting their way through the darkness.

Mac's eyes rose to where they had come from and his heart leapt into his throat. Thousands of tentacles poured from the walls drawing nearer to the Stormbreakers each second. "Go!" Mac screamed. "Hurry!"

A hopeful cry from Anaiya caused him to turn forward. The mouth of a cave loomed small in the distance. "Go!" Anthony shouted, and they did.

Tentacles whipped by and a Harper leapt from the wall. Its maw closed viciously where Celeste had been seconds before. Anthony's blades flicked twice and the creature flew, bloodied and dying, into the opposite wall of water. The mouth of the cave grew closer with each step and the mass of following Harpers did as well. Mac's breath came rapidly. Figure eight, arching light, rushing tiger. Each sword move came unconsciously, saving him from a grabbing tentacle and snapping maw.

The sound of writing tentacles echoed around them as the Harpers caught up to them. For a brief moment, Mac's vision was filled with nothing but thousands of tentacles out of every inch of water. He saw the cave and heard his own voice ringing above the den. "Dive!" He dove blade first and suddenly he was free. He rolled three times and came to his feet. Anaiya was beside him, breathing heavily, and Celeste beside her. As they watched, Anthony exploded through the wall of tentacles. After several rolls, he too came to his feet beside them.

He sheathed his swords. "The Harpers will not follow us into this place. They fear the light."

Chapter 27: The Aquillian Scroll

It was only then that Mac realized the cave they had leapt into was illuminated by a light other than Anaiya's sphere. The ten-foot, curved walls seemed to emit a soft, phosphorescent glow. It was enough lighting to allow Anaiya to release her globe. It winked out, allowing their eyes to adjust to the softly lit room. Mac realized Anthony spoke true as the tentacles slowly faded away, leaving only the darkness outside of the cave.

"Creator's mercy," Celeste prayed. "What were those things?"

"Harpers," Anthony told them all. "Like all fiends, they are attracted to servants of the light, to destroy them." *As well they should.* "They swarm at the slightest trace of blood, and they never stop chasing you when you are in the water, no matter how many you kill."

"So the light here turns them away?" Celeste asked.

Anthony ran his fingers along the wall. "This is a holy glow … a warding. No fiends can enter this cave." *Burn Creator for that.* "It is the entry way to the door where the scroll must rest."

Mac felt the weight of the darkness in the world press upon his heart. "Let's hurry then. We need to get back to New York."

The cave stretched for 20 yards ending in a vertical wall. Mac approached the wall warily. As he neared it, he noticed a triangular notch at eye level. Above the notch was an engraving of the setting sun. He took the key from his pocket, turning it in his hands thoughtfully.

Anthony waited anxiously. This was one of the reasons Mac's life had been required. The door would open only to the Chosen One, and he knew the scroll waited beyond.

The engravings of the spider, eagle and snake stared up at Mac from the key in his grasp. The setting sun sat silently upon the stone wall, it seemed to Mac to be waiting for something. *A puzzle,* he thought, looking at the engravings. *All of the animals on the key live beneath the sun … the spider, the eagle and the snake.*

He thought for a while longer and then moved purposefully toward the triangular notch.

He slid the key into the notch with the eagle pointed up. A grinding noise filled the cave and a circular groove appeared around the notch and key. Gripping the key tightly, Mac turned his wrist. The circular section of the wall turned smoothly with it. He turned the key so that the snake pointed up beneath the engraving of the sun. A click resounded around the group. As the sound faded, Mac turned the key the opposite way, turning the wall until the spider engraving rested beneath the sun.

As soon as the click sounded, the setting sun blazed white. Two beams of light shot from the wall, finding Mac's crosses. They stayed in contact for several seconds then winked out. A crack rippled through the solid rock wall, branching out like spiders' legs until the entire wall fell in a cloud of dust.

Mac covered his mouth with his cloak and saw the others do the same. Slowly, the dust settled, leaving two large, wooden doors standing closed tightly before them.

"How did you know the combination?" Anaiya asked Mackinsi as the group stared at the doors.

"I just knew," he replied evenly. "It was a combination based on predators. The eagle preys on the snake and the snake upon the spider. I guess I was right."

"Thank Creator," Anaiya breathed.

Anthony strode forward and pushed the doors open. Each weighed around 300 pounds, but they swung open silently and effortlessly on blessed hinges. Mac stepped through the doorway, followed closely by the others. A stairway stood before them, leading downward. The holy glow continued down the stairway disappearing into darkness.

Mac led the way downward. Another hour went by as the group continued their descent. Mac's legs ached as the stairs finally leveled out into a narrow hall. *We must be in the bowels of the earth itself,* Mac thought. Somehow the thought intrigued, instead of unnerved, him. In the faint glow of light, murals could be seen on the walls of the hallway, depicting battles between light and darkness.

The air was completely still as Mac led the others down the hall. It ended in another set of doors made of stone. Two depressions in the shape of handprints marked the center of the door. Each had a green cross glistening in its center. Anaiya, Anthony and Celeste looked at Mac, and he nodded. The stone felt cold against his hands as he placed them into the indentations. The doors swung open to his touch and the others followed him into the room beyond.

As they walked through the doorway they all stopped in their tracks. The room was enormous. It stretched out before them for 300 yards and tall pillars stretched 50 feet to the ceiling every 50 yards, supporting its immense weight. The floor was cold marble, dark and rich in color. The room was wide as well ... at least seventy yards from wall to wall. At the opposite end of the hall, between two crosses mounted on the wall, was a marble pedestal.

"The Aquillian Grotto," Anthony murmured in awe. Only yards away now.

The grotto was amazing and Mackinsi wished he could celebrate at finally reaching it but, even in this holy place, the weight of the battle being waged weighed heavily on his heart. "Let's go." The tall pillars passed by like silent sentinels to either side of them as they approached the pedestal.

Anthony had seen a room larger than this once before. He remembered the night of the Gathering well. It had been fulfilling to finally kill his nemesis, Michael. All was falling together nicely. The boy would pick up the scroll, unlocking its power, and then he would steal it. After that, he would slaughter Creator's puppets. *No,* he thought again, *that would cause too much delay. I'll let my puppets slaughter the Stormbreakers. They should be here right about…*

A footfall echoed through the large chamber from the direction they had entered. Anthony spun toward the sound, as did the others. Because his back was to them, they all missed the smile on his face. He feigned to be peering into the gloom.

"Celeste and I will check it out," he said to Mac. "Just make sure the scroll is safe."

Mac nodded silently. If they had been discovered, he had to get the scroll away from Destroyer's minions at all costs.

Anaiya followed Mac closely as he approached the pedestal. She could see the top of the platform was devoid of dust as if it had been cleaned every day instead of isolated for centuries.

"Be careful," she whispered as Mackinsi ascended the steps.

Mackinsi took the steps quickly and suddenly stood before the pedestal, staring down on Creator's greatest gift—the Aquillian Scroll.

***

Celeste rushed toward the entrance of the hall. If enemies had followed them into the sea they had to be stopped. She knew they had to protect the scroll. She felt invincible with Anthony beside her. She had shared her bed with him and now knew she truly loved him. She wished Grady had not hated him so. As she neared the entrance, a shadow moved. Celeste knew it at once. Dimlock!

"Celeste." Anthony's whisper came from behind her. She instinctively turned, and gasped as cold steel slid into her throat. Her eyes went wide with shock and her scream came out as a quiet gurgle. Tears of confusion welled in her eyes as she struggled vainly to speak. Anthony was grinning from ear to ear.

"Thanks for the fun," he whispered into her ear then pushed his blade through her neck, slicing her spine cleanly. Her body went limp, and her eyes dimmed. A single tear ran down Celeste's cheek and then she was gone.

***

The sound of battle turned Anaiya's head just as Mac picked up the scroll. Dark dots swarmed through the entryway at the far end of the hall. Anthony seemed to be holding them, but Anaiya could not see Celeste.

"Anaiya!" Anthony bellowed. "I need you!"

Anaiya wanted to stay with Mac. She looked at him quickly. He was standing completely still, staring into the scroll. *I can keep him safer by fighting.* With a last look at Mackinsi, Anaiya ran from the pedestal toward the swarming mass of evil, and the Stormbreaker in white.

***

As he touched the scroll, the light overwhelmed Mackinsi and for a moment he believed he was blind. Then he was flying through small specks of light. Somehow he knew they were stars. Despite the speed he was traveling, no wind caressed his face. He would not have known he was moving save for the stars. A flash of light rippled before him and he beheld Creator. His hair waved like tongues of sun-fire as he smiled and cast seven specks of light from his hand. The specks spun out, expanding and interlocking. They continued expanding until Mac could see the surface of each. Each was a window to a different land. Mac realized they were the seven dimensions.

The windows spiraled toward him slowly, losing momentum until they began to rotate in the opposite direction. They spun faster and faster, collapsing inward and then merging into a ball of molten glass. The ball stopped before him, hovering in space. Slowly, blue appeared on its surface, followed by green and brown. Patches of white swirled casually across its surface. Mac gasped in awe. The world! It got larger and larger before him and he realized he was falling into it. Creator had made everything with light! All was held together by it and even the darkness was dependent on it, for light formed the shadows that held it together. *Destroyer must not learn this,* Mac thought as he hurled through the atmosphere.

Mountains and forests rushed by him as he rocketed across the sky. In mere seconds he was flying across the ocean. Veritas grew larger before him and the sun dipped beneath the horizon. He saw Anaiya and Celeste below him, on one side of the island, and Grady stalking the streets below him. *Where is Anthony?* He saw himself and Dali go their separate ways and then Mac was rushing toward an alleyway.

He saw the soulburst explode above him and, as he floated around the corner, he saw Destroyer fall back into Anthony Ward. *No!* Denial sprang immediately into his mind. *I couldn't have been so blind!* He felt tears of anger welling in his eyes. Destroyer's swords beat at Grady's opalescent blade relentlessly. Mac saw Dali, dying against the wall of the alley. He jumped as Destroyer plunged his sword through Grady. He moved to help, but found he couldn't. He was merely watching the events of the past. He heard Grady mutter something about what he would do next time, and felt sympathy well inside him. *Poor old man, I'm so sorry. You were right all along. I've been a fool.* He saw Anthony move toward Dali and then pretend to help Grady as Mac, Anaiya and Celeste rounded the corner. Suddenly, the vision shifted. He was hovering above the marble floor of the Aquillian Grotto watching Celeste run toward several Dimlocks. Anthony was right behind her. He tried to shout a warning to her, to tell her that Anthony was the Man of Power, Destroyer himself. But no words would come. He saw Anthony whisper her name. As she turned, he plunged his sword into her throat. Mac felt tears run free down his cheeks. *No, no, no!* Then he was hovering over himself. He saw he was stationary, staring into the unrolled scroll. Anthony yelled for Anaiya. He ordered his creatures to attack him in order to lure her! Mac's heart felt like it had been dipped into ice water. Destroyer was going to kill Anaiya!

Her red cloak flew gracefully behind her as she ran toward her death.

Anaiya! Mac tumbled toward his body and felt the scroll grasped in his hands. He whirled. "Anaiya stop!" One hundred yards from Destroyer she did just that, turning to see why Mac had called.

Anthony saw her stop and growled. He sprinted toward her, katanas flashing.

Mac sprinted too. His bow was instantly in his hands, an arrow nocked. He had to get close enough for a shot.

Anaiya saw the two men rushing toward her. The Dimlocks appeared to be waiting for something. Why were they waiting and not pursuing Anthony?

"Anaiya!" Mac screamed between breaths. "Anthony is Destroyer!"

Anaiya wondered if she had heard right. Had Mac said something about Destroyer? She turned to find Anthony had covered half the distance toward her.

"Anaiya, help me! Come here, Celeste is dying!" Anthony shouted.

Anaiya saw Celeste slumped on the ground behind him, and felt her heart jump to her throat. "No," she whispered, "not her too."

Mac ran as if on wings. Seconds remained before Anthony would reach Anaiya and he was not yet close enough for a good shot. "Anaiya!" he shouted. "Come to me!"

Lost in confusion, Anaiya only knew Mac needed her. She whirled back and sprinted toward him. Mac felt a spark of hope ignite within him.

Anthony howled behind her … feral and savage. Anaiya looked over her shoulder in confusion. Anthony was a mere ten yards behind her. Something evil flickered in his eyes and Anaiya suddenly knew he was dangerous. She put everything into her sprint.

Anthony gained on the running woman step by step. He would reach her first. He knew her death would guarantee Mac's fall. His grief would make him weak. He could hear her rhythmic breath. It was music to his ears. Her cloak came within reach and he did. With his left hand, he grabbed her cloak, jerking her backwards off her feet. His right Katana came slashing down.

Mac loosed his arrow and with a cry loosed another. The first hit Destroyer's falling bade, knocking it to one side. The second arrow spun toward Anthony's heart. The dark man leapt to the side as the arrow barely missed him. The delay bought Mac enough time to cover the distance to Anaiya. He leapt over her, drawing Nightsbane, and, in a flash of steel, green and white, Mackinsi Wrighton engaged Destroyer.

Blades flashed in a whirlwind of singing metal that almost masked the two from view. Anaiya struggled backward out from underneath the spinning blades and pushed herself to her feet—only to be met by a wave of Dimlocks. They flowed around the two men and toward the platform, seemingly not caring about the red-cloaked woman.

Anaiya raced the dark tide of creatures to the platform and, to her relief, arrived first. She spun, putting the scroll to her back. The first Dimlock leapt for the scroll, only to be skewered by Anaiya's blade. She beat another off with the center of her white staff. Her hands moved in blurs as she spun her staff around her body sending the blade to skewer another creature, but the Dimlocks pressed into her, accepting their losses and overwhelming Anaiya's defenses. Mac caught a glimpse of her and then she was gone under a sea of writhing Dimlocks.

Everything in Mackinsi screamed at him to help her, but he knew if he turned his attention from Destroyer, he would be dead before he even reached her. Anthony's blades tried to find his throat, stomach and knees, but Nightsbane met the strikes with the flat and back of its blade, deflecting each attack just enough. Mac was surprised by his own skill. He was able to mirror the Dark Lord's strength and blinding speed. He noticed this unnerved

Destroyer as well. He stole a glance over his shoulder to see if Anaiya was alive and received a deep cut to his forearm. His parry turned Destroyer's next thrust and saved his life, and he felt his hope renewed. He had seen a flash of red cloth and blonde hair. Anaiya was still standing in the midst of the black mass.

The wail of the Dimlocks turned to shouts of glee and Mac felt his stomach lurch as Destroyer grinned from ear to ear. "It seems I must make my exit." He attacked savagely, driving Mac backward. Mac tried to reclaim the offensive, but Destroyer's blades never stopped. Back and back he went.

When the spear pierced his right calf, it surprised him. Somehow, he had not realized their fight had carried them to the altar. He kicked out powerfully. The spear point had not pierced his leg too deeply and it came out as he kicked the attacking Dimlock. He spun quickly, but Destroyer was gone. Mac caught a glimpse of the white-cloaked man as he disappeared into the tunnel at the end of the hall. He knew he had the scroll.

A bullet whizzed past his ear and Mac spun to face the roaring, screeching clump of Dimlocks. Destroyer had the scroll, but Anaiya was fighting for her life. *Creator, forgive me,* he whispered.

Nightsbane swept methodically through the Dimlock ranks, killing a Dimlock with every swing. Mac's calf throbbed with each step and his forearm stung where Destroyer had cut him, but he forced the pain out of his mind. His love was in danger. *I'm such a fool,* he thought bitterly, but he knew he could do no different. Now Destroyer had the scroll, but Mac would not chase him yet. The Chosen One was in love. And that love might have doomed us all.

He spun to the left, catching a pistol-wielding Dimlock by the gun hand. The gun fired harmlessly by Mac's head and his sword hand shot out. The Dimlock's arm snapped, causing it to pull the trigger again. This time, its bullets blew a hole in another Dimlock's head.

Nightsbane arced downward, severing an arm here, a head there. Mac's focus was intense, his objective all consuming. Sizzling bullets passed mere inches from his body, but none could touch him. Black blood pooled around his feet and fell in droplets from his blade. Another Dimlock fell screaming under his blade, and he saw her. He inhaled sharply. Even in battle, her beauty was breathtaking. Her staff was a wheel of shining white, crushing the creatures around her. Even so, he could see that she could not go on much longer. Her pale arms were covered in red blood … her blood, he knew. A trickle ran from under her hair as well. She met his eyes and he saw sadness there.

"Hang on!" he shouted. He cut right and left as Anaiya thrust and parried. They continued this way for several minutes until the last Dimlock fell beneath Mac's feet. The large hall stank of bile and sulfur and the black blood of the Dimlocks was smeared across the marble floor and white marble pedestal.

Mac raced up the steps and Anaiya stopped leaning on her staff and fell into his arms.

"We have to catch Destroyer," she whispered.

"I know," Mac replied, "but right now I have to take care of you."

She shook her head in protest, but Mac's insistence won out. An hour later, the two Stormbreakers lifted Celeste's body between them and began the long trek back to the surface of Veritas.

***

The ships burned in the harbor, their masts pillars of fire in the rising sun. Some had already sunk beneath the waters. Even as the crew dipped below the surface, they were still trying to kill each other, their expressions mirroring the emotions of the Dimlocks inside them.

By the flaming wrecks, Veritas burned. The people in the community had turned on each other. They had raped their women and plundered their homes. Eventually, they had killed one another. Now the inn still burned as if it was a funeral pyre. Veritas had discovered its truth, but they had not been prepared.

The crew stood quietly at the railing of the ship. Somehow the wave of evil had passed them by. The old sea dog grinned despite himself. He remembered the miracle. His ship was blessed. "Keep watch, boys," he growled. "I'm bettin' Miracle Boy will be needing a lift."

***

Mac and Anaiya buried Celeste beside Grady. Anaiya tearfully spoke the words that bound her weapons as her headstone. Her short swords sparkled in the sun beside Grady's shimmering blade. No hand but their own could ever move them. They would mark the graves until the end of time. And that could come very soon, Mac thought sadly.

Everything had burned. The storm had indeed begun and Veritas had not been immune. Bodies lay twisted in the streets. Some still smiled grotesquely, clutching a weapon or some stolen merchandise. The suspicious people of the island had been unable to fight off the Dimlocks. They had been possessed easily, and had complied with the Dimlock suggestions even faster.

"He must have had a plane," Anaiya suggested, "or maybe another ship was waiting for him."

Mac nodded, quietly searching the horizon. Destroyer had the scroll and the Seventh Dimension would soon be ripe for the taking.

Mac looked about him and shuddered. If this could happen so quickly here, how was the rest of the world doing? Would it hold out long enough for someone to find them? In the chaos would anyone even look? "Creator, help us," he prayed.

The sound of oars slapping the water turned his head. "Ahoy! Miracle Boy!"

Chapter 28: The Raging Storm

"Rally to me!" Marcus Stone screamed to his battered group.

The Stormbreakers pulled into a tight wedge formation. Seven others stood with him, they were his unit. Fourteen other units were spread through Los Angeles. One had eight Stormbreakers, the rest seven.

"Archers!" At his command, two of his unit began to loose arrows swiftly. The Dimlocks before them dove for cover, but the fiend kept coming. The Tremorda lumbered toward Marcus and passed people who were frozen in time and oblivious to the war being waged for their very existence.

"Archers, all!" he cried and all seven of his warriors fired arrows at the volcanic beast. The arrows glanced harmlessly off the fiend and a Dimlock got a shot off. One of Marcus' unit reeled backwards. "Hit!" the wounded man cried.

"Fall back!" Marcus shouted. And then they were running through the streets. They could hear their pursuers behind them. Skyscrapers towered like silent sentinels, watching the city go insane.

"Come on, Mackinsi," Marcus grunted between breaths. "We are only delaying them. There is no way we can win this war alone!" One of his unit fell face first to the ground, a bullet in his head. Marcus darted right then left down the narrow alleyways. He had to get his unit to safety. They now had less than 100 Stormbreakers. Thousands of Destroyer's forces were in L.A. A scream rang out behind him and he turned to find one of his Stormbreakers held aloft by a purple tongue. He glowed for several moments then went limp. The tongue whipped back into the shadow of the alleyway.

"Reap!" Marcus barked. His Stormbreakers veered away from the shadow and they continued to sprint. A second later, they emerged from the alleyway and into hell. People were pillaging the city. Twenty yards in front of them a lady put a gun to a man's head and pulled the trigger then, laughing, turned the gun on herself.

The noise in the street was deafening. Glass shattered and people screamed. Gunshots echoed across the asphalt and children wailed. With a thought, Marcus pulled the area slightly out of time. The people froze and the Dimlocks poured from their bodies, gnashing their sharp teeth and screeching. Their yellow and red flecked eyes stared greedily at the six Stormbreakers.

"Creator!" Marcus screamed and the five others took up the cry. They drew their melee weapons and waded into hell.

***

Night had fallen in the streets of New York. There were no Stormbreakers in the city and soon it seemed the blood would be deep enough to wade through. Glenn laughed, deep and harsh, as he sat in his room at the top of the Leviathan building. He watched through his minions' eyes as they slaughtered humans and the few Stormbreakers still scattered across the globe. Several days had passed and Destroyer had returned with the scroll. He seemed pleased with himself.

Mac had been left on the small island of Veritas, without a way back, and two of his companions were dead. Destroyer not only had the scroll and Heartstone, but had dealt with the prophecy. Mackinsi could not kill him if he was stranded in the Caribbean. Glenn laughed again, this time more quietly. Destroyer thought all was well, but he was forgetting something. The greatest dangers sometimes are the closest to you. Glenn opened and closed his fingers on his right hand.

Soon he would take control. At the right moment, all would fall into his grasp.

Chapter 29: Prophecy

Three arrows took up residence in a throat outside of the Leviathan skyscraper and a man fell heavily to the ground. His companion would have shouted an alarm but a slender knife was embedded deeply in his skull.

Silently, like the breath of vengeance, figures slipped through the front doors. Lightning crackled through the black clouds outside and the rain fell heavier. The storm was reaching its worst, but inside the first floor was deathly still.

***

The box opened silently before him and Anthony grinned broadly. Slaver ran down his face. His excitement had been building since he had taken the box from the grotto. He had been very specific in his directions to his Dimlocks. They were never to touch the scroll. They had knocked it into the velvet lined box and had presented it to him.

The time had not been right to open it until now. He needed to be completely focused, rested and prepared. He could feel the world beating like a rotten heart. Tonight was the night he would assimilate the final dimension, and tonight he would attain the power of the scroll.

The candles flickered on the cold stone walls, a myriad of shadows flitting about the throne room. Outside, the storm—his storm—thundered from the heavens. He would defeat Creator tonight. Everything had come together. He looked at the pedestal to the right of his golden throne and beheld the Heartstone. He wanted to go to it right now, to tell … no, command it to absorb the final dimension, but he knew the scroll had to come first. When he gained control of all the dimensions he wanted the knowledge of Creation.

Then he would truly be a god. *And what a world I will create!* he thought with elation. He reached downward and touched the scroll. The paper felt cool to his touch.

The candles blazed in their sconces, columns of fire lining the walls, and the knowledge came. Like a sea, it washed over him, relentlessly pounding and crashing into his consciousness. He saw everything that had ever been. He saw the first ray of light and the first star in the heavens. He saw the creation of the universe, even the events unfolding that very second. His body jerked as the vision ended. He felt alive and more powerful than he had ever been. Slowly, Anthony Ward, the Man of Power, Destroyer incarnate, turned his gaze to his large, wooden doors. "Impressive," he said, his voice like frozen silk. "Prophecy seems to yet have a voice."

***

Mac's arrows worked like passcodes to the floors above, killing Destroyer's guards and allowing him and Anaiya to climb to the next level. They progressed silently, and soon had reached the fortieth floor.

Mac was glad he had not been expected. Destroyer's overconfidence had thinned the guard. Otherwise, he knew they would have had to pass through an army. But the army was in the streets, and Destroyer was all alone.

As the shadows passed by his door, Glenn smiled a wicked grin. "The pawns have come." He felt the edge of Bloodletter and slid it back into its sheath. "Two birds with one 'stone'," he sniggered madly, then, silent as a wraith, slipped into the hallway.

The wooden doors loomed like destiny before Mackinsi Wrighton. *The prophecy waits inside.* He reached to the power within him for confidence, but instead found fear. Anaiya's hand was suddenly on his shoulder, its warmth soothing his racing heart.

"Creator will guide you, Mackinsi," she whispered. "And I will be by your side."

He reached up and squeezed her hand. "What if I lose?"

Anaiya amazed Mac by smiling. "You will not lose ... but if you do, I will slay Destroyer myself."

Mac sighed heavily, and squared his shoulders. "I love you."

"Anaiya's lips met his, and for a moment his worries melted away. Her sweet scent lingered in his nostrils as she pulled back. "I love you too. Now let's finish this!"

Mac smiled at her. She was right of course. He knew Creator would be with him. He counted to three on his fingers and he and Anaiya burst into the throne room, weapons drawn.

The room was much darker than the hallway had been, and it took a moment for the Stormbreakers' eyes to adjust. They pressed together, back to back, and slowly the room faded into view.

Anthony lounged almost lazily on the golden throne. The scroll sat to his left and the Heartstone rested on the pedestal to his right. At the sight of the scroll, a pang of guilt wracked Mackinsi's stomach. *I should have stopped him.*

The candles cast flickering shadows onto the walls and caused the Man of Power's features to shift and slide. His confident smile was unnerving. "It seems the prophecy found us all. Are you ready to face it?"

Both Mac and Anaiya turned to face the Dark Lord. Mackinsi's wrists burned hotly. "Creator has brought me back from the grave for this very moment. He believes I am ready."

Anthony laughed smoothly, his voice echoing around the stone-walled room. "It seems Creator has failed to help your companions up to this point. You only have until midnight before this dimension is ready for me to control!" He rose from the ornate throne. He still wore his white cloak. "I'll never forget how sad Celeste looked as I slid my sword into her throat."

Anaiya's eyes flashed and she moved to step forward. Mackinsi put his hand on her shoulder. "Don't let him provoke you. He wants us to rush in blindly."

"Very good," Anthony chuckled. "At least Creator hasn't placed all his hopes on a complete imbecile."

A crack of thunder shook the building and the rain fell so heavily that its sound penetrated the thick, stone-walled room.

"What hope can you possibly have, Mackinsi? Even now the last of the Stormbreakers are falling in Los Angeles. By midnight this dimension will be overwhelmed by evil. Even if you defeat me, you can't seriously believe the two of you can stop my army. This world is lost, no matter who the prophecy favors tonight."

Thunder roared as Mac's mind swirled. Was Destroyer right? Mac had thought only of facing Destroyer, he had not thought about what would come afterward. If he and Anaiya survived this night, would they have a world to live in?

Anthony saw the hesitation in his eyes. "Forget this petty prophecy, Mackinsi Wrighton. I hold the power of Creation and can give you a role in that future. If you live for me and fight for me, I will give you a hand in that Creation. You can recreate a world you have lost."

Hopelessness threatened to overwhelm Mackinsi. One hundred Stormbreakers could not defeat Destroyer's army, but he would never bend a knee to the beast before him.

A vision returned to his mind of a being with hair like sunlight. He remembered how it felt to be in Creator's presence, to see his face. Mac felt Creator's courage wash over him.

"The prophecy would not have brought me to this moment if the future was hopeless. If Creator gives me victory here and now, in the midst of the storm, I am certain he will cleanse the world of your taint."

Destroyer's eyes hardened instantly and his voice took on a new chill. "That was unwise, boy! I had hoped to work together, to build a new future, but I see now that you are simply one more obstacle I will crush under my feet. Perhaps you are an imbecile after all! If Creator were as powerful as you claim, would he have allowed me to kill Michael, Grady or Celeste? Would he have allowed me to fool you and take the Aquillian Scroll? I think not!" Anthony was breathing heavily, seething. "Creator will help you ... just as he helped Michael!"

Mac felt Creator's peace. "If you are so confident, come down and face me."

Anthony smiled strangely; his eyes seemed to look through Mac and Anaiya, past them. "I believe I will leave it to someone who has thirsted for just that for a very long time. Glenn, kill them and I will restore your precious face."

Mac turned to the doors, still keeping an eye on Destroyer.

"Mac and his whore have come to call." Glenn snickered as he strode into the room. Mac could see the madness flitting about in his bulbous eyes.

Anaiya flinched at his face. "What happened to you?"

"Shut up, whore!" Glenn growled. He took a step toward Mackinsi, easing Bloodletter in its scabbard.

Mac stepped toward him as well. "Glenn, don't do this. The prophecy is at hand. I must face Destroyer."

"Wrong, Mac," Glenn spat, "you will face me! And when you are lying cold on the floor, I'll have a taste of your woman."

Mac refused to be provoked. "Why do you hate me? I have never done anything to you!"

"Creator despised me but loved you! So, in turn, I will despise you and hate Creator. A bit twisted, I know, but when you're crazy, it makes perfect sense."

He stepped closer and Mac moved to his left to distance himself from Anaiya.

"Glenn," Mac entreated, "you were my only friend in those halls of Lathim High. We had so much fun together, so many deep talks, and I trusted you. Will you throw that away for the likes of him?" Mac pointed toward Destroyer with Nightsbane. He had not noticed he had drawn it.

Glenn's face softened for a brief moment. He remembered a deserted wasteland where the sun rose and set within a heartbeat. He remembered fighting. He remembered killing. "Nice try, pretty boy, but the person you speak of is dead. I killed him myself." Glenn unsheathed Bloodletter and its blade ignited into scorching flame. "You are jealous of me! Just like you always have been. I won't let you have my power!"

"I don't want—" Mac began, but Glenn Cross was upon him. In his peripheral vision, Mac saw Anaiya's white staff spinning. "No!" he shouted. "This is between us." Anaiya stepped back reluctantly, keeping a wary eye on Destroyer. Mac raised Nightsbane vertically, intercepting a vicious horizontal cut from Bloodletter. He dove to the right to absorb the power of the blow and came up fighting. The two old friends pivoted and lunged. Black and green cloak alike flared and spun with their fluid movements.

Glenn attacked like a cornered animal, each blow meant to kill. Mac had taken the defensive. "I don't want to kill you!" he shouted as he blocked three consecutive rapid strikes from Glenn.

"Too bad you're already losing. You won't get to kill anyone."

Mac retreated then attacked, each blow rang out dangerously throughout the throne room, but neither fighter landed a strike.

Glenn grinned as he backed Mac into a corner. *Michael's puppet isn't as tough as he thinks,* he thought wildly. *Soon I will have my face back!* Before he killed Mac, he wanted him to suffer. "You fight pathetically, Chosen One. Last time we met, I killed your whore. I don't know how she lives now but, believe me, after I kill you I will make sure the whore dies for good ... after some fun of course."

Mac felt the fire of Creator's power ignite within him. He brought Nightsbane down heavily. The force behind the blow staggered Glenn and his eyes bulged obscenely. "Her name is Anaiya!" Mac screamed and then his blows poured down like the pounding rain.

His arms moved like striking vipers and Glenn struggled to keep up with the torrent. He mirrored Mac's steps and attempted to take back the offensive, but Mac's skill level had improved well beyond his own. *No!* Fear welled inside him and he felt his arms slowing with fatigue. *I can't lose! What about my face ... my face!* "My face!" Mac's blade sliced deeply into Glenn's left cheek, and he wailed.

In several quick steps, Glenn had retreated into the darkness, leaving a trail of blood droplets behind him. Mac stood breathing heavily, his shoulders heaving. Anaiya rushed to his side and both turned to face Destroyer.

"Very good," Anthony congratulated them, "it seems that my puppy has run away. I fear he will be ugly forever." He stepped to the floor and drew his twin katanas. "Into prophecy!" With his cry came his blades.

His right blade snapped toward Anaiya's head and his left toward Mac's stomach. Anaiya's staff met the blow and she spun her blade toward Anthony's chest. He spun to the left and, as her blade passed by and Mac blocked his first strike, the fight began. Anaiya and Mac attacked Anthony with a vengeance. Her staff flashed ghostly white in the candlelight as it struck everywhere except the fake Stormbreaker. Mac's blade fell just as ineffectively.

Anthony's blades moved independently, clearing spaces for him to move into and keeping the Stormbreakers on their toes. Destroyer's demonic laughter rang out, mingling with the crashing thunder.

"Two against one and still you fail. Is this the power of Creator? Michael would be proud!" The battle raged across the throne room, each fighter giving and taking equally. Mac knew it could go either way. As he struck and parried, danced and twirled he heard the tolling of the grandfather clock in the dark corner of the throne room. A chill passed through him. The mournful toll signaled midnight, the shift of the dimension and the coming doom of all.

***

Glenn's facial wound enveloped him in searing agony. Half of it was slicked in blood, and his left eye twitched uncontrollably. The bell was music to his ears, and in the midst of his pain he knew it was finally his time. Silently, he slipped through the shadows behind the throne. The Seventh Dimension was ripe for the taking. He could feel the Heartstone calling for a master, eager to be complete.

He edged toward the pedestal, keeping his eyes on Destroyer. If he could claim the stone while destroyer was distracted, he could use it to destroy him.

He felt the madness swirling inside him… Not madness, genius. That thought almost caused him to burst out laughing, but he controlled himself. *The stone first then the laughter.*

The pedestal was within reach when Destroyer spun low to the ground, sweeping Anaiya off of her feet. She fell gracefully, rolling into a crouch, and Mac leapt between her and Destroyer. Mackinsi's back looked so vulnerable, so tempting. Glenn eased his dark bow from his back and notched an arrow. *The stone before!* Logic screamed. *Just one arrow! I can have the stone after,* he argued back. He watched Mac hold Anthony's katanas at bay under another volley. *Just one shot and we will all know who is the stronger one, who Creator should have favored!*

The candlelight danced in Glenn's slaver as he drew the fletching back to his cheek. "Now you die," he whispered, and released the arrow. As the nock left his grip he saw Anaiya staring directly at him.

The arrow flew straight and true, its black fletching mirroring the dark hate that had launched it, but Anaiya moved swifter. In the blink of an eye, she was next to Mac and in the next she had leapt in front of his body. The arrow made a sickening crunch as it broke through the left side of her rib cage and entered her heart. She fell heavily to the stone behind Mac.

Glenn cursed loudly and pulled the Heartstone from the pedestal. Its power coursed through him as it never had before. With a single thought, his face was restored. "Destroyer!" he shouted. "Who rules the seven dimensions now?" Destroyer whirled to face him. He held out his hand, but the Heartstone did not come to his call.

Mac spun and dropped to a knee beside Anaiya. She was shaking as if she had a chill. A thin stream of blood ran from the corner of her mouth onto the cold stone. "Finish it," she whispered.

"You're going to make it!" Mac felt the tears falling from his eyes. "You have to! I want you to be my wife! I love you!"

Her eyelids fluttered. "I love..." she began, but never finished. Her hand fell limply from Mac's grasp and her eyes closed gently. Then she was gone.

The tears burned hot as Mac rose from beside his love. His wrists burned with a fury he had never before known. His heart burned as well, torn and broken. He saw Glenn and Destroyer were locked in some sort of mental war for the stone. Each had their hand outstretched and the air between them bent and shimmered from the heat of their silent battle.

Mac hardly felt himself nock the arrow, but he felt the satisfaction of its release. As it left his bow he screamed. Two columns of light burst from his wrists to the arrow, igniting it into a flaming green missile.

When the arrow was halfway to the pedestal, Glenn saw it. He pulled his hands toward him in defense, but the arrow of light would not be denied.

Destroyer cried out as the arrow hit the center of the object Glenn had pulled in front of his chest—the Heartstone! The stone cracked and flew high into the air. The arrow continued and hit Glenn in the chest like a truck, its force launching him ten feet backwards and pinning him to the cold stone wall. The green fire engulfed Glenn Cross. He wailed as his body sizzled and cracked and then fell from the arrow as fine, grey powder.

Mac watched all of it with a cold heart and turned to Destroyer. He had lost his love. He would fulfill the prophecy, but he knew that nothing could ever bring his happiness back to him. He knew part of him had died with her.

As he turned to Anthony, he saw the Heartstone. His arrow had pierced it, but had left it whole. It hovered in the air above the golden throne, spinning faster and faster. Mac looked back to find Anaiya, but she was gone. *What's happening?* his mind screamed. Thousands of voices filled the room, softly at first, then louder. Anthony shouted at the Heartstone to come to him, to heed his call, but it did not respond. Faster it spun and then the ink-black surface began to change.

Patches of pure white appeared upon it then grew rapidly. As the Heartstone turned white, it began to glow. The white light grew brighter with each moment until the brilliance of its glow shone like a small sun. With an ear-shattering roar, the Heartstone shattered. Destroyer cried out and covered his face as the light engulfed the entire throne room. The ceiling exploded outwards and a column of white light rocketed into the black night, punching into the clouds and spreading in ripples across the city. The ripples continued to the horizon and beyond.

***

In the streets of New York, several Dimlocks jumped as a flash of white flame exploded amongst them. They shrunk in terror as a cloaked figure stepped out from the flame.

All around the city, cloaked figures seemed to melt from white flames. Thousands of flashes illuminated the city. On each corner, Stormbreakers slew retreating Dimlocks.

An old man came around the corner of a high rise, his shimmering sword poised and ready. He stopped in his tracks as he saw the girl before him.

"Celeste!" he shouted, and then he was running. Grady wrapped her in the tightest hug of her life and used his brown cloak to wipe her tears away. "How … how is this possible?"

Grady smiled. "Only by the hand o' Creator!"

Together again, they turned and joined the army of once fallen Stormbreakers as they took back New York City.

***

It was unexplainable and Marcus Stone was not about to try. The flashes had brought allies— friends he had seen die at the Gathering; Stormbreakers that had fallen next to him years before. "By the light!" he shouted to the cloaked figures. "Let's finish this!" The army's cheer sent the Dimlocks running, but they could not run long from the vengeance of Creator.

***

The light of the explosion faded from the throne room. Destroyer blinked rapidly. Gradually, his eyes adjusted and he noticed the newcomer who had appeared in their midst. The tall, lanky figure stood like a statue. His long, slender katana rested with its tip on the ground. His forest-green cloak swirled in the last gusts of the explosion of the Heartstone. His large hood covered his face, but as he looked up, his blue eyes met Anthony's.

The Man of Power blinked in surprise. "It can't be! I killed you! I saw you die!"

Michael's deep laugh filled the cold room. "I'm back."

His words hit Destroyer like a wall. His dreams were turning to ashes in his mouth. "How—" he began, but Michael interrupted.

"The Heartstone. You created it for evil, but Creator used it for good. Creator infused it with a Power of Light that a creature of darkness could never detect. He used its power to preserve any Stormbreaker killed by you and your minions. When they died, they entered the hidden light of the stone, waiting for the day of the Prophecy … waiting for Mackinsi Wrighton to set us free."

"Anaiya—" Mac began to ask, but he felt a hand on his shoulder. Its warmth was wonderfully familiar.

"Yes," Anaiya whispered in his ear. Mac spun to wrap her in his arms. Fresh tears flowed down his cheeks, mirroring the ones sliding down her porcelain face. "Yes," she said again and smiled.

Mac didn't understand. "What are you saying?"

"Yes, I will marry you." She laughed quietly. "If you'll still have me." His lips were all the answer she needed.

The candlelight flickered knowingly on Michael's face as he stepped toward Anthony. "Now, where were we?"

Michael leapt at the Man of Power and, as Whisper moved like the wind, Anthony's blades struggled to keep up. Michael cut low then high then low again, raining blows at Anthony from every angle, forcing him backward. Purposefully, Michael brought Whisper arching low. When Anthony moved one of his blades to block it, Michael's right leg shot out.

His kick caught Anthony in the face and the Man of Power staggered backward, red blood splattering his white cloak.

The Dark Lord's katanas whirled to make up for his error, but Whisper had already gotten under his defenses. With a snap, it cut his hamstring. He dropped heavily to his knees, gasping in agony. His face was a twisted mask of hate and pain. "I killed you once and I will kill you again!"

Michael stood stoically before him, sword poised at his side. "I think not."

Whisper slashed down, seeming not to touch the Man of Power. As Mac and Anaiya watched, a thin line of red appeared on Anthony's throat, and then his head tumbled from his body. As the head tumbled to the ground, an immense darkness exploded up and out of the body. Destroyer rose up and out, and, with a great flap of his wings, sent Michael sprawling.

"Fools!" His voice rumbled like the thunder. "I do not need a body!"

Michael rose slowly, keeping a safe distance from the raging beast.

"The Heartstone can be remade, and, when it is, I will return and turn your world into a living hell!"

Destroyer raked his long claw across the air in front of him, leaving a shimmering line that widened into a doorway. Strange shapes twisted within, ominous and dark. With a flap of his wings, Destroyer was through.

The three Stormbreakers dashed toward the portal, but Mac made it first. Without a second thought he dove through the narrowing gap in time and space. It closed behind him with an ominous snap.

Anaiya stood still before the place where they had vanished. She turned to Michael and seemed for the first time to realize he was there.

"Michael." Tears of happiness fell as she embraced her mentor, but fear sent others rushing down her cheeks as well. "Where is Mac?" She asked the question knowing she did not want to hear the answer.

Michael held her close. He could feel the world returning to balance. "He is in the world between dimensions, a place Destroyer knows well. It is a land of darkness, like a poor reflection in a cloudy mirror. Reality holds no sway there." Anaiya stepped back to stand beside Michael. Both looked to the spot where Mac had vanished. Michael re-sheathed Whisper and rested his hand on Anaiya's shoulder. "He has followed Destroyer into the Shadow Moor."

Chapter 30: Destiny

Darkness swirled around Mac, like spirits floating without purpose. Tall, grey pillars stood before his eyes, stretching into blackness above him. The only light came from his markings, and they glowed brightly.

Where am I?

The room undulated strangely. Nightsbane felt good in his grasp, a comforting friend in this sea of darkness.

As he scanned the room he noticed it looked similar to the grotto. Its ceiling was lost in shadows, but the pillars were spaced the same way, and from the echoes his landing had made, he guessed it was roughly the same size as well.

Anaiya was alive! The thought nearly toppled him with relief. When the arrow had pierced her chest, the light had flown from his world. Now it was back. His wrists pursed and flickered.

He could feel the power inside him begging to be released … begging to fulfill the prophecy. He was startled as a voice spoke from the darkness.

"Glad you could make it, Stormbreaker!"

Mac turned slowly. It was hard to tell where the voice was coming from. "I came to fulfill my destiny, Destroyer! I will make sure you never return to the seven dimensions. I will end this here and now!"

The laughter that rippled around him was deeper than he remembered it being. A shadow moved on one of the pillars and Mac loosed a throwing knife in its direction. The knife was swallowed by the darkness. Mac never even heard it land.

"Will you kill me with that sword?" Destroyer's voice mocked from all around him. I am a mortal no longer … especially not here. You will soon understand the full power I wield."

"Show yourself!" Mac cried to the darkness. He listened to his voice echo through the room.

"You are such a fool, Mackinsi Wrighton." Mac thought the voice came from his left. He spun and loosed an arrow, only to have it vanish as well.

"The prophecy said we would meet in battle." Destroyer's voice was smug. "It said nothing of fighting again in the Shadow Moor."

Mac spun slowly, but each time the deep voice spoke it was from a different direction.

"When you followed me into the Shadow Moor, you sealed your fate. The laws of reality are different here. I am different here. Now I will re-write the prophecy!"

A three-foot-wide column of flame exploded toward Mackinsi from his left. He felt his hair singe as he leapt backwards into a layout backflip. He noticed too late that he had not pulled his sword up in time.

The flames blasted it from his hands and carried it ten feet through the gloom, embedding it a foot deep into the slimy stone floor.

Mac landed in a crouch, preparing to leap again.

The shadows moved before him and his glowing crosses revealed one of the most terrifying sights Mackinsi had ever seen.

Destroyer seemed to melt from the shadow. He had grown to a height of seventy feet. His dragon-like jaws oozed saliva that fell sizzling to the floor. His black wings were open, adding to the immensity of his form. In each hand he held a katana, each blade over fifteen feet long. Small flames rose from every inch of his slimy skin, giving him the appearance of living fire. It was his eyes that unnerved Mackinsi the most. They almost dripped with hate as they seared into his soul.

Mac knew he could not let his fear distract him. As swift as a falcon, he released two arrows. They flew for Destroyer's eyes, but disintegrated as they hit the creature's fiery shield.

"What now, Stormbreaker?" Destroyer's voice shook the room and his tone was mocking. "You destroyed the Heartstone. Where will you go when I kill you?"

Destroyer inched forward and Mac moved backwards out of range of the invisible barrier. The monster's breath blew steam and sulfur from his nostrils.

He eyed Mac carefully as if he would pause for a moment then, in a movement surprisingly fast for a creature his size, he beat his wings and was upon him.

Mac felt the searing barrier touch his skin and prepared to die. "Anaiya, I'm sorry," he whispered. But then his crosses flickered and the barrier was gone. He saw Destroyer's eyes widen in shock as he saw Mac was still alive. He dug his claws into the ground in an attempt to slow his momentum, but Mac was already acting. Two more arrows flew consecutively, one struck Destroyer in the chest, and another in the neck. Black blood oozed from the wounds and Destroyer roared. Instead of slowing, he rushed headlong like a living earthquake. His right katana moved faster than Mac could see. He felt the flat of the blade smash into him and then he was flying.

He hit the pillar heavily, causing a crack to run up its length and knocking the breath out of him. The pillar shook as Destroyer's steps sent shockwaves through the room.

Mac couldn't breathe. He struggled to pull air into his lungs, but his diaphragm was in the midst of a spasm. Destroyer stopped twenty feet away from him and smirked. Finally Mac was able to take a gasp of air. "So," he rasped. "This is the end?"

Destroyer's laugh was garbled as the arrow in its throat brought blood into his mouth. He pointed a blade at Mac. "Now you die!" A column of flame shot from his hand and down the blade, directly at the wounded Stormbreaker.

As if time had slowed, Mackinsi watched the flames roll toward him and he despaired. *What has it all been for?* he asked himself. A vision answered him. A vision of a woman holding a small child. He stood beside her on a mountaintop as an army of darkness crawled up the mountain from all sides. Anaiya. He knew instantly. *We will have a son!*

The Power of Light rolled through him and he felt himself rise to his feet. He would not die today! As the flames were about to engulf him, Mac lifted his left hand.

A brilliant white column of flame exploded from his palm and met Destroyer's fire. The flames collided with a blinding fury. The force propelled each column of fire against the other where they licked the floor. Sweat ran down Mac's face from the inferno in front of him, but his eyes held their determination. "I will not die today!"

Destroyer's eyes narrowed in concentration. So, it was to end like the Gathering. He had already fought that battle, and he was sure to win again. Slowly his fire gained ground, engulfing Mac's white fire inch by precious inch. The floor sizzled beneath the flame's meeting point, and the roar of the fires was deafening. Destroyer grinned through the blood pooling in his mouth. He was still more powerful. He would still kill Creator's puppet. "Is that all you have, Stormbreaker?" Destroyer bellowed. "I'm afraid it is not enough." He growled and forced his flames closer to Mackinsi.

Mac could feel their angry tongues seeking, reaching for his body, but he had lost all of his fear. He raised his voice above the din. "I know Michael fell to you in a battle like this, but you are foolish if that gives you comfort."

"And why is that, little one?" Destroyer laughed as the flames inched closer and Mac knew he was out of time. The power within was raging and it was time to let it out. "Because I am double marked!"

The fire blazed from his right hand joining the column from his left, and the white flames engulfed Destroyer's fire.

Mac saw fear in the Dark Lord's eyes an instant before his flames engulfed him. He clawed at himself as the flames tore at his dark flesh, and slowly the fire melted into Destroyer's body. For a brief instant, Shadow Moor was again awash in silent blackness, but then a brilliant light appeared. Light roared outward from every pore of Destroyer's body. His tattered wings beat vainly at the air and then, with a crack that split the air like lightning, he exploded.

The wave of white fire spread in a circular pattern though Shadow Moor. The columns of stone disintegrated beneath its intensity.

Mac felt no pain as it washed over him, but, nonetheless, he covered his eyes against its brilliance. A second later it faded away, leaving him once again in quiet darkness. Well, almost quiet. The ground rolled beneath him as large pieces of the distant ceiling crashed down upon him. *Shadow Moor can't exist without him,* Mac thought wildly. He dodged another chunk of stone by diving into a somersault.

"The sword." The whispering voice sounded familiar in his mind. It reminded him of a man with shining hair. He saw a gleam to his left and turned to see Nightsbane still embedded in the stone. As he looked at it, its green crosses began to glow and he knew what he must do.

A column crashed to the floor and the impact knocked him from his feet. He scrambled to his sword and, with all of his strength, pulled up on the handle. It slid as if oiled, and he stumbled to retain his balance.

Pieces of stone fell like hail around him as he lifted Nightsbane high into the air. He swung the blade and cut downward and his hunch held true. A shimmering gash appeared before him, widening to a door.

A sound above him caught his attention, and, as Mac looked up, a column of grey stone fell directly toward him. With his last remaining strength, he threw himself through the portal. He hit hard stone and for a moment feared the worst. But the explosions came from behind him instead of upon him. Somewhere, he heard Anaiya's voice shouting and then everything went black.

Epilogue

The smell of clean cotton pulled Mac from his sleep and, as he opened his eyes, he blinked in the soft evening light. He was in a small room, sunlight streamed in lazily from the window beside his bed. He was comfortable and warm, underneath several blankets, and as his eyes adjusted he saw he was not alone.

Anaiya smiled as Mac blinked at her. "Welcome back."

Mac smiled. "What happened?"

"That's what we want you to tell us when you feel better. But, to us, you fell from thin air into the throne room. You've been out for a week."

A figure moved in the corner and Michael stepped into the light. "You must have used an amazing amount of power, Mackinsi Wrighton. It is good you slept."

Mac reached up to clasp Michael's hand. "It is so good to see you again."

"I can say the same of you, my young friend." Michael smiled warmly. "I have truly missed you."

Mac began to rise, but quickly noticed he was naked. He blushed and looked questioningly at Anaiya. "Where are my clothes?"

Anaiya shrugged her shoulders and smiled casually. "You don't need them right now."

Mac sat up against the headboard, carefully pulling the blankets with him. "What happened with the war?"

Michael answered. "The Stormbreakers annihilated most of Destroyer's armies, but some escaped. The ones that fled have gone into hiding. They will not be a threat for a very long time."

"The dimensions were cleansed!" A familiar voice interrupted from the doorway. Grady walked in followed by Celeste.

Mac felt tears falling down his cheeks.

"Stop yer blubberin'," Grady quipped, "sure you'll get sick of us sooner than ya think."

Mac laughed. "Doubtful."

Celeste smiled as she put her arm around Grady.

Michael took advantage of the silence. "When you broke the Heartstone, you released its hold on us. The stone not only contained the assimilated dimensions, but every Stormbreaker who fell to Destroyer. You brought us back; when we reappeared, so did the other dimensions. They were reborn and cleansed. Their Stormbreakers returned to them as well."

Something tugged at Mac's mind. "What of the scroll?"

"Marcus returned it to the Aquillian Grotto," Michael answered. "It will remain sealed there, and you will keep the key."

Celeste smiled. "You saved us all."

Faces cycled through Mac's mind. The humans who had fallen... Dali. "Not all."

"Many lives were lost, Mac." Anaiya held his hand in hers. "But you kept the rest of the world from dying. You gave Dali's sacrifice meaning."

He nodded quietly. Anaiya's presence was like rose petals brushed along his face or the lingering warmth of a glass of hot cider.

Her love was tangible and he knew he loved her too. His vision of their son returned to him and he almost spoke. *No,* he thought. *Some things are best left to be discovered in time.*

Anaiya looked to the others and cleared her throat. "I believe now would be a good time."

Grady laughed and winked at Celeste and the two left the room.

"What's going on?" Mac asked.

"What you promised me before I died." Anaiya grinned slyly.

Michael took both of their hands. "Let us get you two married." Mac blinked in surprise then looked at Anaiya. She was aglow with happiness. "Are you sure?" he asked. She nodded and Mac felt his heart soar into the clouds.

When the ceremony was over, Michael blessed them and left the room, closing the door behind him. Anaiya stood next to the bed. "I told you clothes wouldn't be necessary." With a shrug, her red dress fell to the floor. Mac gazed on her with wonder. "My wife…"

Later, Mac lay quietly with Anaiya's head on his chest. She breathed softly, and he wondered what dreams were dancing through her mind. It seemed so long ago that he was walking through the halls of Lathim High. So much had changed. He wondered about his parents and his fellow classmates. Had they survived the storm? He would check on them soon. Again the vision returned of him and Anaiya standing upon a mountaintop, holding their child as an army stalked toward them. He shuddered and shook his head slowly to clear his mind. He would leave his troubling thoughts for another day. For now he would enjoy the moment. He brushed a strand of blonde hair from Anaiya's face and smiled. *Anaiya Wrighton … my wife.* It was such a good thought.

He looked out the window and he knew that somewhere in the seven dimensions parts of Destroyer's forces had taken refuge, waiting for the storm to come again.

He would find them and destroy them, and if the storm ever came again he would face it and defeat it once more. But for now he would simply be grateful for his friends and his love. Mac sighed softly and closed his eyes. For the first night in a very long time, he had peaceful dreams.

THE END

When you dream big and have courage,
you can accomplish the impossible.

40223624R00278

Made in the USA
San Bernardino, CA
14 October 2016